The Seven Year Year Glitch

by

DT Mularkey

Drake's Key, Book One

Cover Art by *Najla Mahis*

The Wild Rose Press, Inc.
PO Box 708
Adams Basin, NY 14410-0708
Visit us at www.thewildrosepress.com

Publishing History
First Edition, 2024
Trade Paperback ISBN: 978-1-5092-5845-1
Digital ISBN 978-1-5092-5846-8

Drake's Key, Book One
Published in the United States of America

Chapter 1

Drake's Key, USVI

I expected to make a *minimum* of a billion dollars this week because of the Chairs, the highest stakes gamble on the planet where a player could lose their fortune or leave in a different physical body.

"Good morning to ya, Boss. Coffee black today?" Peaches asked in her soft island lilt. "Here's the mail. The usual except for one letter. It's on top." Peaches was *never* subtle. If a letter was on top, she meant get to it now.

I noticed the letter was typed on a manual typewriter. "Boss, you will die before Sunday sunrise." She was spot on and this note was straight to the point. "Any ideas?" Peaches was aware of everything there was to know here.

"Sure, Boss, always. We all loves ya, but you got a couple of employee contracts to negotiate." Her eyebrows were raised, a sign to pay attention.

Several top managers were due new contracts, and I hadn't even started. Someone may be harboring a grudge because of previous contract terms. Someone may want to leave and kill me as a sweet goodbye. That tightness came to my chest, my natural response to assassination. "Bring me their contracts," I requested.

She rolled her eyes and I realized they were in the pile she handed me. She topped off my coffee and added,

"No time to be combing the beaches for pirate treasure."

As I set the note aside, she handed me the list she kept of past guests who played in the Chairs. Given Drake's history, the writer may be a former guest, someone who lost their millions or even their physical self. It could be a Player for this week hedging their bets in case they lose. More than six Players a year for seven years: where to start? And then there's the walk-ins.

"You might want to keep an eye out for folks who were none too happy with the Chairs. I crossed ones who already went to Jesus, and a few darlins who went to jail." Peaches could read my mind.

The killer, if there even was one, could be someone from my life before Drake's: someone who held a grudge from a case I won against them, or a case I lost for them. On top of that, there was my old mob connection. Wise guys had very long memories and longer networks. Some bodies returned from the grave when you least expected it like Nikko the Knife perhaps…

"You and your family are dead meat hung up for slaughter and skinned alive…" Chills went down my spine… and I twitched and realized I was in my office. I left the mob because of Nikko and I always stood a few feet away when someone had their hand in a pocket.

The red alert note was mailed last week in St. Thomas, Virgin Islands. "Which boat brought this note?" Drake's mail boat went three times a week. Since we are legally U.S. territory, my boat handled mail for everyone on the island, even if they didn't work for me.

"Monday. I was off the island yesterday and just opened it this morning."

I'd forgotten that I asked her to hand-carry banking documents to St. Thomas. The note might have been posted by a resident, a tourist, or someone from Drake's Key, someone on my staff even. This meant the killer could be someone known to me, someone I might never suspect, someone within striking distance at this very moment.

Peaches brought in a fresh cup of coffee. "Darlin' boy. I got you a present and I'll be put out if you don't keep it." She placed a small package on my desk. The only time she bought me a present with company funds was for my own good. I opened the package to find a shiny black taser nestled in red tissue paper. The tissue was a nice touch somehow softening the stunning, or perhaps even lethal, intention of the user. "Already charged. Right pocket. No license needed. Ready for breakfast?" She was a local lady who didn't suffer fools—especially me.

My question was: taser, switchblade, or both? I settled for my familiar blade in my right pocket and the taser as back up in my left.

I checked the note's envelope addressed to "The Boss."

She said, "We buy them by the case, so anyone on the island could have sent it. Now, breakfast?" She was my conscience and my stomach.

The name on the envelope intrigued me. No one used my name. Everyone called me Boss. I doubted any of them recognized my name except for Peaches, Max, Marie, and of course Dex. Someone was going to kill me soon. I always watched for Dex—he seemed too obvious, but the sender addressed the note to me, the Boss.

"Assault in the first degree." Peaches clucked her tongue. "Whoever it is, they picked the perfect time to do the crime." Drake's was a resort, and this was the last week of the season. "We're booked to the roof and our harbor is overflowing. The airport can't park another plane."

"We called that murder in the first in New York," I said. "How many day trippers are here?" I had people who flew in to enjoy our activities, restaurants, floorshow, and casino, but they came mostly for the Chairs. It was a simple game, but the wins and losses were spectacular. A loss could bring a multinational corporation crashing down. Careers were crashed, traded, and sometimes created in the aftermath of the Chairs. Even a life or two had been lost.

"None until the Chairs. Except for darlin' Beryl, Curtis, and Tom, of course." Beryl and Peaches still kept in touch. Tom and Curtis were two of our earliest guests.

If there was a diabolical plan in motion, I had one more stressor: we had taken on extra staff this week, meaning I was extra cautious around new faces. "And how many extra staff did we take on?"

"You'll have to ask Vic. Every bunk is taken. The Key Omelet with mango it is for you." She handed me a bottle of antacids. Yeah, she was well acquainted with my stomach.

It was our big splash. I didn't want to wash up on the beach with the Sunday high tide as the last murder of the season. I had five days to figure this out and no idea who I could trust.

Then there was Rosalie. Rosalie Warren Smith waltzed into my casino last evening, a vision in a bronze-hued sparkled strapless evening dress that showcased her perfect cleavage. She was just as I remembered, and my heart hurt to see her. The downside was she died twenty-five years and three months ago.

****

I was more distracted this week than I've ever been. The cricket match was an unknown and now I regretted I'd agreed to it. This cricket thing guaranteed a lot of faces I didn't know and additional distractions for my security team. And there was the death threat that rumbled across my consciousness: "...dead by Sunday morning."

Today was Tuesday and the Chairs are played on Saturday. My highest blue chip rollers were here or arriving in the next day or two. They brought a ton of baggage, especially their egos. Drake's always employed extra security sprinkled amongst the staff and a few impersonated guests. Some past seasoned escorts picked up extra bucks as security for this event. If you were interested in such things, you could probably pick them out. I speed-dialed my security manager. "Vic, I want a word about the escorts. Yes, all of them."

At Drake's we charged one fee that included all food, drinks, shows, and activities except cosmetic surgery, dental surgery, or special servicing of your boat or plane, or access to the racetrack, and shopping.

Staff arrived at and left the island on a resort shuttle. It probably wasn't too hard to slip onto the island by that shuttle. *I'll have to fix that next season, if...*

I buzzed Peaches. "Do we have our doctors lined up for next year?" As a rule, I had cosmetic surgeons standing in line. Dentists too. They came for four weeks at a time, but with a stipulation. They spent three weeks on my clientele and the rest operating on my staff and my island residents. My island kids had the best dental health in the Caribbean. I never had kids of my own, so it gave me satisfaction to help those here. I got my teeth done here too.

Peaches came into my office. "Boss, I already got a stack of letters from visiting doctors and dentists for next season. Did you want to go through them?"

"Any new ones? Let the doc look them over and make recommendations. Were there any complaints last year?"

"Just about one man who understood better than God what my poor cousin's chin should look like. I hardly recognized the girl. She looked better after the accident than after his surgery."

"Okay. Drop him. Make sure a new doc fixes her chin."

We had a seaport at the resort for guests, and another port five miles away on the leeward side of the island for our cargo deliveries and staff. Guests never used it even if they were aware of it unless they needed a ship repair. That's where all our machine shops and repair facilities were located. "And ask the harbormaster for a boat count, both ports."

Some guests preferred to stay on their yachts anchored at the far end of our harbor. These ships had a tender to ferry people ashore and back. The yachts were draped with festive lights from the masts in the evenings. They tried to outdo each other and were identifiable by their unique décor. It made for a picturesque view from our restaurants, patios, and walkways with the boats bobbing as if waving to our guests.

"Is tonight a full moon?" I asked.

Peaches looked down her nose at me and nodded.

Nights with a moon shining on the water and the lights from the boats were spectacular. We had room service from the resort that took orders to the yachts. Our doctor even made "house calls" if needed. Some guests preferred to dock, and we offered boat slips for them, at an extra fee of course. Those guests liked to be seen as they strutted up to the casino in their finery and jewels.

"How many undercovers are there?" I wanted to be sure we had enough muscle for the Chairs.

She huffed but answered, "I'll ask Vic and get back to you."

Our undercover guests stayed in resort rooms rather than on boats. They ate in our dining facilities since they were always on duty. Some undercovers participated in resort activities like scuba and eco tours around the island. In fact, wherever there was a group of guests, there was security—some live, some digital. A few special undercovers circulated around the casino in pairs or as singles. And, if you checked their drinks, they looked like our specialty cocktails, but they didn't contain alcohol. Of course, they had appropriate wardrobes, and some of the women were goddesses. Who would have suspected a gorgeous woman in an evening dress could break your arm as well as your heart?

Because of the big buildup for our season finale, we had more food and more drink, and more of everything. Our guests expected it for the exorbitant prices we charged, and we didn't disappoint. Do you think those A-lister movie stars and celebrities came here to gamble? Not on your life. No, I paid them. And the Grammy winning singers? Well, they are paid because they perform. And the famous chef who had two shows on TV? All these folks had egos they brought along too.

"And who's our top celeb this week? It's that couple

from Italy, isn't it?"

Who was I really focused on? Rosalie. A deep wound opened I laid to rest long ago. *Why now? Why her?*

****

Rosalie was a sophomore and I a junior when we started seeing each other. "It's funny because your middle name is the same as my last name," I said. We hardly ever mentioned it.

My father belonged to community service groups and was a volunteer fireman. He was a somewhat successful family lawyer practicing in a small town. He'd tell me, "Without the law, we have no society and no justice."

Rosalie's father was the pastor of a conservative congregation. She sang in the choir and taught Sunday School. He visited everyone at the small clinic in town whether or not they were a member of his flock. Her father believed in true charity. "The golden rule says it all. 'Do unto others as you would have them do unto you.'" Oddly enough, he gave all his kids the same middle name—Warren.

Why? It bugs me if I will or I won't ever know the answer to that one.

****

Truth was this last week was getting to be one big headache. Take what happened two years ago. I won't use any names, so let me refer to them as Ego#1 and Ego#2.

Both Egos owned large, extensive, and influential media companies, so they were fierce competitors. They could make or break you if you were a politician. They could launch your star into the heavens if you were broadcaster or TV series celebrity. They could bring your star crashing to earth with the snap of a finger if you fell out of their favor.

Let's say Ego#1 had the majority of his assets in a rather colder climate and Ego#2 had his in a warmer climate. Their domains were separated by the equator but they shared a rather outdated macho view of women. I believed half a world was enough for one man, but neither of *them* did. Sparks flew whenever they were on the same side of the planet. The trouble concerned the personal security they brought with them.

On the west side of the island, less than a mile from the casino, we had a mini resort for our staff and the guests' staff. It included a gym, tennis court, and patio bar by the pool.

Ego#1's bodyguard's sister worked here as a casino dealer, and he took his job so he could visit her for free. The brother was a guaranteed expert to have a client that big.

One afternoon while the Egos rested before their evenings of nightclub shows and gambling, Bodyguard#1 went to have lunch with his sister. She was twenty-two and a knockout, but still a kid in his mind. He went inside for a plate of food and a drink. He probably had more than one drink while waiting for his meal, and when he got back Bodyguard#2 was in his seat talking up the sister.

Witnesses swore the conversation went like, "You're in my seat," to which Bodyguards#2 answered, "Buzz off, ping-pang. Go back to the kitchen. Can't you see we're busy?" Bodyguard#1 set his plate on the table only to see it swept into the pool by Bodyguard#2. Bodyguard#2 picked up a steak knife, stood, faced the other man, and winked. "Hey, coolie, can't you see I'm chatting up this piece of ass. I got plans for her real soon."

"She is my *sister!*" screamed Bodyguard#1.

"Oh, well you'd be the one to ask then," Bodyguard#2 smirked. He leaned in and whispered so all could hear, "How is she in bed? Is she gonna squeal when I shove my—"

Before he finished his sentence, he was a dead man down. Her brother cut the man's throat before he spoke another vile word or the bartender could call security.

Vic interrogated the brother while taking his statement. His sister and other witnesses corroborated his account. His body was removed and taken to our clinic, but Dex and Vic disposed of it later.

I spoke to the two Egos. I called them in together so they got the same story. "Sir, your bodyguard was rudely propositioning a female member of my staff," I said to Ego#2.

He protested, but I'd been through this before. It's much worse if it's their spoiled kid, but a bodyguard usually only rated a token defense.

"When her brother came to the table to sit with her, your bodyguard used racial epithets, made crude remarks I shall not repeat about the brother and sister, and identified the brother as a cook. That was a mistake all around, and he never got to use the steak knife he brandished in his hand."

I turned to Ego#1. "Your bodyguard, sir, gave a statement which was supported by all of the witnesses. It was self-defense without a doubt."

"Gentlemen, this kind of thing is bad for everyone. I worry that some of the dead man's friends might seek revenge. It has happened before." I turned to Ego#2. "Sir, please recall all of your crew and guests and pull up anchor in the next two hours. I can offer to reprovision your boat, if needed."

He nodded, as he didn't have a good reason not to leave.

"And I hope your next visit with us is less eventful."

And now, on top of all the things going on, Rosalie Warren Smith had me twisted in a knot, and I did *not* like that. Who *was* she and what did she want from me?

Our fathers' paths crossed on a regular basis. They were both good men, both good husbands, both good fathers. In a small town everyone knows everyone else's business. The mystery of why these two men didn't cotton to one another was just that—a mystery.

As such, the two families did not approve of our dating. Her parents' rule for Rosalie was she was not allowed to date until she was seventeen. That birthday came around in October of my senior year.

I remember it every year.

Chapter 2

"Dex, Boss asked you to fill me in on Drake's," the interviewer said. "So, I take it you must know it inside and out. If you wrote an ad to promote Drake's Key, what would it say?"

I never worried about this before. It better be good. "Hmm. Here goes. 'What kind o' odds do you need to bet your life? Your life and everything you got.' How's that, miss?"

I'm Dex. I played this little game with myself. So far, I owed me more dough than I'll ever make in this job, but I got plans. I know I'll never get back what I had before, but I'll get something better—yeah, way better. Like I said, I got plans.

"Not bad at all. How did you decide on that? And, call me Peggy." She was writing in shorthand, like Peaches did when we're meeting with the Boss but me, I couldn't read that chicken scratching.

"Thanks. I just made it up. Well, Drake's Key is for people like me, people who made it big and want to play hard and get a thrill to match. The Boss says this private island caters to the top one percent based on net worth. I'm not sure what that means but he says you got more than twenty million bucks. Honestly, most of our guests got way more than that."

"How long do guests usually stay?"

"A guest stays for a day or more, depending if

there's an outstanding extradition warrant on them. The original owner, Duncan Drake, named the place for himself."

"What do they do here, Dex? I've seen guests playing golf and I've seen the deep-sea fishing boats. What happens to the fish they catch, anyway?"

"Did you eat any fish here, uh, Peggy?"

"Yes, I had the wahoo last night. It was perfect. The Macadamia nuts and the soy glaze was to die for."

"You can thank the guest who caught it yesterday. Yeah, our chef does that fish to a tee."

"I see. What else then?"

I wasn't sure what she was getting at. "Do you like the beach scene?"

"I liked the pool and a rum punch. I am going to the lagoon tomorrow to snorkel and work on my tan."

"Someone as pale as you will fry in no time if you don't wear sunscreen. You should o' seen the blisters I got the first year we was open. Now I stay in the shade." I waved the waiter down and ordered mango juice for two. "Well, you could learn to scuba dive, play polo, hang glide, actually dozens o' things. Did you see the floorshow yet?"

"Yes. What about it?" It seemed like *she* was fishing for something, but I didn't take her bait.

"One of the perks for the show folks is plastic surgery. Some guests get plastic surgery, and don't have to leave until they look 'camera-ready.'"

"That all sounds common. There must be something else, something unique here."

I was outta answers. *What was she nosing around about?*

"Have you talked to Rusty at the track?" I asked,

hoping I could send her his way with her questions. "Going as fast as your car will go with no cops around is pretty exciting."

"Rusty? What track? I made out a road when I looked from the plane."

"You did. That's the track. It's for guys who fancy themselves to be race car drivers."

"That doesn't seem like it would appeal to very many people or be able to handle more than a couple of people at a time. Come on. Dex, give. Are you holding out on me? What's your gimmick here?" *She had a sexy smile, but my guess was she was trying to trick me.*

I shrugged. "You caught me. The big draw ain't the beach and it ain't the track. It's the casino what draws the high rollers—"

Peggy interrupted me. "They can go to a dozen casinos around the world."

"…but it wouldn't exist except for the Chairs and that technology, that 'personality transference' thing the Gizmo does. Drake's is the only place that's got it. It sure put a new swing on gambling." That shut her up.

"Gizmo? Personality transference? Is that legal?"

I shrugged. *How would I know if it was legal?* "I never would o' believed it if I didn't see it with my own eyes. Believe you me, you can walk out o' this Drake's a different person than you walked in. Uh oh, I gotta get humping. Boss is coming. Come on, miss. Hurry."

We walked into the casino, which was spectacular even by Vegas standards but classy. "See that big glass chandelier? Boss had some fancy French company make it. It's insured for two million bucks. We put it in storage for the hurricane season. The Chairs are under it."

"Are those birds in the chandelier?' Peggy pointed

up towards the ceiling.

"Hey, you got pretty sharp eyes. Those are Drake's Dandies which are some kinda birds that live here. They're pretty noisy but you can't miss them, all yellow and red with big green eyes."

Peggy walked around the chairs. "These are breathtaking, Dex. Burgundy tapestry shot through with gleaming gold threads. Real gold?"

I nodded.

"They really catch the eye."

"You betcha it's real gold. And the buttons on the front too. That's the idea, and it's my job to set them up."

"Any idea what the Chairs are worth? Just a ballpark number?"

I never thought of that much. With all the Boss spent in here, why steal a lousy heavy chair? "You'd have to ask someone else that. Maybe Yvette, the casino manager, knows. I just set them up.

"See, the Chairs are all alike except for the numbers in plain business envelopes. That way no one tries to end up on a certain chair, and you don't know what you got until it's over. I put the chairs in a circle with the backs together."

"What's this pocket on the back for, Dex? Are the Chairs used every night?" she asked.

"That's where I put the envelopes and we only play once on the last night of a season. But every night we got the wheel, the cards, the dice, and the bones or something else. But for the big stakes, it's the Chairs. That's our end-o'-the-season big draw, our Fourth o' July fireworks, you could say."

"Dex, did you have the upholstery cleaned?" asked the Boss as he joined us." He still called me Dex. He said it sounded like a decks o' cards.

The Boss stuffed ten C-notes in my tux pocket, my traditional tip for the Chairs.

Our head waiter Hugo arrived with a tray holding a small bowl.

Boss said, "Ah, the Osetra Golden caviar." He used a pearly-colored spoon to scoop up a sample of the Russian fish eggs laying on top o' the crushed ice. "Nice. Buttery. Nutty. Clean fish ending. Do we have enough spoons?"

"Yes, Boss. Some of the guests like to keep them every year for a kind o' souvenir. The restaurant manager laid in eight dozen more. We're good."

Boss picked up a frosty glass of clear liquor and sipped it. "Also, very nice. How many Russian vodka brands do we have on hand?" He waved Hugo away. "Thanks. Nice presentation."

"The top six, Boss, ten cases of each. And we got another two hundred o' the glasses already in the freezer."

"Good. I'm going to check the flowers. I hope you are enjoying the casino, miss." Boss winked at Peggy.

"What's next, Dex," she asked.

"This." I draped a fancy 24-karat gold and silk ribbon across the Chairs so's no one will sit on them. Then I polished the mahogany trim until it was as shiny as glass.

"Every night I stand by the door. It's my job to make sure only the right people get in the Casino. We got a reputation to uphold, you know. Admission is by invitation or referral, and I know everyone who's coming tonight on sight."

"Has anyone ever tried to slip into the casino who

wasn't invited?"

"Yeah, sure. One guy's butler put on the guy's tux while his boss was sleeping and tried it. I caught him when he ducked in behind a real millionaire. Me and Vic grabbed him. We played like he was new and so was supposed to meet our Boss. Instead, we took him to Vic's office. When *his* boss came looking for him next day, well, we never hosted them here again. The rich guy was kicked out and wasn't allowed back on the island." We walked past the roulette wheels.

"It takes a while to get an invite to the Chairs. It'll take you at least six months to a year to set everything up all legal-like, check you out and sign the paperwork, plus legal fees, and background check. You might o' heard o' the required, up front five-million-dollar entry fee, twenty million minimum bet. Players cough up their passports before the game. Some o' them will get back the same one, and some will get back a different one, but you'll look like the photo in it."

"How did all this get started?" Peggy asked as she looked around.

"Dumb luck really. Before that though, I'll go back to how I started gambling. By the way, I know Boss is letting you interview people for a book or something all week, but you won't use any names, right? "

"That's correct. I'll use an alias for each person."

"And… as a personal favor, could you make me talk better?" She nodded. "You can? The Boss says I add 'character' to the place but thanks a lot. Can I get you a drink while we talk?" I waved the nearest waiter over.

"Miss, Boss said to give you this fancy French scarf as a souvenir o' Drake's. He hoped you like the red and blue combo. He said to wear it in good health. It's named for that old Greek guy who invented boxing."

"Convey my thanks to Boss. I'm excited he is letting me conduct these interviews." She put the scarf in her briefcase and started to put her notepad in, but I stopped her.

"I don't see how that could be a problem, Peggy. Uh, why don't you practice on me?"

Peggy was probably happy to start interviewing with me because I *am* Boss's right-hand man. Who knows as much about this place after me except for Boss o' course? With a past criminal record, I always gotta be careful what I said. This way I figured I could get it out of the way before she had time to think up questions that could be more complicated.

"Tell me about your family to start with," she asked.

"Sure. My folks was a working-class family in Jersey. My dad Ron was a longshoreman from the day he turned eighteen. A lifelong member o' the ILA, International Longshoremen's Association, just like his dad. See, Ron wasn't ambitious, just wanted a job with a paycheck and no thinking. That last part's why he never made it to crane operator."

"Dexter, loan me ten bucks until payday." I hesitated and he twisted my arm behind my back until I grunted "uncle." He dislocated my shoulder and it hurt like hell, but I didn't say nothing. He rifled through my pockets taking my money and smokes. "Don't tell Mary you little prick." I couldn't get my shoulder back in place and had to walk to the hospital. "Ron was mean and dumb and couldn't do the math so's he let bookies and card dealers do it for him. One day I came home from school and the door was locked. I banged on the door until a man the size of our refrigerator opened it. 'Who

are you?'"

"The new tenant. Scram kid." I tried to get in around him. He stopped me with his fist in my eye. 'Where's my ma?' I bawled. Mr. New Tenant jerked his chin up towards Mary who was sitting on our broken couch on the sidewalk across the street."

Peggy was real quiet and didn't look up at me. I guess she was shocked or something.

It pissed me off when Ron blew the rent on cards, and we'd get the heave ho. "The next time I was high I forgot we moved and was back pounding on the same door. The same guy answered. 'I got what cha want, kid.' Then he kicked me in the gut, and I rolled to the curb.

One thing I remember from that time was when I lost my cherry. I was delivering groceries to some dock worker's wife Evie, a mousey brunette with a perpetual black eye."

It was always, "I'm short this week, kid but…" and she locked the door and lifted her skirt. I was fourteen. I never said no, but I kind o' think that's why I don't trust women. I'd rather pay and know where we stand right up front.

"Evie did hound me to get a GED, and that turned out to be the best free advice anyone ever gave me. One day after I dropped off her groceries and my pants she said, 'You're getting better in the sack than my old man, Dex. But you got a get away from here, kid.'"

"Doing what? I got no skills, and I can't join the ILA."

"Finish school."

"I already quit,"

She said, "Get a GED. It's almost as good as a diploma."

"I try not to think o' the time the cops came and got me to ID Ron." I needed a swallow of coffee before I hit the next part. " It was Officer McCarthy who said, 'Your SOB dad stiffed the wrong bookie this week. We can't find Mary, so I need you to make the ID. Come on.' He took me to the morgue.

Chapter 3

"Is that him, Dexter? Is that your dad?" Ron's face looked bad, like rotten hamburger.

"What happened to him?" I asked. I couldn't look away.

"McCarthy said, "They broke all his fingers. Then the bookie's goons beat him to death. Don't lift the sheet and look, kid. If it's who we think, they like to tie a guy down and use a baseball bat starting at his feet." I didn't hear the rest o' it.

"I could still see the scar on Ron's neck, the one from a knife fight the year before."

Evie's old man guessed Ron was the one servicing his wife. I never said nothing, just let Ron take it. He beat me plenty, so's I figured he was guilty o' something and deserved it no matter what the reason.

"Yeah, McCarthy. That's him. That's my dad Ron.… That's when I dropped out o' school."

No big deal. I didn't have many friends then and still don't. It was all me and ma after that and my sister Linda. My ma, Mary, worked her ass off. Looking back, I guess I don't resent her blowing cash on smokes and lottery tickets, if that's the best thing you got going. I still hate the beatings she gave us kids when she was high or drunk.

"Not long after Ron croaked, we ended up on welfare."

Peggy was shaking her head as she wrote this stuff down.

"Ma got TB bad. She didn't have no insurance from the ILA because her and Ron weren't married legal-like.

"'Where you taking her?' I asked the social worker."

"'County hospital,' he said. Mary smoked until the day she coughed up a lung and died." *The county put Linda in foster care. I don't know where she is now.*

"That's pretty grim." Peggy looked like she was gonna cry.

I nodded. "Know what's the one thing I liked about my life before Ron died? Funny question, right? The movies. Nobody much bothered about me, so I had lots o' free time." *I had to find some way to make dough and stay outta trouble.* "I worked a deal with the movie manager."

"'What can you do, Dexter?' he asked me.

"'What cha got?' I answered. 'I seen the ushers emptying trash and running the vacuum. I can do that.'

"'How 'bout mopping and cleaning toilets? Got any problem with that?'

"Since I'd eat for free and I was used to eating every day, I told him I been cleaning toilets since I was six. It was my specialty. I was fast at doing the mopping and collecting trash, so he'd let me sit in on a movie. If he said, 'There's a sports movie coming on, Dexter. Theater one in ten minutes.' I'd say no thanks and keep on mopping. But if he said, 'Paul Newman's in Theater Two in ten,' well then, I was there."

The waiter topped off my coffee and brought me seconds on pie and one for Peggy.

"I only watched movies where you went somewhere or had an adventure o' some kind. Or someone escaped from somethin' or a western. Paul Newman was my go-to guy. I still watch reruns o' *Cool Hand Luke* or *The Hustler* when I have time. I tried eating fifty eggs, but I didn't make it. Puked my guts out, but if I'd been in prison, I bet I could. I liked *The Hustler* the best. You know the story—big loser, the comeback, the big score." *Just like I'm gonna' make soon.*

"After I dropped out of high school, I looked into a GED and the Navy. By the time I was seventeen I passed it. Yeah, I know. I forged Mary's name on the Navy consent form. I was big for my age, so no one looked twice. Anyways, that GED got me into the Navy. I left Jersey and never told anyone. I got three squares a day, a bunk to sleep in with a pillow and blanket, I never thought about what I was gonna' be doing 'cause someone always told me. Since I was a big guy, swabbies picked on me. Now, in spite o' my family situation, I'm a pretty easy-going guy. I don't mean the Navy Chiefs 'cause that's their job. I mean the other guys who want o' show how tough they are. I don't take that from nobody." I hadn't remembered this in a while and was gettin' worked up. "The first time we was doing boxing in PT, that's like gym class, I was matched up with a smart-ass New York car mechanic named Ratso 'cause he looked like that guy in that movie 'bout the cowboy hustler. Ratso was harassing me for weeks."

"*Midnight Cowboy?* Is that the movie you mean?"

"Yeah. Anyways, 'What cha got, oilcan?' I said hoping to rattle him. He threw a bunch o' punches that I mostly knocked away, but I let a couple connect. A cut opened under my eye and started to ooze a little." I got a scar from that. *I always lie and say I got in a bar fight.*

"I blinked like I was having trouble seeing. Ratso

fell for it. He let his hands down a smidge. He was feeling cocky. I could see him smirking like he had me. That smirk was what I was waiting for. I punched him square in the face. He spun out and face-planted on a steel bulkhead—that's a wall on a ship."

Ratso always moved to the other side o' the passageway when we ran into each other.

"He never said as much as one word to me after that beating. Neither did a lot o' shipmates, but I didn't mind. Did I mention that movie theater shared an alley with a YMCA? I did their mopping and trash for boxing lessons and a couple o' bucks between movies."

Peggy laughed like I told a joke or somethin. "It sounds like you were a go getter, Dex. How did you like the Navy?"

"I ate good in the Navy. I tried to eat things I never had before. Found out I hated salad—weeds and leaves, as I called it. I avoided spaghetti and noodles. You would too if that's what you ate every day growing up. I ate all the meat they'd give me, same for eggs, I loved broccoli, peas, baked potatoes, apples, and bananas. I was still getting use to the taste o' coffee, but I drank a lot o' milk."

She said looking at her empty pie plate, "I'm afraid I would eat too many desserts. How about you?"

"Sweets weren't hard to come by growing up. I swiped candy from the movie theater. But when they served soft ice cream, or real ice cream on board ship, I'd load up. I still love lemon pie. Anyway, the next time we did boxing in PT, coach Tyson, who'd done all right for himself on the All-Navy Boxing Team and had a flat nose that proved it pulled me aside and asked, 'How would you like to box on the ship's team? You didn't just fly off and pound that guy who'd been harassing you. You stayed calm and got the job done. That's what it takes.' I said, 'Why not. It'd keep me out o' trouble.'"

It did for a while. I was pretty good compared to the other guys, and hard to take down. Pretty soon, they was betting on me. Some o' them was making money off me and how was that fair I started thinking? So's, I started betting. First just on me. Then on other guys. Then on every guy. I got busted enough that the Navy kicked me out. *But I didn't do anything stupid, like some idiots who got caught cooking drugs on board ship.*

"Finally, me and the Navy split. I got a general discharge." I didn't get a bad record, and I was lucky the Navy didn't kick me off the ship in a foreign country. Oh, yeah, my face looked like I went through World War II without a helmet. No one would mistake me for Paul Newman. "What I had was some cash and this tattoo I got in the PI—that's the Philippines. It's a pair o' snake eyes dice on my right arm 'cause that's my shooting arm. Life's a crap shoot, so why not? Well, miss. What else do you wanna know?"

"Tell me a little about yourself and what you do here at Drake's."

"Me, Dex, I'm forty-three. The ladies ask me if I'm George Clooney's brother. I always laugh at their joke and say, 'Yes ma'am. The good looking one.' I usually get a good tip from that line."

"You seem to be everywhere at once, Dex."

"That's 'cause I work hard and put in long hours."

"I see, but I notice you are always very dapper looking."

I didn't know what "dapper" meant, so I guessed she was talking about my clothes. "Thanks. I speak a little street Italian and I'm polite to the gentlemen and kind to the ladies. I don't own a pair o' jeans. Boss's orders. My leisure wear is silk shirts and slacks, mostly 'cause I never know when I'll run into a customer."

"Always on the job? What do you do for fun? What do you do on vacation?"

Vacation? I'm always on the hustle, looking for my big chance and payoff. I never took a "vacation" in my life. Vacations are for suckers. "I gamble for fun. I get a couple o' months off every year when we shut down for repairs at the end of our season."

"Well, you look very fit. How do you keep in shape?"

"Boss makes me lift weights and jog with him. We both like to work out on the punching bag. Helps with reflexes and coordination. That's why I look good in the tailored tux I wear for work."

Peggy wagged her head. "I wish I did that. How did you and Boss get together?"

"So let me tell you about the Gizmo first. It'll make more sense that way. Refill on that drink?"

"Yes. The Gizmo? I don't know what that is."

"How about a lobster sandwich? And a piece o' lemon pie? I didn't get lunch yet."

"That sound delicious. Thank you."

I waved for the waiter. "Swell. It's on the house, just so you know. Miss, the Gizmo is why gamblers come to Drake's. It's the real story at Drake's Key Casino."

"What's the story on Drake's start, Dex? How did it happen?"

Peggy picked the right guy 'cause I know everything that happened before Drake's got started. "I'll tell ya but keep it to yourself. Boss keeps his cards close to his chest, and I ain't tired o' this job just yet…It started over ten years back. Now, picture New York City, but the kinda rundown part. Imagine orange neon lights blinking outside o' sleazy hotel's dirty cracked window. On the other side o' that window was a dark smoky room. I don't smoke myself, but some o' the others did." *That's one addiction I don't want because o' what it did to my ma.*

"I remember that game like it was last week. I was sitting at a round table with a naked bulb hanging from the ceiling by a ragged cord.

"Five guys was playing poker with me. Everyone had a glass o' whiskey or something sitting by their hand. The ashtrays filled up fast. The game has gone on for nine hours, and I already emptied most of the pockets there.

"This girl named Luscious came over and took the empty plates from the sandwiches she brought two hours ago. 'Want anything?' she says bored-like while she popped her gum and twirled her hair around her finger.

"Button, who already lost his shirt to me, says, 'Another Jack and Coke,' but she emptied the ashtrays and sat down and ignored him. She knows I only paid for booze when a player's got cash on the table.

"I can't remember much o' their faces 'cause o' the smoke and 'cause my eyes were on the cards and the money. I got my sleeves rolled up, so my dice tat shows. I rub my tat for luck when I'm playing. I got a greasy hat pulled down low so's my face is dark from my nose up. The brim keeps the light out o' my eyes, and it's harder for the players to read my face.

"Three guys are out—out o' cards and out o' money. They're sitting back in their chairs smoking and yawning. Even so, they keep their eyeballs peeled and on the table. Across the table is a dude with bushy white hair that glows like a halo from the light. He looks like that famous scientist riding the bicycle and sticking out his tongue, but he's not him. He just reminded me o' him so I called him the professor.

"There's a cracked leather sofa in one corner where Luscious sat and filed her nails and painted her lips when she wasn't serving up drinks or flirting with the guys who had cash. She was walking her skinny legs around serving drinks. Short, short skirt, big rack—not for me, for the other guys. I'm running the game and she's my secret weapon.

"I pat Luscious on the ass for luck. So far, it's working. I played with most o' these guys before and they know I ran an honest game—almost. I asked her to bring me a gin. She'd bring me a glass o' water though because in *The Sting* Paul Newman says you always drink gin with your mark so's they think you're stupid."

"Charming," Peggy said.

"Yeah, I know. There's was a pile o' money on the table. Three men were out, and a fourth was sweating. His tie snaked around his neck like it was choking him. He looked from me to the money and over to the professor. The professor was low on cash but still in, but I ain't sweating none, and this guy with the tie knows it. He leans back and slapped his cards down. 'Fold,' he sneered as he pushed his chair back and whipped off that tie.

"It was down to the professor and me. He took out a white handkerchief and wiped the sweat off his face. It looked like he wanted to surrender. I could see he's desperate to call my bet but, like I said, he's out o' cash.

He reached in his pocket and brings out a document o' some kind. Seems he was some kind of professor, after all. 'I've got the damnedest invention in modern history, Drake. It's worth millions, probably more.'

Everyone laughed their pants off.

" It's his first time at my table, see. The dude don't know my rules. I says, 'I don't take paper from nobody.' The professor says he has a working prototype. I don't know what a 'prototype' is, but he used the word 'working.' I says, 'Oh yeah. What does it do?'

"The professor wipes off his glasses with his tie and cranes his neck forward like one o' them big birds that don't fly. He says, 'It switches people into different bodies,' in a drop-dead serious voice. Now he's looking at me straight in the eye, and he don't look like a bullshitter or a crazy guy.

"Someone says, 'Like in *The Fly?*'

Everyone laughed even harder.

"And he says, 'Not like *The Fly!* Better. You keep your own personality and memory but move into a new body. Let me give you a demonstration.' This guy looked as serious as a bookie rubbing out a bad bet. 'What have you got to lose but a few minutes of your time?'"

"I'm a gambler. I knew a sucker bet when I saw one, but I felt like a stretch and a piss, so I says, 'Okay. Show me.'

"Three men and the girl stayed and guarded the table. I left with the professor and Vic, one o' the players. Me and Vic go back a long way, so I trusted him.

"Vic's a big guy like me but he's got brown eyes with a scar through one eyebrow and an undecided moustache that don't know yet what it wants to be. Nice hair though. Vic knew Luscious was with me, and I trusted her with the money while the others were there."

"Where did the professor take you?" Peggy asked.

"Hold on. I'm just getting to that. We get in my car. Vic drives and the professor gives directions pointing to show Vic when to turn.

"'Left at the gas station…' the professor says, '…then, over the train tracks and turn right.' I was lost. Finally, he says, 'Pull up in the alley behind this luncheonette.' Vic parked by a padlocked metal door. The streets were empty so's we got to his lab in less than fifteen minutes.

"We must o' been near the river 'cause I smelled it. I never forgot that slimy garbage smell.

"The professor took out a bunch o' keys and says, 'Follow me.' He took us up in a squeaking freight elevator that smelled like cat piss to the second-floor o' this old warehouse that smelled like moldy cheese. We got off, walked around the corner, and he unlocked a rusty steel door.

"It looked like we was in some kind o' storage room because it was jammed full o' stuff I don't know about—coils o' wire, batteries, wood, metal tubes, boxes o' giant clock parts, even glass and computer pieces. There was a cot with a scummy blanket and pillow in the back, and an apple crate for a table. A flea-bitten rat was finishing off what looked like a cheese sandwich. The place made my skin crawl.

Chapter 4

This place reminded me o' the professor's lab in *Frankenstein,* you know with Boris somebody, but in the middle o' the lab was the Gizmo."

"Finally, the Gizmo," Peggy said with a scratch on her notepad.

"Yeh. I laughed at the Gizmo, thinking this is a pretty fancy hoax, but the professor just kept working. The Gizmo looked like he swiped a couple o' fancy phone booths. They had glass fronts so you could see in or out, and the glass had a fancy swirly design. They each got a seat covered in beautiful cloth, real swanky looking.

"The professor flipped open a box hanging on the wall like those fuse boxes and threw a switch. Right away noises started like…like in the movies, like in *Frankenstein,* like things were starting to turn and soon—real soon—there was a steady humming sound. It's like the room had a heart and it just started beating. The hair on my neck stood up like when I stood outside in a lightning storm. I felt the electricity surging through the air. My palms sweated.

"Between the booths was a fancy wood panel all shiny and covered with old-looking brass knobs and dials and colored lights. It looked complicated.

"'We wait two minutes while the Gizmo warms up,' the professor announced. A big clock in the center o' the panel counted down the time. It looked like the fancy dial from the clock at Grand Central Station—you know the one with all the X's and V's instead o' numbers. You know—when you go in the door at 42nd and Park Avenue. Over the clock in fancy letters, it says "*tempus fugit*." Vic says that means 'time flies.'

"All our eyes couldn't help but stare at that clock. Then it was ready.

"The professor pointed to a square green button on the left side o' the clock and there's a round red button on the right side.

"'Does it matter who gets in which box?' I asked. I don't know if my leg is being pulled or if I'm getting driving lessons, but I knew my shirt was kinda wet.

"'No, it doesn't, but there always has to be someone in each booth,' he says, cool as an ice cube."

"'Anyone?' I says.

"'Yes, anyone. But you must always wait three minutes to use it again. And no one should go through it more than twice. Ever.' He shuddered when he says that, and his voice cracked. 'Now, when we get in the booths….' and I stopped him right there.

"'I ain't getting into one o' those.' What kind o' sucker does he think I am? 'Finish explaining to me how to run this thing,' I says. Funny. He was so calm, like a proud papa showing off his baby. But me, my hands started to shake.

Peggy was hooked on my story. "And? Come on!"

"The professor says, 'When we got into the booths and the doors are closed, a yellow light will come on in each booth. There,' he says as he pointed to a light over each door. 'When the countdown is done, a bell rings, and the Gizmo is ready. Push the green button. That's it.

The Gizmo counts down two minutes, the red light comes on, a bell rings, and you're done.'

"It sounded too simple. Did he think I was an idiot? 'What if someone opens the door to get out before the two minutes is over,' I asked.

"The professor shook his head. 'That can't happen. The doors stay locked while the device is in operation. The red-light flashes on, and…Ding! A bell rings. It's ready,' he said."

"Vic and me stood there for a minute looking at each other. 'Vic. Get in the booth. I'll make it worth your while,' I says.

"Vic looked at me with a smirk on his face. '*Bona fide* IOU, Dex' he asked. I nodded and Vic says, 'Then sure thing. This ought to be good.'

"I guessed Vic thought this Gizmo was a joke, and when nothing happened, he was gonna rough this frizzy-haired hippie up 'cause Vic joked all the way there about the professor's hair. Then Vic put the cherry on the cake. 'Here, Dexter. Hold my wallet,' as he winked and handed me his cash and brass knuckles.

"The professor gets in the other booth, but before he closes the door he says, 'When the countdown is over, press the green button. Got it?'"

"I nodded and waved for him to close the door. The yellow lights come on. Ding! The countdown is over. I press the green button." I stopped to catch my breath and sip coffee.

Peggy said, "You can't just leave me it at that, Dex. What happened? What about the Gizmo?"

Peggy took up her pencil and looked at me. "Ready, Dex?"

"Yeah, sure. So, Vic and me got back to the poker

game after an hour. Someone said, 'Where's the big shot professor?' and I says, 'The old professor demoed the Gizmo for us. It worked. Vic *is* the professor now.'"

Peggy's eyes bugged out. "Really?"

I nodded. "Someone else asked, 'Then where's the real Vic?' and I snorted, 'Getting a haircut,' which he was. I accepted the professor's bet. We sat at the table again. Two o' the other guys left already. It seemed weird 'cause now it was Vic's body and voice but the professor's words and mind." *I don't know why Vic ain't collected on that IOU yet. I know he ain't forgotten. How could he?*

"Cards were dealt. I ain't never been so shook in my life. I ain't sure if I wanna win or not. I looked at my cards. At first, I'm shocked, but I won with black aces and eights."

She choked a little. "The dead man's hand." *Maybe she was superstitious like me.*

Yeah, the 'dead man's hand. "Just like Wild Bill Hickock, but we don't draw no guns for a shootout in this game." *I sluffed off the idea this win was unlucky.* "Being superstitious, I rubbed my tattoo saying my good luck charm worked. The professor never looked up when he signed the papers. I stuffed them in my pocket."

"'You'll need these,' he says as he handed me a keyring. I noticed a little brass plate that said 'Gizmo.' 'The instructions are in the drawer in the console between the booths, he says.'"

"'And how do I fix it if it breaks down?' I asked."

"'That's all in the manual,' the professor says. 'Just watch the clock and you'll be okay.'"

"'Watch the clock. Got it.' I picked up the cash on the table and stood to leave. I stuffed a big tip between those tits on Luscious. The professor, now in Vic's body, sits with his head in his hands just staring at the green felt tabletop. Someone put a gun on the table by the professor." *Maybe even me, I don't remember.*

As I closed the door, I heard a shot. I never looked back. "I needed to find Vic. We had to move the Gizmo somewhere safe. It took me a while to figure out the best way to make money off the invention. It was a pain moving the Gizmo around. I needed the players to come to me. Then, one night in a room in New York City, I took another sucker bet. Poker again. This room was fancier. I'd moved up to a better class o' clients. I was doing swell, but I worried I was a one-trick pony. I moved into the big time like I never imagined existed. Me and Vic met the Boss." *That should keep her busy.*

"I have to say 'Wow!' I've never heard a story like this. And as they say, the rest is history," Peggy sputtered.

"You got that right. Nobody else can compete with Drake's when it comes to a big gamble and a bigger payoff."

"And it actually—it actually works? This Gizmo works?" Peggy looked like I told her I used to know the Tooth Fairy.

"Yep. No lie."

"And it doesn't hurt or damage anyone?"

"Nah. Take my word for that." *At least not as I remember.*

"Could I get a peek at the Gizmo. You've got my curiosity riled up now." She looked at me with a big smile and even bigger eyes. She had to o' seen the Gizmo on display in the casino lobby.

I had to think about that for a couple o' seconds.

Boss didn't say nothing about that to me. "Yeh, I don't see how that'd hurt anything, but no pictures."

We got up and she said, "Dex, would mind showing me your lucky tattoo?"

"Sure thing," and I started to push up my sleeve. Then I remembered and let go o' my sleeve and lied, "I don't have time right now. Catch me later. I just remembered I gotta be somewhere."

I left her writing in her notebook. I needed to duck her in case she asked me again about the Gizmo and my tat.

####

"I'm Ledger Warren but everyone calls me Boss, owner of Drake's Key. I've asked my staff to cooperate with you in your research and Player interviews. Do you have any concerns?"

"Yes. Is there a way I can come and go without being seen? I've never interviewed people of, uhm, the *caliber* of some of your guests. I'd like to avoid any unwelcomed attention."

I squelched a chuckle. "I understand. I'll introduce you to the Maze. It will help you get around more securely. Dex can help you if you get lost. I don't anticipate any risk on your part, but you may be right. What shall I call you?"

"That's great. My name is Peggy, Boss."

"Yes. Of course." *She had the curves, blonde hair, and sultry voice that reminded me of singer Peggy Lee.* "Where shall we start?" I kept my life private, an old habit from my mob job. I patted my pocket to check I had my taser.

"How did you acquire this island? It's huge."

"It is big. This island was privately owned. I did

some legal work for a wealthy client. He didn't want it to fall into the hands of his future ex-wife. My fee was rather stiff, so we settled on the island." *We stiffed it to his wife: he charged me one dollar to buy it, and I charged him one dollar in legal fees. We were both satisfied.*

"I can see that happening. How did you decide to build Drake's?"

I planned how to best dodge this question. I left my job with the mob on good terms. I'd kept my nose clean, but I hated Las Vegas. Too phony. Too big. Too many grudges to be settled at my expense. But I did understand it. "I was changing careers. I wanted something I could control yet be entertained and able to relax. A resort seemed the answer and the island the ideal place. I met Dex who owned the thing that made us unique: the Gizmo." *A simplified version but technically true.*

"Dex mentioned the Gizmo. Will I have a chance to see it up close?"

"Perhaps. I'll see what I can do."

"How did you settle on the resort name and who was Boss?"

Dex believed he should get the privilege, but I was adamant he was fumbling the Gizmo for peanuts by running a penny-ante poker game. I couldn't let him fumble this chance. I fronted the cash for construction and all startup costs. Dex settled for a seven-year contract as my manager with a big payout at the end. I named the resort after him as a consolation prize. I hoped his story was the same as mine. "We cut cards. I won. Perfect for a gambling establishment, don't you think?" *My deck, of course.* Afterwards we rolled my dice and transferred bodies, just in case any old enemies showed up. I assumed my enemies were a wee bit smarter than his.

"Come, let me show you the Maze. You should talk to my department managers for more detail about our operations, and of course talk to the Players for the Chairs; you have two scheduled interviews after lunch, don't you? The Maze was designed so staff could move around unseen by guests. The same idea as a waiter disappears around a corner and returns with your order. It's the 'skeleton' of the resort. It curves and branches out but is enclosed by the public spaces of the main buildings. I can cross over from the casino to the dining room in minutes." *Guests see me when I chose to be seen.*

Peggy said, "This should be fun. Lead on, Boss."

The Maze is the secret to efficient management and superior customer service. "Here's a layout of the Maze. Sorry, I can't let you have a copy. We're *here* in my office." I pointed to a location on the layout. "No photos. I wouldn't want your readers to get their curiosity up. "I drew an imaginary circle on the map. "My office, the casino, and the Gizmo are all clustered in one area."

I drew a second circle. "This area includes the Consolation and Waiting rooms Players use after the Chairs. We get a few sore losers so we can contain them better here."

"And for my interviews, where will we be?" Peggy asked.

"For the interviews you'll be using a Waiting room and a small private dining room that is next to the backstage dressing rooms." I pointed to a different area in the Maze. "You'll bump into waiters and entertainers but be sure the interviewees leave by the main door, and then you go out the *hidden door* to the Maze afterwards."

I passed her a remote control. "You can find that door in any room by pushing the green button. Usually the door is opposite the main door. Push the button again in front of the hidden door, and it pops open. Be sure to close it securely as you leave. Give it a test."

"So, I push the green button…Oh, I see an arrow. That's clever. The arrow always points to the door no matter which way I stand," Peggy remarked. She walked to the wall the arrow was pointing to. One push of the button again and the hidden door sprung open.

I said, "Let's go into the Maze."

As Peggy closed the door to the Maze, she noticed a green light indicating the door was secure. Each door was marked by the name of the room in fluorescent letters.

"Maze doors with a blue light are men's rest rooms and pink lights are the ladies, just in case you need one. Hall lights are standard full-spectrum white light day and night. If you want to enter your interview from the Maze, you can see on the camera if it's empty. Look, my office is empty. If it's empty or someone like me or Dex is inside, push the button and go on in."

"Good idea. Look before I leap."

"I suggest you arrive early and come in through the hidden door. If you have any trepidation about it, ask me or Dex to stay with you. If you really don't feel comfortable about one of the Players, just skip it. We'll make up some excuse." I walked Peggy to the busiest part of the Maze. "The kitchens are in the central area. This makes provisioning easier. You may have noticed the halls are wide. We use a forklift to bring in supplies. The dining rooms, lounges, and bars are on the outside of the kitchens. I think this is about all you'll need. Any questions?"

"Maybe later. This'll get me started."

We walked back to my office. She pushed the button, and my door opened.

"Let's go back in," I said.

"Talk about seeing behind the curtain, the Maze is amazing. You are a wizard. I only have one question. Are the dressing rooms open all the time?"

****

"'A dare devil oceanic salvor, Player Ten recovered a Spanish King's treasure from the briny deep. Now she's mining for gold on dry land. Welcome, Captain Ten.' I asked Boss to say that. Advertising for my company. I'm always looking for investing partners," I said.

"How did you get started? Aren't old shipwrecks dangerous? Call me Peggy, please." the interviewer asked.

I looked at her pale arms and face. *She looked like a ghost next to my brown body.* "You look like you've never been in the sun. I was born on Summerland Key. Are you familiar with the Florida Keys?"

She nodded. "Yes. I was there once on vacation in Key West. Very hot, scenic, and a bit eccentric."

I laughed. "Your memory is correct. My dad ran a shrimp boat, but I ran into local eccentrics every day." *I grew up crewing for my dad.* "My favorite class in school was history. I used to lay awake at night imagining the Spanish Main, pirates, and treasure. In my dreams I was the Red Witch of the gunboat Red Devil. The next night I was the Spanish captain of the *Vela d'Ora*, the Golden Sail, outrunning Blackbeard."

"Did your dad catch anything else, Captain? Spanish treasure?"

"Hardly. His boat was the *Half Shell*. He joked that half of what he dragged up was old shells rather than shrimp. My brother Howie used to crew for him when school was out, and my name is Rhonda."

"Okay, Rhonda. Tell me about working on a shrimp boat. That job sounds hard and dangerous."

"It *was* hard work. It made me stronger than many of the boys, and I learned to not complain. If there was a problem, we had to fix it pronto. That was a life lesson for me. One day the winch was acting up and dad was slammed by a lobster trap. He broke two fingers. He taped them together and kept on working. He didn't get to the hospital until almost dark."

Peggy whistled. "Wow. He sounds like a tough guy. Was he a tough captain?"

"Not really. But Dad had one unbending rule: when he was docking the boat, no one was to jump onto the wharf to tie up. Instead, we would throw a line to a linesman on the wharf. One day the linesman didn't show. Without even thinking, Howie jumped to the wharf. He missed and fell. Before Dad could react, the boat crushed Howie against the pilings." *He was twelve years old.* Every year I drop flowers off the dock where it happened. "That crushed Dad too. Howie was his heart. Dad was just a shell of a man afterwards. He kept running the boat to support our family."

"I'm so sorry. It must have been hard for you on the boat."

"No. I never crewed for Dad again. He wouldn't let me." I believed he and mom didn't want to take the chance of losing another child.

Chapter 5

When I was a teen, the scuba shop owner next door taught me to fill tanks, repair equipment, and to dive. I was a natural in the water. I moved up the ranks and became a professional scuba instructor in no time."

"That sounds like a lot of responsibility for a kid. And dangerous."

"The danger wasn't in the ocean; it was right on shore." The red in Peggy's scarf was the same color as the blood I spilled that night when I was eighteen. "I was in the shop alone getting everything set up for the next day's charter. It was hot and sweaty work, so I had on my bikini." I looked away for a few moments in silence.

I was offered kindness when Peggy said, "You don't need to tell me anything you don't want to, Rhonda. You really don't."

"I know. It's something I tried to put behind me…One of the new dive masters, a local redneck who'd been leering at me and making dirty remarks for weeks showed up. I noticed him hanging around on the dock, but I ignored him. He was scheduled to work the charter. He came in and locked the door. Without a word he yanked off my top. He got my arm twisted behind me, bent me over, and raped me." *I was shocked at how quickly the anger returned.* Other than the cops, I've never told anyone about it.

Peggy waited again and handed me a tissue.

"I guess he forgot what the trip was the next day. When he let me go, I grabbed a loaded speargun from the counter, turned to face him, and shot him square in the heart." *I could have gone for his groin or stomach but I worried the doctors might save him.* "I put my top back on, called the cops, did a rape kit, and filed a report. It didn't bother me much, but I did go to counseling for a while." *I swore then that no man would ever put his hand to me again.* The interviewer was quiet at this admission of my rape and the killing that followed.

I continued, "After that, I've was named the Red Witch Rhonda because I was a killer at spearing big fish. I always wear my knife on my leg, even out of the water, even today."

Peggy's voice quivered as she said, "I...I can't even imagine..."

I looked her in the eyes and admitted, "I've never forgotten the look on his face, but I've never missed a minute of sleep over it, nor have I had to fend off another drunk. I always have my knife in my purse if not on my hip."

We both were quiet after my admission of killing a man. I looked away and dropped my voice. "When Dad passed, Mom and I scrambled to support ourselves. She worked in a factory cleaning fish. I worked full-time in the scuba shop and waitressed in the offseason. She had to sell the boat, of course, and all dad's gear. That wasn't much after the loan was paid off."

"How did you get into treasure hunting?"

I beamed at her, grateful for a change of topic. "One day on a dive off the Carolina coast I spotted sunlight glinting in the sand. That area is treacherous because of hurricanes and strong currents so *famous* for shipwrecks.

I picked up two gold Spanish dollars—pieces of eight—minted in 1498. "Those coins set off a gold fever in me. I still own them. Imagine owning money that's more than five hundred years old and still valuable today."

"Spanish shipwrecks off the U.S. coast? Didn't that gold come from South America?"

"Absolutely right. But if you're in a sailing ship you have to follow the highway available to you to get home." Peggy looked puzzled, so I said, "Ocean currents here from the equator are warm and flow north. Spanish ships sailed from the different ports of South America to Havana and consolidated their cargos.

"So?"

"Off Cuba they caught a ride in the Gulf Stream going north along Florida, past our east coast, Canada, then curving east across the Atlantic. Ships from Britain, France, Spain, and India were there to pillage and loot them all the way. That was the start of the real pirates in the Caribbean." This got her attention. "When the current reaches the British Isles, it cools off, turns right, and surges down past Spain. This way you're getting an easy ride. The wind and the waves carry you back to home sweet home."

"Like airplanes prefer to fly with a wind behind them?"

"Exactly, because those ships didn't have engines. Ships from Spain got on the return current going south to Africa, then swing north along South America, so round and round they went. Canvas sails and ropes and a good tailwind. The thing is after the gold and loot petered out, Britain and Europe sent trade goods to Africa. They traded for African slaves and took them to the Americas. There they traded slaves for money and sugar. We know how that turned out."

"That's incredible. And it makes so much sense from an economic standpoint," Peggy admitted.

"Well, it's all too real when I come across a sunken slave ship. So many skeletons, so many manacles. It makes me cry." I stopped for a moment as the *Canterbury* shipwreck flooded my mind. I didn't touch a thing, but the ship and cargo still haunted me. *Especially the children.*

"I signed on with a famous treasure hunter to get a share of the find. Being smaller than the men, I could stretch a tank of air and stay down longer. I almost got a case of the bends from that. The captain put me back into the sea with a full tank of air. I hung on a rope at fifteen feet below the surface until the tank was dry. Probably overdid it and I sure got cold. Back on board I filled up on hot coffee and soup, and I skipped the next dive. I scooped up so much stuff in one trip all that was left was some silver bars for the afternoon scavenge," I said with a gloating smirk. *Those guys had to scrape the bottom to find that much.*

"I get shivery just thinking about being in cold water. But now you work for yourself, don't you?"

"Yes. I found investors of my own. I researched a shipwreck off the coast of South America loaded with emeralds, diamonds, rubies, and sapphires. The ship was off course from where it was reported. I spent *mucho* time translating old Spanish ship logs and diaries and found it three years later."

"Where was that?"

I smiled my Mona Lisa smile. "I have never officially reported the location." *Because a certain country will claim ownership and I say, "Screw them."*

They didn't take any risks or lose two divers. I have the longitude and latitude memorized because that's where Manny is. Manny, the only man I ever gave myself to willingly. Manny—trapped and killed on the shipwreck that made me rich and famous. *It seemed a shark trailed my life and every sailor knows that's bad luck.*

Peggy brought me back with, "What does your mom think of your career? She must worry."

"She's in a nursing home. Mom's a piece of sea glass—smooth and hazy on the outside, sparkly on the inside but I seldom see that anymore. She thinks I teach scuba lessons."

"I see. My dad is the same. I appreciate your analogy to sea glass. Yes, very appropriate. What's your plan if you win in the Chairs?"

"I don't know. My life has run out of luck and everything I care about. The sea is all I know. I've considered writing an autobiography. Make me an offer."

"You're asking the wrong person. Have you met the actress who's in the game? She might give you some advice. What if you lose? What if you end up in the Gizmo and come out in a different body? Even that of a man?"

I had put my life in a bottle and was casting it into the sea in the Chairs. I didn't know which shore I'd wash up on. I couldn't say I've had many good experiences with men.

"I guess I really haven't considered that. I'd still have my mind and salvor skills... but me as a man?" *Now that might be a problem.* "Well, if I can pee in a wet suit while stripping an underwater shipwreck, I can learn to pee standing up."

Peggy laughed. "Thanks and good luck whatever you do. Personally, I love to see strong women out there doing what they want."

****

Max was in the Lizard Lounge talking to Jack Bollar. He booked Jack's client Jamie Justice for this last week of the season at Boss's request.

"Jack. Are you and Jamie settled in?"

"We're fine, Max. You have very nice accommodations for the help. It would have been easy to scrimp on that like some resorts do."

"Boss knows everyone works hard and earns every penny and perk they get. Bad food means bad service, and more trips to the Doc. It's one of the things I admire about him. Is there anything you guys need?"

"Jamie's in rehearsal right now. Once they get the arrangements to work, I think he's good. If he needs some help on a costume—a broken zipper or a ripped hem—who would we see? I think he might need a seam stitched up."

"You asked the right guy. My wife Marie is the wardrobe mistress. Does all our costume design too. Let me …" Max flagged down one of the waitresses. "Sally, it's slow just now. Could you show this gentleman over to wardrobe for me?"

"Wardrobe, sure thing, Max." She twinkled at Jack, "Ready, sir?"

"Give me a couple of minutes," Jack answered.

The men stood. "Jack, I'm sorry I can't walk you over myself but I've a got a venomous snake to find before someone else does. Sorry. See you at the show. Tell Jamie I'm looking forward to his act."

Max left but Jack sat down and enjoyed the show on

the wall. The gecko fascinated him as it changed colors and blended into the scenery. "Clever, so very clever," he whispered to himself.

****

"Peggy *ji*, I know family money doesn't play in the Chairs. Sadly, I'm the last in my family, but it's my chance to get out of acting. I never wanted the life I've had. The Boss will say something like, 'Player Eleven says he'll turn the Chairs into a Bollywood musical. He dances better than I do. Watch for his next film coming soon. Good luck, Player Eleven.'"

"It's just Peggy, Mr. Khan," the interviewer said.

"Yes, my lovely, but *ji* is an honorific I added to your name as I would in India. It's like 'miss' or 'madam.'"

She blushed, "I see. Thank you for the culture lesson. You were saying?"

"My grandfather was the first generation. He started as nothing but grew with the Indian movie industry. The top movie star in the world—based on number of fans, is Indian. Did you know that?" *Movie star number one is not me.* Movie fans think we are who we play on the screen. Once we are set in a certain role, that's all they want to see. *I'd rather be a normal spoiled rich Indian guy who's out of the public eye.*

"I didn't know that. Again, thank you."

"Of course, my dad is the one I feel sorry for. He had three therapists on speed dial." *My poor mom. She never imagined who would ring the doorbell next looking for him.* "Have you ever seen an Indian movie…? Yes. Then you know there is no shortage of gorgeous women who want to be stars. My father tried to 'audition' every one of them." At the end, those pills didn't help him, and women lied about what a great lover he was to get cast.

"I have to admit, I sometimes get confused about which wife *was* my mother." *I say it as a joke, but I don't laugh.* "My nannies were my family. I've got brothers, sisters, half-siblings, stepsiblings; it's just all so confusing. Producers would never cast us as one big happy meddlesome family. Like all of my siblings, I went to English boarding school. It seemed a vestige of colonialism, but I didn't have a choice. I spent holidays and vacations playing small parts in my father's or grandfather's movies. The beggar boy or the shoeshine boy or the spoiled brat son of the star." *No rehearsal needed for the brat role.* "However, to show what a hypocrite I am, I speak like a proper English gentleman. I *can* play a decent game of cricket—"

"Cricket? They play cricket in India?"

"Indeed, we do. I'm signed up for the cricket match. I can't do more than two days but I'm sure it's just an exhibition game, so maybe only one day. It's exhausting. Are you coming?"

"If I have a break. I've never seen a cricket…uhm, did you say cricket *match*?"

"Yes. Where was I? Oh, yes. Even more English is I drink my tea with milk, and I shop at Harrod's in London twice a year. I adore a rainy day so I can unfurl my Swaine Adeney Brigg Men's 'Whangee' umbrella and swoosh it around."

Peggy laughed. Perhaps she visualized me as an Asian Gene Kelly splashing through a Mumbai monsoon.

"What was your childhood like?"

"I grew up on sets with production assistants looking after me. They fed me, taught me, made sure I

49

memorized my lines and actions, and I was on my marks." *No stage mother for me.* "My mother was on another set somewhere working on her career. I was just a prop in her life and an anchor to my dad's money if things went wrong."

"Was there a flip side to being from a famous family?"

"What? The flip side? I see what you mean. Sure, there was a flip side. I never had a friend I could trust. I got whatever and whomever I wanted, and no one ever said 'no.'" *Except my parents when I asked for a little of their time.*

"I'm on my third wife and sometimes call her by the wrong name. For sure I have trouble telling which of my kids I'm talking to."

"That's a shame. Do you see them much?"

"Not really. They all have trust funds, so they don't bother."

"What are your plans if you win, or if you lose?"

What will I do if I win? "Good question. I think I'll create the world's largest movie industry in my hometown. My goal is to have at least half of the Hollywood Oscar nominations go to Indian nominees. Won't that be fun? Those black and white American actors trying to pronounce brown Indian names? I might even change mine to the longest name I can legally just to screw around with them."

Peggy laughed. "But, if you lose, then what?"

"What if I lose? If I trade bodies in the—what is it called?"

"The Gizmo."

"Well, my wife will have a better love life, so she probably won't complain even if she notices. If I don't transfer, I'll still have my name and face and continue to crank out the same drivel until I die on set playing uncredited Camel Driver Number Three."

Chapter 6

"How will your fans feel about that?" Peggy asked.

Yes, what about my fans. "My movies, my dad's movies and my grandfather's movies still play on TV and in theatres. They can see me anytime they want. I get paid all the same."

"But if you transfer, won't the 'new" you get that paycheck?" Peggy asked.

Well, yes. But I have a kind of trust fund that is more like a bearer bond that pays to whomever has the account number and password. Only I know that, and I *do* get to keep my memories. "Probably, but I am a resourceful guy. Back to my fans. Do you think I have ever once gotten a fan letter begging me to play a tortured soul? Have I ever gotten a Facebook page comment asking me to play a poor farmer who traffics his child to an old rich paedophile to save the family?" *Here I go again.*

"No one has even asked me—me, born Indian—to play Gunga Din or Mowgli, or even do the voice in the cartoon version. Have I ever been a character who told a lie or killed a beggar just for fun?" *No. I am trapped in a life that is not mine no matter how many times I play it.* "Do you think always having a happy conclusion, always getting the beautiful sari-wrapped woman with a red bindi mark on her forehead, always being loved and kind and having people grovel at my elbow, do you think that is a good life?"

"It sounds like paradise to a lot of people."

"I wouldn't know. I've had all that and I am the most miserable person I know. I hope I can beat the opposing cricket team to a bloody pulp!"

****

Peggy was made comfortable in front of a large screen TV on a wall painted as a jungle in the Lizard of Oz Lounge. She jumped when a large gecko unexpectedly flicked out its tongue and licked its eyeball.

Dex laughed. "That thing gets me every time. Don't worry none. It's just a computer thing… a whadda ya call it?" he asked the bartender.

"It's a holographic projection. Sometimes this jungle comes alive, but nothing bites," the young man said.

"Yeah," Dex said. "We made this video to introduce our guests to Drake's Key. I got to duck out to check on something. Order whatever you want. Tell 'em Dex is comping it." He waved at the barkeep and pointed to Peggy.

She looked over the menu while half listening to the video and watching the bartender deliver food to two men partially hidden by a screen. She recognized one as a Player from China.

Narration: "Welcome to the world's largest candy store: Drake's Key." The video gave a bird's eye view of the island surrounded by cobalt-blue waters shading to turquoise then to aqua nearest to shore. Steel drum music played softly.

"That's a great shot. I considered the colors might be enhanced but that's exactly what I experienced flying in," she whispered. She jumped as leaves on the wall nearest her moved ever so slightly. Goose bumps rippled across her neck.

Narration: "You'll find secluded private white-sugar sand beaches and shady palms dancing in the breeze." The view swept over athletic nude and seminude sunbathers laying in lounge chairs. Bikini-clad snorkelers splashed by.

Peggy laughed out loud and talked to the video. "Oh gee. I forgot my speedo and sunscreen."

The bartender nodded and suppressed a smirk.

Narration: "No one should ever get 'rock fever.' This island covers one hundred square miles." The plane flew towards the far end of the island where mountains sparkled from fresh-water lakes and hot springs.

Peggy fanned herself with her hand as she sketched a rough outline of the island.

The bartender set Peggy's drink down. "Enjoy this while your order is in the kitchen. Just wave if you want a refill." He glanced at her sketch as he passed.

"Thanks."

Narration: "The natural shape of the island creates several very different ecosystems set up as nature preserves." The plane flew across spectacular waterfalls. Over the rain forest a cloud of yellow and red parrots clattered from the trees.

Peggy jumped at the raucous chatter of parrots over her shoulder. One came into view on the opposite wall causing her to spill her drink as she noted the geographical terrain on her map.

Narration: "The parrots are Drake's Dandies, unique to this island."

A cool breeze ruffled her paper as she made notes of the seaports and airports.

The bartender delivered Peggy's food. "Just so you know, miss, there wasn't any charge. Dex said that to impress you." He rolled his eyes as he put the plate down. "And drink refills are unlimited. Is that map going into the book?"

She laughed like a conspirator and shrugged. "Maybe."

Narration: "Drake's casino, nightclub, lounges, and Michelin star restaurants are all located in the main resort under the dark-blue roof. If you need a quiet minute or religious counseling, the light-blue roof identifies our chapel." The plane flew past bungalows, rooms, and the sports center.

More features were sketched and noted on Peggy's notepad. She turned to the waiter. "Do you know if they conduct funerals at Drake's?"

He shrugged. "Sorry, I don't know. That map is very detailed. You could be a spy," he quipped and returned to polishing glasses.

She paused the video and took a bite of her sandwich. "Do you mind if I ask you a question?"

"Shoot. It's the last week. Ask me anything."

"How long have you worked here and what do you do during the season break?"

He stopped polishing glasses. "This is my third year here. I leave the island and go back to a resort in Canada my parents operate. This year, I got an offer on one of the yachts in port. I like to travel and they're heading to places I haven't seen yet."

"You must like it here if you come back. What attracts you to Drake's?"

"Besides that Boss treats his staff well? The chances for extra tips are— between just us—are enormous." He winked at Peggy.

"I was told everything is covered. Where do the tips come from?"

"Oh, honey. I work the early shift, so I have evenings off. I'm a great dancer, I'm discreet, I'm young, and I take cash."

Peggy was struck by a sudden moment of clarity, and her face reddened. She swiveled back to her drink and the video as he snickered. Her face and neck flushed even deeper.

Narration: "Our sports facilities are at the periphery of the residences. The golf club, marina, and private airfield are near the main buildings."

She could discern the distinctive sound of tennis balls being swatted. Her map was detailed, and she turned a page to make additional notes.

Dex walked into the lounge with Max. It looked as if they were arguing.

Max kept shaking his head "no" and Dex kept putting his hands up as if surrendering. Max left and Dex walked over and talked to the bartender.

Narration: "Does snorkeling, sailing, kayaking, paddle boarding or windsurfing appeal to you? Private lessons are available." The video showcased tanned, well-muscled helpers in bikinis and thongs demonstrating the equipment.

Peggy laughed and murmured, "I need to be hanging out at the staff quarters more."

Narration: "For you scuba divers, we have a decompression chamber and a private sunken pirate ship to explore."

She glanced towards the windows to glimpse a second Player from South America rise and shake hands.

The Players exited together through the patio door.

"For you shoppers, Drake's features a small, exclusive shopping complex under the green roof." The video showed a slow pan past high-end branded stores.

Peggy smoothed down the red and blue Hermès scarf draped around her neck. She murmured, "I didn't even have to fight the 'crowd' to get this."

Narration: "For those of you who prefer to hunt for the perfect memento, our shops, jewelers, and tailors open at noon and close at 1 AM. Our international banks are open twenty-four hours a day by appointment." Shoppers were fitted for a Gucci tux and a woman's Philippe Patek watch.

"Maybe Boss will gift me with a Rolex next time," Peggy joked to herself.

****

Dex put an iced tea, a fried shrimp sandwich with spicy chili sauce and chopped mango salsa, and a lemon meringue tart on the table and sat down by the interviewer. He used the remote to pause the video. "What do you think? Any questions so far?"

"This is a pretty upscale establishment you have here. Who made this video for you? "The special effects in this bar make me feel like I'm in a theme park or the bird house at the zoo," Peggy answered.

Dex chuckled, "Let's just say a well-known Hollywood movie director stayed here for several weeks for free. We like our guests to view it before they come, but most are only interested in just a few o' the attractions so they can make appointments in advance. Of course, it's more interesting watching it here, don't cha think?"

"Appointments such as?"

"Such as…" he replied as he started the video and turned to his lunch, avoiding eye contact with her.

Narration: "Confidential and personalized cosmetic and dental services feature world-famous doctors. You stay out of public spaces until *you* are ready to be seen." A pristine medical suite was shown with masked and gowned staff. "The recovery suites offer room service meals."

Dex stopped the video, leaned towards her, and said in a low voice, "You'd be surprised the docs who call us offering their services. They get a free week for every week o' services. Plus, they have their evenings off. I get my teeth cleaned and fixed twice a year." He paused for a moment and considered his next words. "Uhm, we have a new thing that's not on the video." He scanned the empty lounge and cleared his throat. "I say this 'cause it's for ladies only. I don't really understand it but there's some kinda laser treatment that…uhm…makes lady parts…like new again. It's named after some girl in a play about teenagers who kill themselves. I think Leonardo DiCaprio played in it, but I don't watch snuff flicks. Anyway, I know about this laser thing from Yv… uh, a lady I know, in case you want to write about it." He started the video again as he returned to his sandwich.

Peggy suppressed a smile but not her rapid eye blinks.

Narration: "Recuperation suites are spacious, private, and camera-free. Our emergency medical clinic is open 24/7. At Drake's you can stay close to the resort, or in a villa with an ocean view and uninterrupted privacy." The plane flew over tan-roofed bungalows near the resort, and pink-roofed villas set apart.

She asked, "How many weddings and funerals have

you had here? I notice there's a chapel, so I assumed…"

Dex hit "Pause." He winked and made a show of wiping his mouth with a napkin. "Ten weddings. I couldn't say about the funerals though, miss. A few people have brought ashes we dump at sea, but bodies? I would have to dig into the files for that, and probably can't get to it for a while." He gulped his tea.

Narration: "Villas have quarters for your staff and a garage for your limo. We are committed to preserving our environment. In addition to Drake's Dandy we have unique orchids dubbed Drake's Candy." The view panned through protected rainforests before diving into an underwater view of a rare red and purple oceanic nudibranch named Dex's Dancer undulating like a fan dancer over a coral head.

"What about the staff? Where do they live?"

"You know I think most o' our guests don't get to this part o' the video but it's next."

"That's okay. I'd like to see it."

"Be my guest. Do you want a refill?" He waved at the barkeep and pointed at her drink. "No charge."

Peggy nodded but avoided looking at the barkeeper.

Narration: "Much of our fruits and vegetables are home-grown by local families. They run our aquacultures farms where we work with experts to farm clams, oysters, conch, grouper, lobster, and shrimp right off our own shores." The scene swept over farms and moved to aquaculture pens in the ocean teeming with fish and shellfish, and a shrimp hatchery thriving in a repurposed mangrove swamp.

Narration: "Our staff have quarters near the resort where they enjoy a pool, gym, and amenities." The scene showed happy waiters and recreational staff splashing in the pool with a bar. A volleyball game was underway in the background.

Narration: "Staff brought by guests are also welcome to use these facilities."

Dex stopped the video. "The rest is just about how we generate our own electricity from …uh…vertical axis windmills and water from a waterfall, really just the engineering stuff. You should see Chet if that interests you."

" Oh, and about how the roads are mostly off-limits for guests. And the racetrack, that's Rusty's job." Dex stood as he finished.

"Okay, Chet for engineering. Rusty for the track. Got it. Who was the man you were talking to before? Should I talk to him?"

Dex looked puzzled for a moment. "Oh, yeah, that was Max. He books all our entertainment, so you should interview him. I didn't catch your name before."

"Peggy, just call me Peggy. Thanks, Dex. I've got another participant for the Chairs to interview soon. Oh, could I see your famous lucky tattoo now?"

He looked towards the nearest door. "I really gotta get going, but look, if you want any company for those interviews, let me know. Some o' these guys don't know what a boundary is."

Peggy pursed her lips together and looked down. "Thanks for the offer. I'll keep it in mind." She picked up her notepad and purse and left. The bartender gave her another wink as she passed. She'd never interviewed an African diamond tycoon. He sounded like a real gem.

****

Growing up in South Africa my parents taught me to be polite and to address people by their names. "What shall I call you?"

"Peggy is just fine." She had an air of confidence that was unexpected.

"Miss Peggy. What a pretty name. How are you today?"

Her head tilted up and her eyes met mine. Her look was very direct. "Thank you, sir, for asking. How can I be anything but happy to be on this beautiful island with an interesting job. Please, be comfortable," she said and waved at a chair.

I said, "In answer to your previous question, Boss will announce, 'Player One is a diamond king from South Africa. It's his first time in the Chairs. Those cuff links and shirt studs are real.'"

"Have you seen the Chairs before?"

"Yes, I was astounded at the risk. Yet, here I am."

"Are you a seasoned gambler? Is that why you're here?"

I shrugged as even I was not sure why I was here. I have gambled but only with my life. "Gambling for pleasure or money, I have never done. Perhaps because I have lost everything I cared about. Perhaps I do not care if I live or if I die. Whatever the reason, I am throwing my fate to the stars, and I will be content with the outcome."

"That's a surprise. Please tell me about yourself, whatever you think might be of interest to readers."

"People call me Gogo. Not because that's how I operate, but it is my actual name. I think I am around forty-five years old. My mother was never clear on the date. Like everyone, I did not pick my parents, nor they me, nor where I was born. My mother said I was born in the Republic of South Africa, but she wasn't certain as to where. I feel sure it was in the interior of the country because my father was a diamond picker. He worked in open pit mines, standing in mud and water for ten hours a day, for less than a U.S. dollar. When he wasn't digging, he was picking through mud and dirt looking for raw diamonds." *He came home so dirty I could not tell his skin from the dirt.* "My mother said as she scrubbed his legs and feet each night, 'I never want my children to have to work in this way.'"

"Did you work in the mines as a child?"

"No, never, but other children do even today. I picked May 10 as my birthday to honor Nelson Mandela. He was sworn in on that day as our first Black president. He showed me what hard work can accomplish. Later that day Nelson said, 'Political division, based on colour, is entirely artificial…'" *I believed perhaps so was economic division, and I never looked back. I doubt he would appreciate how different my path to success was than his.*

"Gogo, your English is beautiful. Was it your first language?"

"Oh no. South Africa has eleven official languages, of which I am fluent in four, and I can haggle in a couple more out of necessity. We spoke Southern Sotho at home, but my parents encouraged me to be a teacher. 'Gogo, you are a very smart boy. You must grow up to help boys that are not as smart as you. Please learn to speak English so you can talk to all boys everywhere,' my mother said. I am sad to say my sisters were not equally encouraged, and they lived hard, short lives as many women do.

Chapter 7

"Somehow my mother scraped enough together to pay my school fees each term but learning to be a teacher was upon my shoulders. I had to leave home. My teacher helped me find an academy where I could study for two years for my Certificate of Teaching. He said, 'Gogo, it will be hard but do not be afraid. You are a good student. You will be a great teacher.'

"Once I found where the school was, I looked for a job. Being a strong young man, I found one milking cows."

"Cows? You made enough to survive doing that? That makes me ashamed to think I waited tables and never accepted how lucky *I* was," Peggy remarked.

She seemed to be a self-made woman. I admired that.

"Yes, I did survive. The old farmer had a herd of twenty cows. Marauding rebels killed his son. I slept in a shed and they fed me two meals a day. I got up in the dark to milk the cows and clean out the dung. I walked three kilometers to school. After school, I ran back to the farm to milk the cows again. After the cows I went to the river to bathe being careful not to end up as the meal of a crocodile before my own evening meal. Last, I studied until I fell asleep. Every day. For two years. When I left, I said, 'Thank you, sir, for my job, but I must go to my destiny as a teacher. *Sala hantle.* Goodbye.'" *I hope I never see another cow up close in my lifetime.*

"Tell me about your experience teaching."

"My academy helped place me in a rural school where I taught with one other teacher. I tutored the boys and she tutored the girls. It was natural that we would marry. We had three children, a boy and two girls, all beautiful to us and precious. Life was hard but we were happy." *Happy. I can't remember how that feels any more.*

"Your family sounds lovely. Did your wife come to Drake's with you?"

I held up my hand for her to stop. I continued with, "We were happy until about ten years later when *they* came while I was at school. Evil came to our life and changed me. A band of terrorists came to my house. They kidnapped my son." *My sweet baby girls were raped to death.* "Some of the men believed in the virgin rape cure for HIV. They raped my wife because they could." *They at least killed her and saved her from the shame.* "I was the one who found them that infamous day. I was the one who dug the grave, I washed and wrapped their bodies, and I buried my babies in their mother's arms for ever more. 'Jesus loves the little children, all the children of the world, red and yellow, black, and white…' I sang my children's favorite Sunday School song as I buried my precious family. I said my *last* prayer over them."

My soul cried out to join them and I almost did as the scars on my wrists will tell you. An odd thing happened as I waited while my blood dripped onto their graves. "My heart demanded revenge, not just for the men who did this but against life itself. Life that is so cruel, life that taunts us to think we can rise above it, and then it crushes us." *I stopped my blood loss and considered how to craft my revenge.* "First, I needed money. Teaching school was not going to get me the kind of money I hungered for. I was not a criminal…" *At least not yet,* "…but I had an idea. I changed my name and went to the conflict diamond mines in the Congo." Peggy wrote as I spoke. She did not interrupt me again.

I learned from my father what to do. "There is always some pilfering, but the trick is to act stupid, the trick is to do something dangerous, the trick is to wait. After a few weeks of the grinding and precarious work, I found a raw diamond worth stealing. Now the methods of concealing such a stone are well known. Where would you hide such a find, Peggy? Where would you hide a stolen diamond?" Gogo asked.

Peggy looked startled at my question. "I…I don't think there would be many options."

"Correct. I made it a habit to save bananas when they were available. I waited until it was time for a short rest. I stuffed the stone, about the size of my small toe, into a piece of banana and swallowed it. And then I would wait until the workday was over to empty my bowels. After six months I had a small cache of stones."

"I'm amazed you weren't caught."

"It wasn't due to luck. What I did sounds easy. In truth, some mines had x-ray machines and they would randomly test workers. I waited until the x-ray machine was 'not working' because I had surreptitiously disabled it. The next day I would act a little suspicious to ensure they x-rayed me. In this way I was never caught. To be safe, I always quit and moved on before being too greedy."

"Is that usual for stones to be stolen by miners?"

"No, very common. They know miners steal small stones. They have little huts set up in the towns to buy them back, but at a ridiculously low price. I waited until I had a cache of stones, and I went to the city."

"So, you *could* sell them?" She looked up at me as she asked the question.

"Yes and no. Raw stones are not ready for market, so I found me a woman to do some rough polishing. Then I found a cutter. Do you know why diamonds are so sought after? Because of '…diamonds are a girl's best friend…' and 'A Diamond is Forever.'"

"Oh, I never thought of that. Demand. Good old supply and demand."

"Exactly. A perfect cut on a diamond is a small sculpture, a masterpiece that reflects light. It sparkles like a tiny house made only of fresh washed windows with a brilliant light inside." I took out a cuff link and handed it to her. "A perfect emerald-cut, five karat, white diamond set in platinum. Custom made. The set cost me fifty-thousand dollars, but I ask you to turn it and see how the light is reflected and sparkles."

While she looked at the stone, I could not resist an explanation. Once a teacher, always a teacher my teacher taught me.

"A diamond is made of carbon, just like coal almost. Because of the arrangement of the atoms a diamond is the hardest known natural material on earth. The arrangement allows for only a few ways to cut a stone, and a cutter must know them all. He must know how to shear the stone along those tiny light-reflecting planes. One slip and the stone is worthless. Finding a cutter was the key to my revenge." *I found Jacob. He worked in Amsterdam and New York but, like me, had fallen on harsher times.* "Our first batch of cut stones allowed me to buy more pilfered stones from exploited miners, and our business expanded overnight.

"Since the issue of conflict diamonds drew outrage from abroad, the major owners 'solved the problem' and concocted a scheme to launder their products." *In certain African countries—where rebels used the profits to bankroll their anarchy and terror—stones are still available, bigger, and more valuable because of the trouble to fake their legitimacy.* In truth, blood diamonds still exist." *I should know. That's my game.* "Now I have had a great deal of revenge and I need a change."

"Will you continue with your diamond business should you lose? You still have the knowledge and contacts, don't you?"

"I don't know the answer to that. I am open to other opportunities."

"If you win, do you think you will transfer bodies?"

"If I lose but don't transfer, so be it. I have never seen a white or yellow man who wanted to be black, so it won't happen." *I had enough diamonds on me to start again.* "If I win and I switch into a person who is basically good, I will try to be good again." *If I switched with someone who is not so good, well, I feared a leopard doesn't change its spots so easily.*

"And if you come out as a woman?"

"Ah, a woman. I greatly admire the women in my life. Perhaps I could take my wife's place and teach again. That would have pleased her. Have I settled your curiosity, my dear?"

"You have an extraordinary story, Mr. Gogo. Whatever happens. I sincerely hope you find a more peaceful life."

"Good. If you think of something else, just catch up with me on the beach. I'll be in the shade with a cool drink. Who knows? I may meet a like-minded lovely lady."

"Thank you. Don't get burned."

****

I expected Peggy, and she was right on time. "Hello, Peggy. Peaches told me you were coming. I took the liberty of ordering us tea."

"May I call you Max? I've used my voice all day and I really need that tea." She sat across from me and drank her beverage down immediately. I refilled it.

"I can't help but notice your makeup. It's very professional. I notice details like that in my business."

Her face colored as she said, "My aunt has her own salon. She keeps me up to date on the trends. I spend way too much time in front of a mirror."

She opened a notebook. "Max, tell me about your role here at Drake's. What kind of people come here, in your opinion?"

"As the Impresario at Drake's, I see all kinds of guests come to the Starlight Nightclub. Some people are nightlife people. They like the glitz. See that man at the table to our right with the blue tablecloth? What do you see?"

"Hmm, I see a man in what I would consider a designer tux. There was one similar in your shopping arcade."

"Good, and designer haircut. And his lady?"

"She…she's covered in diamonds, has a very plunging neckline and high slits that…"

I finished her thought. "…leave no secrets hidden?"

Peggy nodded at my description.

"That's the new money people, the younger crowd that wants attention and drama, that's got to post on social media or be on the news or their lives are 'ruined.' I'm not sure why they come to Drake's. We don't allow the press here."

"Really? No press. Oh, sorry to interrupt." She seemed familiar.

"Then there's the people who have earned their money but respect themselves and treat others as they themselves appreciate being treated." I nodded towards a couple at the table in front of us. "What do you see there?"

"Yes, I see what you mean. That's a classy tux but a classic too. He looks at ease in it. I'd guess he's had it for a while. The woman...I notice *her* rather than her outfit. It's lovely but I see an inner beauty in her face and eyes."

"Yes. You do have an eye for detail. These women wear their gowns rather than the other way around. The ladies still have hidden secrets and know how to keep their man in thrall because they listen and have something to say."

"Ah, the old money," she said.

"And lastly, and fortunately in smaller numbers now, we have the tech stars, the young people who don't know what to do with the money they have much less know how much is enough; they just want more." I nodded towards a couple two tables away.

"I'd need my sunglasses if I ran into him in the daylight. And is that...a printed tee shirt under his tux?" she asked.

"Yes. As you see they dress without any direction in mind or conscious reflection."

"The cool kids," she smirked as she hit the nail right on its head.

"Exactly. To continue, we have floorshows that alternate nights in the Starlight. One night we'll have a headliner our older crowd appreciates. Guests can dance to the music without looking like they're having a reaction to their lunch. Look at the couple by the Starlight neon sign. This is where couples come to dance close and personal with their arms around each other and whisper sweet nothings. This is where couples come to celebrate an engagement or an anniversary. This is where you imagine you could bump into Cary Grant or Rita Hayworth as she looked in *Gilda*, or royalty. In fact, we have a South American king and a Russian count here this week."

"I loved Gilda. She was a knockout. I love to know what I'd look like in Rita's dress?."

"Enchanting, I'm sure. Now, about our décor. The ceiling of the Starlight is a map of the night sky. It's programmed to mirror the stars on a clear night, even if it's cloudy or raining outside. It shows a dimmed moon, planets that are up, and stars. No satellites though."

"I have to see that. A nightclub under the stars and no wind and rain to ruin my hair."

I nodded and checked my watch. "When we have a special occasion the ceiling stars are replaced by simulated fireworks. During the day, this room is a dining room called The Shores, with sliding screen doors to allow in breezes and the salt air. The ceiling undulates as waves of ocean water—cobalt, turquoise, and aquamarine that breaks onto a sandy upside-down shore."

"That sounds very romantic and relaxing."

"That's what we aim for. For the second type of nightclub guests, we bring in those singers and performers who are pushing forty—again—who are tired of tours and big venues. Stars who want to sing a song to people who will appreciate it. Think music of the 1990s to early 2000s. Think faster dance steps where you never touch your partner even if you have one. Think dances that evoke expensive sneakers, jogging suits, and ripped jeans with a tee shirt, not that we allow any of that.

"With our third type of guest, we encourage them to go to the Coco-Go-Nuts patio restaurant. These guests think formal means a *black* tee shirt. I ran into one of their wives earlier shopping. Her dress was so short I worried she just forgot her skirt, but no. When she stepped up on the revolving beach towel kiosk, I could see she wasn't a *natural* blonde." Peggy stifled a laugh at my description and possibly my indignation, but both were accurate. "For these guests we book in stars who won a TV talent show and cut a record and then went nowhere. There's no shortage of those folks, especially when you count all the world copycat competitions. The headliner tonight won *Sweden's Got Talent* last year.

"Tomorrow night it's the winner from *India's Got Talent*. Now that lady can sing and is gorgeous. She'll go somewhere if she gets a better agent. I'm putting her in touch with someone I know from Mumbai who is here this week with his wife to watch a cousin in the Chairs."

Peggy looked up wide-eyed. "Really? I love Indian movies. Who's the movie star in the Chairs?"

"I really can't say, but you might recognize him when you see him. As I was saying, the nights are a time to relax and slow down at Drake's. Except tonight we got

71

a special request. It's a wedding anniversary and I've booked a legend to sing a particular song to the wife. Excuse me, please."

Chapter 8

As Impresario it's my job to handle introductions. I wave to my wife standing in the wings. "Ladies and gentlemen. I'm Max, your announcer. I hope you've been enjoying yourselves." There was a polite amount of restrained applause. "Tonight, we're helping a very special couple celebrate their thirty-fifth wedding anniversary."

A spotlight fell on a ringside table. A man still handsome with a tanned face and wavy white hair raised his glass. He was joined by an elegant lady with piles of silver curls supporting a small diamond tiara. She waved and leaned in for a polite kiss. The crowd approved with an enthusiastic round of applause.

"Dale and Leonard, we have a surprise for you tonight." A magnificent cake was wheeled across the dance floor and up to their table. It took our pastry chef two days to bake and decorate it. It's three feet tall and supports a garden gazebo. The Drake's Candy icing orchids were so realistic that I bent over to smell one in the kitchen. The candy Drake's Dandies parrots perching on the second layer looked as if they could fly off. "Wow! Our pastry chef outdid himself on this cake. It's almost a shame to eat it. That gold color is edible gold. I didn't even know that was a thing until I got this job. Will you all join me in singing 'Happy Anniversary' to our celebratory couple."

The band started up, the crowd started to sing, at

least most of them did, but they clapped with more warmth at the end. The cake was wheeled to the side. "Our love birds want all of you to celebrate with them. Your own wait person will be happy to bring you a piece of cake and a flute of champaign to your table. Just ask for either or both." Another round of applause was offered up. The chef made extra icing flowers, so each slice of cake will get a piece of Drake's Candy. "And now Dale, Leonard has requested some of your favorite songs. Singing them is Mr. Ritchie Moran."

The band began playing the song intro and Dale's face lit up.

As the curtain opened, I announced, "Mr. Ritchie Moran!" Ritchie stepped forward, acknowledged the applause, and launched into one of Dale's favorites, "Lady" that brought tears to her eyes.

I noticed my wife Marie still standing in the wings. She loved Ritchie but wasn't looking at him. She looked at my interviewer. I stepped over to her. "Marie, it's Ritchie Moran. You remember him, don't you?"

"What's Peggy doing here, Max?"

"Peggy? She's working. Do you know her?"

"Working? Oh, I was worried she needed me to fix a gown. I've been so busy that I haven't had time to get to it."

"What?"

"Don't you recognize Peggy Lee? Why didn't you tell me she was singing tonight?"

I looked at the strong resemblance between our interviewer and the famous singer, but I was sure the singer of "Fever" died almost twenty years ago. *Marie! It's getting worse. I found Marie's assistant to take her to her offstage office.*

Mr. Moran sang for half an hour, and no one left the room. I rejoined Peggy at her table halfway through his set. "Who would be crazy enough to leave while a consummate professional was so close and so charming?" I asked her. Encores went on for almost as long. Then Ritchie joined Dale and Leonard for a piece of cake and conversation with his fans. "Yes, evenings are the time to relax after a day of fun and sun, Peggy. Would you like to meet Ritchie Moran?"

****

Rosalie. I couldn't get her out of my mind. She was an earworm, a song my brain couldn't forget. *Our first "official" date. I was so proud picking her up at her door. Before that date, our folks said, "Not that boy, not that girl," over and over. After that date we were punished so we never said who we were seeing. We just met somewhere else.*

Kids were experts at overcoming the challenges proscribing their behavior often fueled by an overabundance of hormones. We spent a great deal of time together. Before school, after school, Saturdays in the park. At football games in the fall. At baseball games and track meets in the spring. At every school event we could escape to, we'd sneak off to find an unlocked classroom, only to appear apart before the doors were locked. I question now if we fooled anyone.

Scott found me in the Maze near the kitchen as a waiter finished taking my order for a sandwich and pot of coffee.

"Boss, we got… an emergency…you need to… know about," Scott coughed up. "It's Mr. Stewart."

We hurried through the Maze to the clinic. Mr. Stewart laid on a bed, his face contorted in pain.

Doc said to me, "Mr. Stewart has a bad reverse ear squeeze. I'm putting him in the hyperbaric chamber and pressurizing him to get the squeeze to reverse."

"Has he signed a release?"

"Yes, just now."

"Then what are we waiting for? Mr. Stewart looks none too sporty at the moment."

Doc and his nurse helped their patient up and into the next room. They laid him on a bunk on his left side in the chamber and spread a blanket over him. Doc lowered the head of his bunk slightly. Nurse Barbara sat on the other bunk holding a sweater. Doc closed the door securely. The nurse had a button inside the chamber to call him if she needed help. Doc turned on the compressed air, gradually increasing the pressure in the chamber until it was the equivalent of thirty feet under water. The occupants were feeling the heat generated when air was first compressed. Even better, the increased pressure was relieving the pressure in Mr. Stewart's ear. With that look of relief that only the cessation of acute pain can bring, his body relaxed and he gave a thumbs up sign to Doc. Doc continued increasing the pressure.

"What happened, Scott?" I asked.

"According to the dive shop, Mr. Steward made two dives this morning before lunch. During the surface interval between dives, the divemaster was talking to Mr. Stewart about night dives. He showed pictures of the orange-ball anemone to him. He wanted to see one. He also heard of the parrotfish sleeping in its nightgown. After that he signed up for a night dive. They were down about fifty feet for just under an hour, which should have been fine. He noticed ear pain as he was coming up, so he stopped at fifteen feet and tried to clear his ears. His nose started bleeding. He used up his air and had to surfaced. They got him here fast."

Doc pulled me away from the chamber and said quietly, "Boss, I found out he checked out a tank after lunch and made a shore dive off the wall-end of the beach. No telling how deep he went or for how long. He overworked his ear drums today."

"He's damned lucky he doesn't have the bends, which is why I wanted to put him in the chamber, as a precaution," Doc said.

"I agree. You're following a decompression cycle as if he has the bends, and that will alleviate both problems, right?"

"Yes. I can't use his dive computer to set the decompression time since he didn't use it for all the dives. I'm assuming a worst-case scenario and using Navy Diving protocol. Sixty feet for four hours and forty-five minutes. He hasn't complained about any symptoms of the bends, but those can be delayed. Since he got the ear squeeze coming up, it could just be a fluke or just because he's a middle-aged man whose ear drums don't flex as easily as they used to. When he came in, he was only complaining about his ears and his ulcer. It's all in his chart in case the police ask."

"Do you see any negligence?"

"Not on Drake's part. He's an experienced diver, but he should have reported his afternoon dive. If it had been me, I'd have cancelled the night dive. I'm not going to release him until I'm sure he's A-OK."

"Good. If he dives again, remind him not to fly for twenty-four hours after his last dive. I don't remember if he flew in or was a passenger on a guest's boat. Is the nurse okay in the chamber? It will get chilly in there."

"That's why she took in a sweater and blanket."

"I'll drop by tomorrow." I left and went to my apartment. I showered letting the hot water relax my muscles, and I poured out a night cap. "I'm curious if what happened to Mr. Stewart was meant for me. No, I'm just being paranoid because of the note, and it's probably just a hoax," I said aloud to convince myself it was so. But still, I taped my taser to my left hand.

****

I awoke to a jangling phone; it was Doc. "Boss, get over here ASAP. Big, big problem with Mr. Stewart."

Seven minutes later I knocked on the medical clinic's locked door. "What's up?" I said as I saw Doc's face was ashen and drawn.

"I put Mr. Stewart through the protocol. He fell asleep in the chamber. When I opened it, the nurse got up, but Mr. Stewart didn't. He's dead."

I felt I had been slapped in my head. "You're sure… Do you have any idea what he died from?"

"I am *certain* that he is dead. At this moment, I can't see anything that happened from the diving that would cause death unless he had some underlying conditions or some medications he didn't report." Doc's hand was shaking as he sipped from his cup.

"Go back to when I left and tell me what happened."

Doc sat down. "Mr. Stewart was conscious and alert, remember?"

"Yes."

"He asked for something to eat after you left because he missed dinner, so he must have been feeling better. He ate a sandwich and had a cup of coffee I passed through to him."

The nurse added, "That was kind of you to send that

78

food over to him, Boss."

"What? I didn't send any food over to him,"

"Really? The waiter said it was *from* you."

"No. That's wrong," Doc added. "The waiter said it was *for* Boss."

"For *me*?" I paused and then remembered ordering the sandwich and coffee. "I've got a bad feeling, Doc. Can you do any tests to check for poison or anything unusual? That'd show up in his blood, wouldn't it?"

"Probably, or maybe. Depends on what it was. I've got to report this to St. Thomas, you know."

"I do know. Do what's required and call me if you find anything or not. I need to know if it was an accident, or not." I walked through the Maze directly to the kitchen and found Hugo. "What happened to the food I ordered last night? Did you deliver it to my apartment?"

"No. I was aware you got called to the clinic. I got someone to take it over there."

"Just to be sure, you carried it with you when you went to find a waiter?"

"No, Boss. I left it over there on the counter with the order ticket with your name. When I found Derek, he picked it up. Hey, Derek, come here."

"Yeah?"

"Derek, did you see anyone around my plate when you came for it?"

"No, Boss."

"And you delivered it straight to the clinic? No stops? No one talked to you?"

"No. Did someone complain about the food?"

"You could say that."

****

"I don't understand what the big deal is about how

the Boss introduces me. Do you have any ideas?" I asked the interviewer.

"Most likely he will say you are a young widow of a Greek shipping tycoon and you get seasick. 'Welcome Mrs. Five.'" Peggy said. "It's to give the spectators an idea of who you are."

"Is that it? Widow? Seasick? Survivor would be more like it. Listen, everybody who doesn't have money thinks it solves everything. I know complaining that I only bought fifty new dresses from this year's Paris fashion shows is not sad news. I spent more time buying those dresses than I spent each year with my parents growing up. The day I was born my picture was in all the newspapers: Greek Shipping Tycoon Delivers New Heiress. Two days later I went home with the nanny while mommy went to a Swiss spa to "get her figure back." I'm not sure when my father checked on me, since he was off negotiating a shipping deal with some Asian antique dealer. Finances before family."

"You were born into an extremely wealthy family. Didn't you get everything you wanted?"

"I found out from the nanny that daddy insisted on a DNA match before I left the hospital. Neither were role models as parents go, would you say?"

"Tell me about your life growing up."

"Nannies the first few years. Periodically dressed up and paraded out for holidays and the press." Peggy didn't seem surprised at this statement. She's probably seen it before. *It was the standard for every rich kid I went to school with or socialized with.* "Shipped off to Le Rosey Swiss boarding school at seven,. That's why I speak English so well. All my classes were in English, but I took French and German, and I learned Italian from my nanny."

Now Peggy nodded; I went to the best schools and she was adequately impressed.

"The school had a campus in Gstaad where I polished my German. My parents had a house there where they could ski and not be bothered by the nouveau riche. They multitasked by setting eyes on me for an occasional meal. My nanny lived in Gstaad even if they weren't there. When I was at the winter campus she would take me home, to the house in Gstaad, on weekends. I have fond memories of those weekends. We read to each other. When I fell ice skating, she would kiss my hurt. We sat by the fire at night and sang songs, we played hopscotch, and we talked for hours. She let me stay up and ask the cook to fix whatever I wanted."

"So the nanny was a big influence on you?"

"Of course. When I wasn't in Gstaad, the nanny would travel every other weekend to visit me at the main school campus. She brought me new clothes and my favorite sweet baklava and would take me to movies or the zoo or to tea. She was my real family. She's the only person I can say that I ever loved. She died last year. Now there is no one."

"I'm sorry for you. Why did you marry at eighteen? That seems very young."

"That wasn't a wedding…that was a merger. At eighteen Daddy sold me off to the highest bidder. In my case that was the Hellenic Maritime Line. When they merged with daddy's line, they became the world's largest ocean-going shipping company. However, I was daddy's only child, so I had a bargaining chip: sex, my sex in particular. The owner of HML only had two sons, but they both had very black reputations in their treatment of women. One even killed his girlfriend. They paid off her family handsomely, they say. Women were *not* elbowing each other out of line for either of them despite their money. If they're used to paying for sex, what's my price? What's in it for me? I learned to play their game early."

"Their game? How did that come about, the wedding, I mean?"

"Daddy made me an offer I couldn't refuse. I got enough money in wedding presents to play in the Chairs. I never gambled before, and I wanted my father to clearly understand how I much I despised my arranged 'marriage.' I only had to produce an heir to keep the company shares in the family, so I blew the wedding cash he planned to use to expand his fleet. I was positive I would never get to spend it anyway. It was deposited in *my* Swiss bank and I came to Drake's as fast as I could.

"My honeymoon was on my groom's second largest superyacht. It's almost too small to sail around the Mediterranean, but I didn't see much outside of his bedroom. He didn't complain that I wasn't a virgin, but he did gift me with my first rape and beating as a wedding present. I only had to survive sex with my 'husband' until I produced a child. I got a sweet two hundred million in the bank as baby gifts, and his family is raising the kid."

Peggy's face became very serious at my admission. "Was your husband excited about being a father?"

"How would I know? I was never with him after the birth. Wait, make that after the conception. He stayed away for so long I forgot what he looked like." *That's a lie.* I will never forget what he looked like. I recognized what his handprint looked like too.

Chapter 9

"And your child. Do you have her now?"

"No, I do not. I'm glad that his parents have the child. Of course, they are the ones who raised him, but I didn't have a choice. I fool myself into believing they changed their childrearing habits. I avoided being in the same room with him for my own personal safety and sanity even."

"There was a published rumor of a reconciliation at one time last summer. Weren't you supposed to be on the yacht that went down?"

Both of our parents were pushing for the reconciliation thinking it would leverage loans to remodel some older ships. "Yes, I was. It was supposed to be just us two. But I found out he had invited two female 'guests' along. The year before one of his 'guests' went missing in the middle of the Atlantic. 'Oops,' was all he said." *I didn't want to be the second.*

"It was well known that I get seasick. My family teased me over it, being the daughter of a man who owned so many ships. I ran out of medicine, so I elected not to go. At least it looks like I'll make it to thirty and now I'm making up for lost time. The best part is daddy can't do a thing about it."

"Which daddy are you referring to?"

"Doesn't matter. Pick one."

"Do you regret not having custody of your

daughter?"

"I do know that I didn't have good role models for what a parent should or could be. I was bought and sold under their watch. I don't have a friend who was born wealthy who hasn't killed themselves, or at least tried to, and who isn't as unhappy as I have been. But, since my child is cared for, and my despot of a husband has been deposed, I am helping myself to everything money can buy."

"What will you do if you win the Chairs?"

"Buy a football team, or maybe a hockey team. Plenty to keep me warm there."

"And what if you lose? What if you end up in a man's body?"

"I've got assets that Drake's won't claim. Enough to live a very comfortable life. Since I know my libido is really in my brain, I expect that would transfer too. So, win-win. I'm curious to see if the experience is the same. I hope I won't be disappointed."

"What are you doing besides gambling at Drake's?"

"Lessons. I've signed up for everything that includes a sweaty young Apollo, and you are keeping me from Ruslan who is teaching me to ice skate. *Da svidania.*"

With that I, the beautiful and still young, and I am happy to say rather horny, Greek widow stood up and walked out. I still had windsurfing and sailing lessons later to enjoy.

****

Peggy was meeting me in a few minutes. I'll talk about behind the scene side of the entertainment at Drake's. There was a rap at my door. "Come in. Hello, Peggy. Sit down. I'm used to interviews so feel free to ask me anything, darling. How's the interviewing business going?"

"Hello again. As to my interviews, so far so good. And if I may I say so wild and crazy."

"You must be at Drake's. That's it to a tee."

She laughed and drank some water. "Max, could you start by describing your job here on the island?"

"Of course. You are gorgeous, by the way. Your face looks familiar. My wife identified you as Peggy Lee in a reincarnation."

She shook her head. "Maybe I am, but more likely it's maybe not. I really like her music. But go on."

"I'm in charge of entertainment at Drake's. If you were a tiny bit older you would remember me. You'd have seen pictures of me with my famous clients, mostly show people. Mostly singers and dancers but a few others. Some are still working, and I book them here when they want a tropical vacation."

"How did you get started in the entertainment industry?"

How did I get started? Do you think I grew up wanting to be a talent agent? No way, I wanted to be a star! I wanted dance lessons and singing lessons and costumes that sparkled and had feathers. What I got was an industrious mom and dad who taught me to drive a tractor at age eight. By then I was feeding chickens, shoveling out manure, and scraping it off the soles of my boots before I went to school. *In hindsight, it wasn't too different from being a talent agent.*

"Well, Peggy. I sang in the church choir and played a wise man or a farm animal in the Christmas play. One year I was the angel of the Lord. When I appeared to the shepherds, I forgot my lines, and never got another speaking part." After-school chores kept me from ever trying out for school plays or talent shows, but I got to play football." A "real man" played football my dad said, so I got to do that on top of my chores. *At least football promised me a way off the farm if I was good enough.* "I went to college on a football scholarship. I took music appreciation and performing classes as electives. That's how I met performers I managed when they were just starting out. I could speak the lingo of entertainers. My teachers networked with people in the business, so they were my door to my first jobs in the industry."

I got an injury on a hard tackle from a college lineman who objected to my attempted touchdown. I never got that touchdown, I never sang, I never danced. However, like everyone who did perform, I waited tables and tended bar to pay my bills in New York. I didn't go back to the tractor and barn; I had enough brothers and sisters to take over the farm.

"Who was your first client, and have they ever performed here?"

My first client? Debbie. You don't really want to know about her. She was a freelance hooker I recommended to bar patrons in town for a convention. When she got a gig dancing in the chorus of a Broadway play, she dropped hooking until the show ended and she wanted to eat again. But Debbie introduced me to Mario and Marie, a dance duo that I booked into bar mitzvahs, then night clubs, then supper clubs, then finally TV cameos. When Hollywood became hungry for talent, I rode their coattails for a while. After a couple of years, Mario ran away with Thomas to start a dance studio in San Francisco, and Marie ran away with me.

"I got lucky with the Tango Twins. Mario and Marie

could make your glasses steam up when they danced the tango, and make you forget about Fred and Ginger when they danced anything else. Mario was dark and handsome, so the ladies loved him. No, they haven't booked here. They got tired of the road, so they retired to teach ballroom dancing."

Marie and I have been together a long time. We had three kids almost all grown up now. This job let us put them in private school. *She was waiting for me by the staff pool right now,* so I checked my watch.

"Am I keeping you from anything?"

"Uh, no. Rehearsals start soon. I attend all of them. Guests don't pay to see sloppy footwork or missed notes, right? Then I'll look over the new costume designs for next season." *In truth, Marie is my costume designer and wardrobe mistress.* She's great at it. I never have to look for a missing button or a ripped seam. She can make thirty-four-A breasts look like thirty-six-Cs, and she can pad my biggest pansy's pants to make him look like a porn star.

"Max, do you ever interact with the guests here?"

Why would I want to do that? The men either ignore me as one of the help or mistake my on-purpose limp wrist and make a pass. The worst are men who think that they can pay me to make passes at their wives. *In any case, that aspect of the job would be lose-lose if I didn't have Marie on my arm.* "Not really. I introduce the acts so everyone knows me. Schmoozing is a part of *my* act, but I keep everyone at arm's length so there's no hard feelings."

"You must be good with names and faces. Do you ever have a guest who wants to perform? Do you let them?"

Peggy seems so familiar! I racked my brain because I never forgot a face. Do I ever get a guest who wants to perform? *When don't I?* Too much booze and Mr. Tycoon thinks he croons so great in the shower that he'd sound like Sinatra in our Lizard Lounge.

"If that happens, I sign them up for a couple of private coaching lessons beforehand. If they still want to perform after on-camera video sessions, I make sure they are sober before I introduce them to the crowd. A few embarrass themselves, but it rarely gets that far. I let one guy sing to his wife on their twenty-fifth wedding anniversary. I'm glad I did. He didn't make it to twenty-six."

"That was sweet. So, it's not all around-the-clock gambling, booze, and decadence after all." Peggy cracked. "What do you do to relax?"

What did I do to relax? "When I'm not with Marie, I escape to the rainforest. If you haven't been there, you should go. I'm an amateur herpetologist, more accurately a saurologist I'd say, since I study lizards. I coauthored an article for *Caribbean Herpetology* on the effects of climate change on the reproduction rate of geckos on the island."

"That's a surprise. How did you get interested in *that*?"

It's always a surprise, isn't it? When I'm in the forest I can be that kid riding the tractor, who stopped to play in the creeks and caught frogs, and salamanders, and newts or whatever I could catch in one of my mom's canning jars. There's not a lot of entertainment on a farm for a kid and I wasn't interested in having carnal relations with our milk cow. *That little hobby of mine led me to a biology degree.* "This island also has a couple of unique snakes, and one or two of them that I think are poisonous. I've been doing a little research about their venom, but I'm not ready to publish yet."

Her eyes quickly scanned the room and she started to speak but I said, "It's so quiet there compared to here. Beautiful birds and butterflies. I designed the Lizard of Oz Lounge. All the lizards painted on the lounge wall are indigenous to this island."

"Uh, cool. I've already been there. The gecko kept me very entertained. Is he trained?" We laughed over her joke. That lizard scares the bejesus out of some people. A little farm boy joke on my part.

"How is it working for Boss?"

Peggy wanted to know a lot of things I wasn't inclined to tell her. *The truth was I met Boss through Marie.* When Boss worked for the crime family, his boss liked to frequent a supper club where the Tango Twins danced every couple of months. Boss called his boss John. This club usually booked an old 40's tribute orchestra, and John was a fan. They also played for the Tango Twins when they danced. Boss noticed Marie and after a while he started sending flowers and inviting her to dinner. *She said no for a long time.* She finally gave in to a date. They kept it very low key. *She told me the Boss usually just wanted to talk, but she did most of it.* Maybe he was tired of being alone. Maybe she was too because she and Mario were never anything but dance partners.

"Boss is great. Very professional. Our guests get what they pay for. The staff earn a good wage with amazing benefits including a health plan. We get room and board, and the food is gourmet. I'm having crab salad for lunch today at the staff canteen. How's that for a perk."

"Great. I love it too. Tell me about your entertainment staff."

"We have a six-month season, so some musicians and dancers work that whole time. They give private lessons in our rehearsal studio when we aren't having group yoga and dance classes for guests. I rotate the main attractions. That's one way our guests decide when they come to the island. Some come just to see the Chairs, but most don't care about it. They book a trip based on their personal schedule and who I've booked into our venues. Some guests come more than once a season just for the entertainment."

I started seeing Marie while she was still seeing the Boss. *She said it was "pity sex" with him.* It wasn't long after that we started sleeping together that she and Boss broke up. We got married a few months later. We wanted to be together and she was pregnant. I never count the dates. *All my kids are my kids and always will be my kids.*

"About the time Boss got this island, Marie and I were in New York and went back to the old club for our anniversary." *Boss was there alone, and we asked him to join us.* One thing led to another, and he offered me the job here. I get to pick all the performers, the headliners, the celebrities we pay to come and circulate. *People come to me now to book themselves or their clients.* "We met through a mutual friend, Peggy. It was dumb luck really. We were in the right place, at the right time."

"How would you describe your celebrity entertainment employees in general?"

"Say, Peggy, I do need to get somewhere. If you need more, leave me a message and we'll meet again. Oh, be sure to catch the show. Our female impersonator act is so 1960s. This crowd loves it." I never did figure out where I'd seen her before. That'll keep me awake tonight. That and what to do about Marie.

****

"Ladies and Gentlemen," announced Drake's sports manager Scott. "Please find a comfortable seat in the shade. Welcome to the first cricket exhibition match at Drake's. I expect anything can happen. I suspect some of you are already fans of the game." A small spectator section offered a smattering of applause.

The Boss picked a spot to put up his chair. It gave him a great view of the field, the stands, and the road. Boss, Dex, and Rusty were in their seats and sipping a cool pineapple juice. They wore slacks and sport shirts, their Drake's casual uniform. A loud bang came from the direction of the road. "What was that?" Boss asked as he jumped up and scanned around their position.

Rusty said, "Just a backfire, probably a local truck. Do either of you fellas know anything about this game?"

"This better be good. I'm starting to regret it, Rusty," Boss said as he sat down.

Dex waved to one of the snorkeling guides passing out cards describing cricket. "Looking at this card this game seems a lot more complicated than baseball. It looks like the pitcher's mound place is called a 'pitch.' I guess that's where the action is."

Boss stated, "This match was Scott's idea. He noticed a lot of guests come from countries where cricket is king. A vestige of English colonialism, I'd guess. It's popular in the Caribbean," he said as he scanned the crowd. "I sure hope he was right. It's not looking too promising right now."

Scott continued, "Those of you who are new to this

91

game, take one of the laminated cards. On one side you'll find the Laws of Cricket as established in 1744. That card can be used as a fan if tropical breezes fail us."

"So we have eight guests who jumped at the chance to play in this match," Boss said, slipping his hand into the pocket holding his taser.

Dex noted, "Two o' thems Players for the Chairs, Boss. Maybe they think it's their last chance to play this game."

Rusty said, "Since 1744? Why do we have baseball instead of cricket?"

Scott announced, "Our teams come from across the Caribbean, and the fans are rabid. First out of the gate we have the Patriots in green shirts representing St. Kitts, Nevis, and the rest of the Leeward Islands." The Patriots slow strutted onto the field to a live Reggae band playing Bob Marley's "Get Up, Stand Up," took a lap of the pitch, and strutted over to their green benches. Resort staff joined in the dancing from their seats clapping to the beat.

"The opposing team is the Zouks who represent St. Lucia and the rest of the Windward Islands. Their shirts are yellow. I hope none of you are colorblind!" The Zouks danced out onto the field to live steel drum music and took a lap as well, and more guests stood and joined in the dancing and clapping. The team headed for their color-coded benches. The band played "Yellow Bird" that floated through the air as both teams danced on the sidelines.

Scott announced, "As a bonus, we have eight guests from Drake's who will be playing as subs for our teams. Four will play for the Patriots and four for the Zouks. All eight assured me they grew up playing cricket and are eager to get to it."

Chapter 10

The crowd cheered as guest players in green and yellow shirts ran out onto the field waving and joined their teams.

From the edge of the crowd Peaches walked nonchalantly towards her boss.

Boss said, "Scott assured me there would always be at least one guest on each team playing at all times. Those guys paid to be here. I'm paying the teams to be here."

Peaches sidled up behind Boss's chair and leaned in. When she put her hand on his shoulder he flinched and a cold sweat covered his body. He caught a whiff of her perfume and his eyes widened. She leaned in and whispered in his ear, "Boss, bodyguards to your left and right. My cousins Tiny and Bobby."

He exhaled sharply and nodded and she strolled back to the stands. Boss took out his handkerchief and wiped sweat from his face. "Hotter than I expected," he explained.

"Geographically, Drake's lies in the Leeward Island chain, but today we are neutral territory," Scott said, and then he took three minutes to describe the basic goal and play of cricket. "Guests and spectators, the game begins. Captains, come to the center of the pitch for the coin toss." Scott's contract was up for renewal. He needed this cricket match to be a success, or he'd be looking for a new gig.

Boss recognized the CCR rock classic "Run Through the Jungle" playing on the steel drums. "Huh. That never would have occurred to me." He caught a glimpse of Tiny not eight feet away, all two hundred and seventy-five pounds of him.

Rusty stood to stretch. "Do they play any country songs. That might be interesting."

Dex stood up and repeatedly jabbed his finger towards the field," Boss! Look. Look who's doing the coin toss. It's Vic. What does he know about cricket? I'll be damned. Vic."

As Drake's was in the Leeward Islands, the Patriots served as the home team leaving the Zouks' captain to call the toss. Vic took a coin from his pocket and held it up for all to see; the sun glinted off its gold surface.

Scott announced, "The coin the umpire will flip is a new U.S. one-ounce gold eagle worth approximately two-thousand dollars. Drake's has promised a gold eagle for each run scored. The total will be split between the teams and goes to local charities of their choice."

The crowd clapped loudly and added whistled support at this announcement.

Vic flipped the coin. The Patriots won and their fans roared approval. They opted to bat first. The players ran out to their positions and the first bowler started.

"There's Mr. Gogo at bat," Boss said.

"Yeah, and that Khan guy is in the field," added Dex. "Funny how different they are but they both play this stupid game. So, what happens now, Boss?" The bands kept playing on the sidelines.

"I guess we clap when the spectators clap." Boss shifted in his seat and almost missed seeing Bobby wearing a palm leaf hat, but Bobby was watching him.

Rusty added, "Good plan. It's never this quiet at a NASCAR race. It's much simpler— cars pass, cars break down, cars crash, an ambulance takes a driver, a wrecker tows the wreck, the race starts again. Repeat."

The noise level built. More golf carts parked nearby. More carts came and went depositing additional guests and staff and groups of locals. The crowd become noticeably bigger. Boss was sweating and watching the crowd more than the match. Five minutes later Boss understood that more people showing up had to stand. Since many of the staff worked primarily in the afternoon and evening, this was their free time. They brought horns and whistles they blew when scoring occurred, when the reggae band played, when the steel band played, and they blew them whenever they felt the urge. Tiny was blowing his heart out but never took his eyes off Boss.

The Boss called the kitchen. In less than five minutes ice cream carts parked on either side of the field and began passing out frozen coconut, mango, and chocolate ice cream treats. At each end of the field cold drink carts dispensed a never-ending supply of Caribbean beers of various names, soft drinks from every continent, and a truckload of cold water.

"Want a beer, Boss," Rusty asked.

"Don't mind if I do. Bring the local brand…get one that I can open."

"Me too," Dex added.

The teams played enthusiastically in the warm May sun. Screams of joy greeted each run. The reggae band played more Bob Marley. As the crowds' enthusiasm increased so did the players who put on a show twerking and cartwheeling between plays.

Dex pointed across the field. "Boss. Look!" Dancers from the floor shows appeared in their feathered and spangled costumes and danced to the bands like carnival cheerleaders. The teams kept playing, the crowds kept cheering, the whistles blew, and the beer disappeared.

Boss moved his chair away from the encroaching strangers. Dex and Rusty followed.

"Is there a problem, Boss?" Rusty asked.

"No. I just like a little breathing room." Boss asked, "Anyone getting hungry?" Both men nodded as Tiny and Bobby kept within easy distance of Boss.

Smoking hot grills were parked near the stands. Cooks started grilling skewers of shrimp, lobster, and chicken. Another grill cooked skewers of veggies and pineapple and glazed bananas and warmed up Johnnycakes.

The steel drums played "Red, Red Wine." The reggae band played "Island Girl"—at the same time. It started to look as if every guest and most of the staff were at the game. More of each were standing, swaying, or dancing to the music. They moved from their seats to the sidelines. There were lines at the grills, beer carts, and anything offering food or drink. The trash cans spilled over. The crowd hardly noticed when the cricket match ended, but a huge roar went up at the announcement of the amount raised for charity.

Boss grinned. "That prize money will be worth every cent. Great public relations for us, great help for the residents. Keep track of where that money goes and who it helps, Dex."

Loud bangs went off behind Boss. He jumped up and pulled his sheathed knife out of his pocket. Dex and

Rusty jumped and put their hands over their ears. Tiny and Bobby closed in on Boss. They all discovered firecrackers were being thrown onto the playing field. Boss's face flushed as he quickly closed his switchblade.

The firecrackers signaled when the party really took off. The cricket players grabbed beers and food and danced with the staff. Guests danced with one and all and chatted with players about equipment. Players signed autographs and took selfies with fans. Some even signed the laminated cards. Scott networked with the managers and danced with the chorus girls. He danced with Livy and Diamond and even Peaches.

The bands took turns; one played while the other ate, drank, and danced. Vic and security dressed as umpires circulated and kept things to a loud roar, never letting it get too rowdy or dangerous. They kept the smell of pot to a minimum. Only one spectator was taken to the Doc for stitches from a thrown beer bottle, but a couple of staffers were transported to their rooms to sleep off too much fun.

"It's a good thing we had a light activities schedule today. I don't know if many guests or staff would have shown up," Boss remarked to Dex as they mopped sweat from their necks and faces.

"Yeah, I get the party, I just don't get this game. What's the bet, and how would I know if I won?"

****

It was painfully evident that everyone had a blast, which Boss noted as he returned to the safety of his office, trailed by Tiny and Bobby. Bobby sat outside Boss's office beside Peaches.

Tiny stayed by the backdoor to Boss's apartment.

After too much of a good time, the island's two

school buses showed up, collected the cricket teams and their bands, and drove to their waiting planes. Staff and locals accompanied them by honking their car horns to the bands still playing as the buses rolled away. The noise gradually faded, and the soothing ruffled sounds returned of island breezes sifting through the palms.

By early afternoon most people had tired or drank themselves out. Gradually the crowd staggered away, but they left one hell of a mess: bottles, cans, paper plates, ice cream wrappers, cigarette butts, napkins, colored feathers, sequins, laminated cards, and some unrecognizable objects as well. Boss returned with Tiny and Bobby in tow to survey the damage.

"Damn, NASCAR hasn't got anything like this, Boss," a slightly staggering Rusty slurred. He smelled of beer and had chili sauce dribbled on his shirt. A few sequins and feathers stuck to the sauce.

Dex said, "I still don't know who won. Who do I collect my bet from?"

Boss said, "I have a *bad* feeling this was a success, and we'll have to make it a regular end-of-season event. I'd better tell Scott." Tiny and Bobby still shadowed him. "God bless Peaches," he mumbled as he chewed an antacid.

While Boss, Dex, and Rusty surveyed the carnage, Diamond, the Lottery Queen staggered up, and screeched out, "Hot damn, now that was a paar-tay!" She grabbed Dex, laid a big smooch on his lips, and covered them with bright orange lipstick. The look on his face was one of panic. Then she passed out, slid down the front of his shirt, and rolled out cold onto the grass.

Vic said, "Well, Boss, it's officially over. The fat lady sang." The men rudely whooped it up over that crack. Vic's pager beeped. He stepped away, spoke on his phone, and waved at Boss.

Boss looked at Diamond on the ground. "Dex, see the lady gets to her room safely will you," and walked over to Vic. A golf cart stopped so quickly in front of the two men that the driver almost left the cart.

"Get in, Boss. It's the Gizmo."

"What about the Gizmo?"

"Someone broke in with a crowbar and wrecked the control panel."

"Do we know who it was?"

"Yes, Boss. One of the Players. We got him on camera. Twitchell."

Talking about being caught reminded me of one night at a basketball game. Mr. Herman, the principal, spoke to me as I walked out of the bathroom. "A bit far from the gym, isn't it?"

I noted Rosalie exiting the girls' bathroom closer to the gym. I didn't want him to turn around until she was safe. "There was a clogged toilet in the boys, and I drank too much iced tea tonight. I really couldn't wait, Mr. Herman." I could tell I wasn't in trouble.

"You're a good kid. Are you still planning on law school?"

"Uh, yeah, after…" I watched Rosalie hurry into the gym. "…after the Army. Well, see ya, Mr. Herman. I can't miss my ride."

If they had cameras in schools back then we would have been busted for sure.

****

Chet, my chief engineer, met us at the Gizmo. Two security people were stationed at the ends of the hallway. Vic, Chet, and I went into the display room. The curtains were normally open to allow guests to catch a glimpse of the famous Gizmo, but someone had closed them. Broken glass from the Gizmo covered the floor, but the window was intact.

Vic sighed. "He sure did a number on the control panel."

I replied, "Yes. I've seen Twitchell on the golf course. He has a powerful swing. Why do you think it was a crowbar?"

"It was a preliminary guess by security, but so far we haven't found one."

Bits of control knobs dangled from the panel. I flipped the power switch on the wall. It was obviously targeted. None of the lights on the panel lit up. "What do you think he used?"

Vic, a man of few words, opined with a poker face, "A three iron."

Chet snickered. "I'd say he has a terrible hook in his swing. Well, Boss. Plan G?"

I nodded. "Chet you do the work yourself. Vic, no one outside of us three knows about this. Keep the curtains drawn." I added, "Chet. No hurry. 9:00 PM the night of the Chairs is fine. If anyone asks, say it's routine maintenance."

Vic added, "I'd cancel that golf game with Mr. Trevino, Boss."

****

I called Scott in when I got to my office. *I needed to nail his new contract down as soon as possible.* One less disgruntled employee who might have written the death threat. I had many comments from guests after the match: "That was a smashing idea, Boss," and "The best time I've had in years," and "I can't buy that at any other resort. Sign me up for next year, old chap." The grounds crew was still cleaning up the mess, but my staff was the happiest I've seen them all season, maybe even for any season since we opened. *I've got to follow up on this, but when? Now or never!*

There was a knock on my door as Scott peeked in.

"Scott. I need to talk to you."

"Yes sir. What did you think of the cricket match?" he said as he sat across from me.

I kept behind the safety of my desk. "Honestly, boring. The only thing I've been to more boring was a polo match…"

Scott's face fell. He started to talk through clenched teeth when I cut him off. "…but after the teams came on, and the music started, and the staff showed up, it was an unmitigated success that everyone loved." Scott's scowl stretched into a grin. "What do you think about doing it next season, but on purpose with some planning as a fund raiser for island charities?"

"Absolutely." Scott's head was nodding slowly.

"Can you bring in a cricket celebrity or two to circulate for a few days ahead of the match and give talks about their careers and cricket in general? Or maybe, bring them in during the season to promote the last week. And not just Brits. Indians, Aussies, anyone known to love cricket." Scott's face looked about to crack from smiling so hard. "Isn't May prime cricket season? Can we get a live video feed and run it in the sports lounge?

"Get with Max. Let's bring in Caribbean reggae and steel drum bands to play at the outdoor areas and at a monthly shindig for the staff at their pool. Rotate the bands to share the work and income." I was loading his plate. "Could we use the cricket pitch for our kids to practice when we're not using it? Is that feasible? Maybe have a camp in the offseason?"

Chapter 11

Scott's mouth fell open. "That's incredibly generous, Boss."

I waved my hand. "I know it's the end of our season this week, but could you work up some ideas over the break and email them to Peaches?

I said, "We'll want some construction for permanent bleachers, team shelters, and restrooms. I'd say that rates a twenty-five percent pay raise, wouldn't you?"

"Geez, yes, Boss. To all of that. Thank you so much."

I stood and extended my right hand. The taser was in my left hand inside my pocket.

"Great job, Scott. Really. Great job. Thanks." I let out a huge breath. I'd though I had neutralized any threat I anticipated from Scott.

No sooner did Scott leave than I got a call from Doc. "Boss. My preliminary analysis is Mr. Stewart had a kind of reptile venom in his blood. There weren't any snake bites, so on a hunch I tested the coffee. It contained venom."

"You're sure? Snake venom? In *my* coffee?"

"Yes. The crazy thing was the venom normally wouldn't have killed him. But, since he had those cuts in his mouth and an ulcer, the venom got into his blood stream and did him in."

The coffee meant for me. Poison by someone who

believed all poison was the same. The note wasn't a hoax. I started pouring my own coffee after the Doc's call.

****

Looking back, I'm sure it added up to more time together than if Rosalie and I had been allowed to date. I never understood the rules for football or who was on the team. I "liked baseball" in the spring. I ran track and Rosalie came to root for "the team." Track was easy. Being as track was an individual sport, I had few contact injuries, for the most part an occasional pulled muscle or hamstring. *The rules were easy. Be the first across the line, just like life.*

I still followed that rule, and so far I was winning.

****

Vic called. "You've got the see this security video, Boss. I'm in the control room."

I walked in a few minutes later. Vic was alone. "What do I need to see.?"

"I reviewed the video from the camera in the Maze by the kitchen at door K3. Watch this. When the video starts Yvette stands just inside the door. Look how she keeps holding her head like she's got a headache...Then a man walks up to her, but we can't see who it is...They talk...The man takes something from his pocket and gives it to Yvette...Now they move slightly out of view, but I suspect he gives her a quick kiss and leaves... Now see that cup across from her, that's your coffee...She takes whatever the man gave her, opens it, and pours some into your cup of coffee." Vic paused the video.

"Yvette? My casino manager poisoned me and killed Mr. Stewart instead?"

"Boss, it's not true that women use poison more than

men do, and poison is tricky. In this case, I don't think she was trying to kill you. Watch what happened next...Yvette turned sideways to the camera and poured the rest of the poison into her own cup and drank it. "

I shook my head. "I don't understand what's happening."

"I got an idea or two that I need to check out. If I had to guess, it looks like the man tricked Yvette into poisoning your coffee. But—and this is a big but—he wanted Yvette dead too. Maybe he came in, discovered the coffee with your name on it, saw an opportunity, and took it. Yvette was supposed to die to eliminate a witness."

"But she didn't."

"And I bet she doesn't have an ulcer."

"Ah, I see." I paused for a moment and picked up the phone. "Doc, do me a favor. Call Yvette in and test her blood for the venom that killed Mr. Stewart. Make up some excuse about a sick guest who might have exposed her to something. Get back to me as soon as you have results. Oh, do you know if she has an ulcer? Got any idea who Yvette is seeing, Vic? If he was in the Maze, it was probably an employee."

"I'll make some inquiries."

"And check Dex and Rusty's alibis for that time. " *Where did that venom come from, and who is trying to kill me?* I started to leave but stopped. "This venom...it might be local. Talk to Max about that."

****

Vic walked over to the costume department where he found Marie sewing on a sequined button. "Marie, I brought your favorite bagel with cream cheese and a pot of tea. Do you have time for a short break?"

She looked at Vic for a long moment, then sudden recognition showed in her face. The Boss had authentic New York bagels flown in twice a week. It remined her of home and her kids. They sat at a table in the shade.

"You must be busy. Lots of last-minute details?" He spread cream cheese on a seeded bagel.

"No, Vic. You know I keep ahead with the sewing." She poured the tea.

"You were sewing just now. What are you working on? One of Yvette's gowns, which are gorgeous by the way?" He passed her a bagel half.

"No, one of her nightgowns. It got torn. I am making it right as new."

"Yvette is always dressed like a model from Paris, isn't she? How did she damage a nightgown?"

"Dex did it silly. He's just as careless with his clothes. He dropped it by on his way to the gym."

"Dex brought Yvette's nightgown to you?"

"Yes…I'm sure it was Dex. I don't understand these young people. Dex said he was a friend of Yvette's, and she gave him benefits so he was giving her one. Isn't what we always did, help our friends out?"

"Sure did…Marie, did Dex say he and Yvette were friends *with* benefits?"

"Friends with benefits? Yes, I think that was it."

Vic leaned back in his chair and chewed his bagel. "That certainly was thoughtful of him." When she finished her tea, Marie got up and left without saying goodbye to Vic, but he didn't mind. "Some friend. Some benefit," Vic said to himself as he took a bite.

****

Peggy and Player Number Eight entered the room together 'cause they came at the same time. I made the formal introductions. The interview was be rescheduled 'cause the Lottery Queen got drunk at the cricket game and passed out cold. Here she was five hours late. Max and me had done some business while we waited.

I asked Max what Boss would say about Player Eight and he told me, "The Boss will say 'Player number Eight hit two giant lotteries in one year and she says she's on a roll. Welcome, Ms. Eight.'" *She's sporting a solid gold grill and her kids are at home eating hot dogs, unless family services got 'em.* Boss said if she didn't play here, she'd play somewhere else.

Here came the two women. I said, "Ladies, we'll be leaving to allow you two some privacy for your girl talk. Can I have anything sent in?"

"Mr. Dex, you got some Wild Turkey? I'll have two shots over ice. And some o' them concky thingies with ketchup. I never knew it was so hot on an island. 'Minds me o' Houston." Peggy asked for iced island tea and conch fritters too. "And, hey Mr. Dex, I ain't no lady. I'm a full-growed woman, or didn't you look?" She winked at me. I nodded, and Max and I escaped to place their order.

****

The Lottery Queen moaned and held an icebag to her head. "You go to the party, girl? It was the best thing so far since I been here."

Peggy answered, "Yes, for a few minutes. What name would you like me to use for you in my book?"

"Anything just so it ain't too loud. Joyce, my mamma, always call me 'trouble' but I found out last year the name on my birth certificate was Jewel, so *I* picked 'Diamond.'" She grinned a grimace that stretched her face sideways so far you could see every karat of her grill and inset diamonds.

She sat up straight. "I see there's an African brother in the Chairs. You interviewed him yet? Can you hook us up? Just not today. There's twenty bucks in it for you."

Peggy choked a bit and said, "What people tell me is confidential. But you'll have to meet him yourself. Diamond, what is it that you want people to know about you?"

"Damn, girl. I guess it's that I am a big, Black woman who ain't afraid o' eating and I got more money than Aretha."

"Aretha? That's a quote if I ever heard one. Do you mind telling me how old you are?"

"No. Do you mind I'm not too sure o' the answer? Probably thirty-something."

"Okay. How about winning all that money? How did that change your life?"

"Well first thing I found out is the U.S. tax man takes about half of that money. Then I found out every friend and cousin I ever had wanted to be my bestest friend as long as I paid. And every sorry-ass man that ever touched me wanted to come home to his sugar mamma and manage all that money for her. I guess my answer is I don't have anyone I can trust who don't expect me to pay for them."

"Do you shop much?"

"I got a couple o' cars but I don't have a license. I got me a regular appointment at a salon twice a week for my hair, and my nails. I bought me a mink coat. I keep it cold at home so's I can wear it at supper. I got all new clothes for my kids."

"I see you have eight children. Who's taking care of

them while you're here at Drake's?"

"They's the reason I'm here. The big one's sixteen and two of thems hers. I left her some cash to feed them all and buy diapers."

"How old were you when your first baby was born, Diamond?"

She looked out the window to the beach. "I don't know. I was a baby myself when Joyce's boyfriends started messin' with me. The first two babies got flushed down the toilet. Joyce said they was a miss carriage. That sounded like I done somethin' wrong, but I didn't. Her men did me wrong, miss."

There was a knock at the door. A waiter came in with a tray. Diamond swallowed her drink in one gulp, ordered a refill with more ice for her icebag, and attacked her food.

"Diamond, how long did you go to school?"

"That one's easy to answer. Never."

"Never? How was that possible?"

"Let me explain. My mamma Joyce is a white woman and there's lots of men who want some of that. She grew up on welfare just like me, so she didn't know no better than me about school. Even if she wanted it, her mamma didn't let her go. She stayed home to cook and mind the babies while her mamma worked as a cleaner.

"Joyce left home when she was fourteen with nowhere to go. The streets are mean to kids, so they caught her up in some bad things. She ran away from that, but nothin' changed and then I came along. She didn't know no better on raising kids and changing your own life than I do.

"I was having my mamma's life until I hit the Jackpots. I know I ain't no fit mamma. How could I be?

I never been a child much less a woman."

"What will you do if you win the Chairs?"

"I don't care if I win. My bet includes my kids. I hope whoever wins my bet changes my kids' lives. I hope they know what to do for them. I hope they knows how to loves em 'cause I sure don't. I didn't have a choice on being a mamma. They need someone better than me. I need someone better than me."

"Diamond, you're going to make me cry. Are you sure about this?"

"My bet's already in Boss's pocket. I hope them Chairs or Boss do right by my kids."

"Don't you want to reconsider this? Are you sure?"

"Uh-huh. I think it's the best thing for my kids and for me. I think about it every night while I'm trying to get to sleep. I just want to learn how to be a person from now on. If I make a mistake, I don't want to hurt no one but me."

"You mean you are playing in the Chairs to give your kids a better life? And maybe you too? That's beautiful and sad at the same time. And—you are sure?"

She nodded.

"So, no plan to get married?"

Diamond shook her head. Tears rolled down her plump cheeks.

Peggy passed her a tissue.

"The saddest part is it don't matter whose body I be in, it's still me and that's like my mamma always said: trouble."

"Well, what else is left to say?"

The women sat quietly and polished off their meal. The waiter brought Diamond's drink order and ice. As she put more ice into the icebag she asked, "Peggy, how about that football player? You meet him yet? Could you hook me up with him for a hundred?"

Chapter 12

Dex and I were catching up by the pool. We liked to be out where the guests could see us from time to time. Our waitress brought us drinks: an iced hibiscus tea for me, and an iced island tea with a slice of coconut banana cream pie for Dex. "Anything I need to aware of, Dex?" I nodded to a frequent guest who walked past.

"One of the yachts lost an anchor last night, Boss." Dex slurped his tea, a sure sign he was nervous.

"In the guest harbor?"

He nodded vigorously. Another sign. "Yeah. I sent our hoist and crew over there. It's in fifty feet of water, so I don't see a problem getting it. Our guys did notice something, uh, odd."

"Which boat is it? Who's the owner?"

Dex pulled a scrap of paper from his pocket. "It's the *Canopus*. It's a charter from the Bahamas. It was here last year twice. And the year before that."

I sensed a problem brewing. "Spit it out."

"The boat had some kinda pods mounted on the outside of the what cha call it...It's tied up at dock number twelve."

"There are pods mounted on the hull below the waterline?"

"Yeah, Boss. Know what that means, don't we?"

"Indeed, we do. Is he smuggling something in or out of the island, or is he really on vacation? If it's one of the

113

first two, or even both, we need to stop it. Keep a surveillance camera on the boat. If there's any activity, send out the RPV."

"Boss, that RPV thing. What's it again?" He barely nibbled at his pie and Dex loved pie.

"Remotely piloted vehicle. It's an underwater drone with cameras. That's how we caught that Player last year dumping his wife's body on the bottom of our harbor as he left. One more thing. Have Vic contact U.S. Customs in St. Thomas. See if there's anything on the owner of the *Canopus*. They might need to get involved. Is that it?"

"Vic already called them. They should be here soon. Uh, no, Boss. You really got to see that female impersonator Max booked. She can do anyone. I'm gonna ask her if she can do that Frankie girl."

"That Frankie girl?" I didn't remember a Frankie girl.

"Remember she sang with that group from Jersey, the Four Reasons."

Oh, that Frankie girl. "Frankie Valli? Maybe next year. This is the last week, and her show is set, isn't it?" I suppressed a chuckle.

"Yeah, you're probably right. One more thing, Boss. The Lottery Queen is coming on to some of our staff."

"Has she hit on you, Dex?" I momentarily flashed on her smooching Dex at the cricket match. I couldn't resist yanking his chain.

Dex paled. "I wouldn't call it that, Boss, cripes. You were there. I had nothing to do with that. But two of the Escorts mentioned her."

This was not a new problem at Drake's, but it was my job to protect my staff. "Escorts? If those guys can't handle her, why are they working for us?" If escorts can take down a Player unhappy at losing, they should be able to avoid a lonely Player during a normal day.

"Right, Boss. I didn't think 'bout it that way. Those guys do seem to be staying away from the beach and pools. Uh, I'm gonna talk to Vic more about that boat. I'll have it moved to the boatyard at the cargo port."

"Good idea. Explain to the owner that our hoists and repair shops are over there. And have Vic or security ride along to be sure it doesn't leave." Dex swallowed his last bite of pie, downed his tea, and left, knocking over his chair. *He was in a hurry. Why?* I chuckled, "Frankie Valli and the Four Reasons. Ah, yes, I remember her well." *It was the best laugh I'd had all week.* I appreciated what Dex lacked in couth he made up in cunning. Did that include poison? It seemed too subtle for him. Could he think I wouldn't expect something so out of character? *Or was I giving him too much credit?*

I'm doubting if I gave my own folks enough credit lately.

Rosalie was a sweet kid. Idealistic. Warm. She liked me holding her hand. But as much as I wanted more, and as crazy in love as we were, I respected her. My dad taught me that.

We talked a lot. We were fortunate, and we were grateful for it. Neither of us came from a family where there was abuse or alcoholism. My dad on occasion talked at dinner about helping kids escape a bad family situation. Her father on occasion presided over the burial of a child who did not escape.

"Gosh, Rosalie. Let's never let that happen to any of our kids," I said one night. "We'll never let them go." She kissed me to seal our future pact. We never doubted

our parents loved us and wanted a lot for us. Because of this, we respected our families and did our best not to disappoint them.

****

"Hey, Pepe. Did you get a chance to look over the shutdown schedule?" I was checking with my stage manager on our procedures for closing down our entertainment venues after the Chairs, the floorshows, and entertainment end at 2:00 a.m.. All guests have to leave by 3:00 p.m. the day after the Chairs. The lounges and pool bar serve breakfast and lunch for those who didn't sail away or fly off during the night. "Yes. This looks good. Keep me updated."

Peggy arrived at my office as we finished. "Hello again. Are you getting a chance to rest or is it all work, work, and work?" I asked.

She cracked a weary smile. "I would be resting if it wasn't for the one thing you forgot to mention, Max."

I was well aware of what she meant. "More work?"

"Exactly. I have met some very—no, let me say extremely—unusual people, almost seemingly from a different planet." She didn't know how much of an understatement that was. "And some do nothing but zone out."

"Yes, some people just want to sit around and loaf. I call them our lounge potatoes. Some seem to occupy bar stools and armchairs so I long I'm tempted to watch for roots to start sprouting."

"Have you tried watering them and installing sunlamps in the lounge?" she joked.

"At least they'd get a tan for free to show the folks at home," I cracked back.

"I guess they don't care what the weather is, do

they?" She was doodling in her notebook.

"No, not really since they can stay dry and get back to their room. We've got the Lizard and the Sports lounges open twenty hours a day. Sadly, we had guests who'd be at the bars 24-7 if we didn't close to clean them. They fill up more on rainy days because outdoor activities are cancelled. But we have folks who are here alone, or who don't want the fuss of a tux, or who just want to drink. And that's okay as long as they behave. Come on. Let's check it out."

"I talked to a couple of guests and I met one or two that fit that description. Didn't want to talk about much other than what *I* was drinking," she said.

"Let me show you the Lizard of Oz Lounge first. I'm pretty proud of it." We went through the Maze and in through the back.

She looked surprised as I opened the rear door. "Aha! The hidden door is in a wall behind the bar. So this is where you keep clean glasses, bottles of liquor, all the things you need in a bar but don't want to clutter up the place. I see again why the Maze is so important. I was here earlier. Dex showed me the introduction video, and I had a *lovely* chat with the bartender. It's a great place and it fits in perfectly with the island."

Walking around the main lounge I spotted a quiet nook and we sat down under a large green iguana. Pointing to the lizard I said, "I painted that one myself. We won't be noticed here." I recognized a Player and a young woman I didn't know talking in the darkest corner of the lounge. I was nosy about what mischief was cooking when she rose and slapped him as she left, but I realized Peggy had asked me a question.

"I'm sorry. What…?"

"I read that some iguanas actually swim in the sea and eat seaweed. Will I run into them on the beach?" She had a white-knuckle grip on her pen.

"Almost true. There are marine iguanas that eat algae, not seaweed. Fortunately, they only live in the Galapagos west of South America."

Color returned to her hands. She looked at the iguana on the wall. "But in here they are all fake," I assured her.

"Then it's lovely. I'm more of a city girl so the idea of things with more than two legs terrify me."

"Some of the guests like it. They want to experience the rainforest without the possibility of walking into a spider web or crossing paths with a reptile."

"This is a bar," she said, "but I don't see any TVs with sports on them. I'm not sure I've ever been in a bar without sports." The bartender served us our food, and I swear he winked at Peggy. She was pointedly ignoring him. He walked away smirking. *I wonder what that's all about.*

"This is a piano bar. During the morning we have recorded music, but in the afternoons and evenings we have a live pianist." *I come here to dance with my wife.* I caught Peggy watching the walls rather than talking to me. It's part of my job to make all of our guests comfortable. As soon as the fritters were eaten, I said, "Now let's go over to the sports bar. " I led her out the back through the Maze to our second lounge, Drake's 19th Hole.

****

"Wow! The 19th Hole is a change," Peggy said. " Not a Lizard in sight. I expected a lot of golf-related décor. I see wall-mounted big screen TV's, required as usual."

"Yes, but each guest gets a set of noise-cancelling ear buds or a headset to use while they're here. Other guests can easily carry on a conversation, or an argument, over the game. We do have a few golf souvenirs. Here's the set of clubs used by last year's winner in the U.S. Masters. He's a regular. Boss put in a special putting green the champ could configure to match any course on the tour. Even soaked it down once to simulate a rainy day."

A loud roar of laughter came from the bar. Diamond and the former NFL player Livy were surrounded by a squad of men trying on a Superbowl ring. NFL highlights played on the TV.

Peggy turned to me and continued, "That's amazing. How about tennis?"

"Men or ladies?

"Ladies, of course," she said with a shake of her finger.

"Singles or doubles?"

"Singles." A look of doubt crossed her face.

"Grass or clay?"

"Uh, grass."

"Wimbledon okay by you?" *I knew that would get her.*

Peggy's eyes widened and her head swiveled looking for a clue. She pointed to a trophy case and went to it, her high heels clicking on the wood floor. "That's…that's the Venus Rosewater Dish." She leaned in looking at the names along the edge. "What? She won last year! How did you get this?" she said so loudly her voice cracked.

"Boss has supported Wimbledon financially for

years, so he has been a great fan and I'll just say he has 'friends' in high places."

"But, but…," she struggled to speak.

"If you play, you might take a few lessons the next time you're here with a former Wimbledon champ. Boss is very generous to our guest professionals."

Peggy's breathing was hard. I assumed she might need to catch her breath, so I changed the subject. "Let's go over there." I led her to a table in front of a Lamborghini Aventador on the wall. I signaled the waitress.

Peggy said, "The floor and wall are painted to look like this car skidded up the wall. It's so realistic looking." She leaned over to touch the car and jerked back her hand. "It's real! Is that a real race car?"

"Yes, it is. Sad story really."

"What happened? Was it an accident?"

"You should talk to Rusty about it. He knows more than I ever will."

"That sounds like *not* an accident. Rusty? At the track?" She made a note.

"Yes, have you interviewed him yet?"

"Tomorrow, and now I can't wait."

More raucous laughter came from the bar, so we moved towards the exit to the Maze. "Max, how do you find this stuff much less acquire it? Collectors pay obscene amounts of money for these things."

Max said, "I know. It's the usual networking method. Guests who know someone, guests who are professional themselves, and what we find people are interested in. I suppose I'll have to add memorabilia for cricket now, after that spectacularly surprising match we had."

"I experienced it," Peggy said. "It was a wild and crazy time."

"Really? I didn't notice you."

"I was in disguise. Easier to melt into a crowd that way. Max, have you talked to the former NFL player in the Chairs yet? She might have something to donate."

"That's a great idea. If she wins big, she might feel like leaving us a souvenir. I can't imagine what she might still have. Does anything ring a bell?"

****

Rusty

I wasn't sure why she was interviewing me. Boss said she's talking to the Players for the Chairs but now he wanted me to talk with her. *Does he know about the new track offer?*

"Peggy, is it? I know a little about you already. I'm surprised you wanted to interview me. Not all our guests care about the track. Please sit down, ma'am." This lady looks more like a big city gal than a track rat—my nickname for hardcore racing fans.

"Thanks. To be honest, I know nothing about cars or racing, so let me ask about you. What's your background, Rusty?"

"Sure thing. I have a double degree in mechanical and in motorsports engineering from a college in North Carolina."

"Why North Carolina?"

"If you want to do racing you got to go to a southern school because that's where most racing fans live and where more racing teams have their headquarters." I pointed to my shirt. "See this, and I apologize for being so casual, but you caught me on my way to the gym. It reads 'I got tickets to Bristol.' NASCAR started in the

Appalachian Mountains when illegal moonshiners were trying to outrun the government agents, but it's all legit now, so I am hardcore NASCAR."

"This island seems like a strange place for a track."

"It does seem so. The Fast Track has everything to do about the need for speed. Some guests are into high end fast cars. They love to put the pedal to the metal with no cops around. We also have hours for our guests who cycle. It gives them a great workout with spectacular views. With an island this big, Boss figured there was space for a two-lane track. Ours is twenty-five miles long."

"Twenty-five miles? That seems more like a highway. Where does it all go to?"

"I'll show you the layout of the track. It's this way."

As we walked through the door she exclaimed, "Is that a scale model of the track!"

"Yes ma'am. We use it to acquaint our drivers and spectators with the layout. In front of us are the garages where we are now. As you leave the tarmac here and turn right or left onto the racetrack, you'll see the start and finish lines painted on the ground." I pointed to an area near us. "Next you enter a short straight-away that lets you pick up speed before the first turn by a set of palms trees, if you are turning right. I'll just assume for the rest of my explanation that you're driving in this direction. The track's got sharp turns, a couple of tunnels—here, here and there—straightaways, bridges, a pretty good hill over there to climb at the other end of the island, and a figure eight with an elevated crossover—here in the middle of the island."

"That seems complicated and dangerous."

"Yes, but we designed those features to minimize

the noise near the resort and the homes of our employees, and to have very little impact on the ecosystem. Also, they provide a challenge worth what we charge. That means the track is a moneymaker."

"That's good, isn't it?"

"Yes, ma'am. It keeps me in the black."

She nodded. I turned back to the model. "I alternate the direction weekly to keep things interesting. The track doesn't have lights, so people don't drive at night, except my boss."

"The Boss drives at night? That seems odd, and again, dangerous."

"He never drives over thirty miles an hour and has the whole track to himself. He says he

likes to keep his driving skills up. I think it gives him a chance to be alone."

"Do you have drag racing, Rusty?"

"No, we don't drag race here. It's more of a blue-collar sport."

"I see. So how does it work when a guest wants to use the track?"

"Every car owner rents a garage and supplies their own tools and crew. There are accommodations with a kitchen and catered meals. The crew can use staff facilities at the resort on their time off, if they get any. Drake's charges extra for track access and the owners need to show proof of adequate life insurance and an iron-clad indemnity for Drake's if a driver wrecks or anyone is injured."

"Has that ever happened?"

"Boy, howdy, has it ever." Peggy's eyes widened at Rusty's remark about track injuries. "That sounds serious. Was the driver badly hurt?"

Chapter 13

"Well, yes. We close in May but that's not exactly true. That's when we close the casino and the resort for the high rollers. A week after the Chairs, we open a smaller, but still pricey, resort with reduced amenities. The casino is a few slot machines, but no live tables, no celebrities, and the kitchen is much smaller. This lets us maximize the assets here and to keep our local staff fully employed. Last May we had a guest with a four hundred-fifty-thousand-dollar car. One car."

Peggy listened closely after I mentioned the price tag.

"The owner didn't mind the move to a smaller suite because his wives had gone home and he could run his car as much as he wanted. Now there is a story about that car, and people still remember it being in the business news."

"Was that the royal family member? Wasn't that an accident?"

"That was him. He had a deal go bad. His partner lost half a million and the car owner, Abdul, claimed he lost the same amount because he foolishly invested for them in a scam. Then Abdul shows up with this car."

"What kind of car was this?"

I said, as I shook my head, "There's only four others like it in the world. A Lamborghini Aventador. The most amazing car I've ever seen. That car pumped out seven hundred-thirty horsepower with a top speed of two-hundred-seventeen miles per hour. Abdul said he got it second-hand. Maybe—but I do remember that the oil pressure gauge wasn't working right. His crew waited to make the decision because they wanted to change out the gauge. Abdul ignored the mechanics. It's a two-day job. He was in a hurry. He told them to fill up the oil and have it ready at 6 a.m.." *That's what they did.*

"Bright and early, he showed up, strapped in, and took off." The track has cameras all along the garages and the course so we can monitor everything. Abdul drove like he was on fire. Middle of his third lap, his engine blew. He ran out of oil. The engine got so hot it threw a rod through the block. That means the engine is kaput. Abdul was miles away from the garage and near a beach, so he shifted into neutral and rolled to a stop. He got out swearing and beat and kicked the car. I can show you the video. Then he walked to the beach and sat under an apple tree. He never questioned but that someone would come and get him. He ate an apple, and it started to rain so he scooted back under the branches and leaned against the tree.

"Thirty minutes later, his crew drove up in the wrecker and hitched up the Lamborghini. He ignored them so one guy went down to talk with him but he came back screaming. Abdul was dead and all covered in horrible, oozing blisters." *I never want to see that again.*
"Our doctor was still at the resort, so they took Abdul to the clinic. The Doc took one look and understood what happened. Abdul's mouth and tongue were swollen and blistered because he ate an apple from that tree. The tree is called locally the death apple. Anyway, sap dripped down on him with the rain and blistered his skin and

where it soaked through his shirt when he leaned back against the tree.

"The Doc asked the crew chief, 'Did you see the tree he was under?' The guy said yes. 'Did the tree have a big red X painted on it?' Again, 'Yes.' The Doc said, 'Without a doubt, the Manchineel tree killed him.' Abdul picked the most poisonous tree in the world to sit under. It killed him in a painful and gruesome manner."

"Gruesome is right. So, it *was* an accident. Why have poisonous trees here at all?"

"The tree was here first. It's a native and it helps prevent beach erosion. Most places have a sign or paint some part of the tree red to warn people. Abdul ignored the red paint warning just like he ignored his oil pressure gauge. If he had stayed in his car, he'd be alive today."

"Here's the thing about Abdul. His brother-in-law, the one who lost the money in the scam, flew from the Middle East to claim the body. He seemed real chummy with the crew mechanics. Abdul mentioned to me at dinner the night before that all his crew were relatives, cousins of his brother-in-law. He said he didn't trust them and worried they might sabotage his car. That's why he didn't let them replace the oil gauge."

Peggy asked, "Could someone sabotaged the car, whether they meant to kill him or just wreck it?"

"Well, I'll have to think about that…but could someone tamper with the car? The easiest thing I can think of would be to get someone to slide under the car, remove the oil plug, drain the oil, and replace the plug. That would work to sabotage my car, but not that Lamborghini."

"Why not. A car is a car, isn't it?" *No ma'am, it's not!* I had some explaining to do.

"That Aventador has a ground clearance between four and five inches. I don't know of anyone who is skinny enough to slide in under that car sitting on the pavement much less do any work on it. The crew just arrived, so they didn't have their hydraulic lift yet. But is there another way to lift that car up a foot? Hmm. Let's walk over to the garage. There's something I want to check on." We left my office and walked into the first garage. There was my answer in the corner. "The answer to your question is maybe. We have these hydraulic rolling jacks to move cars." I pointed to one by the wall. "It's possible a guy could have jacked up that Lamborghini enough to get under it. They did bring all the actual tools they needed with them."

"So, someone could have done it then?"

"Yeah, but there's another problem. It would take more than one person. This car has an undertray, a sheet metal cover across the underside to make it look cool and protect it because it's low to the ground. I know for sure there's a removeable panel in the middle for maintenance." I skinned up my knuckles on one before I was a driver. "They'd have to remove that panel and that's a lot of screws and bolts. You'd definitely need a helper to keep track of the hardware and different sized tools." *This was getting interesting. How far could I take it?*

"And then what?"

"Next? This baby has, I think, three, no, four oil plugs in the pan, but one plug isn't easy to reach, so you'd have to skip it. However, you could drain a lot of oil out through three holes. The oil spec for the Aventador calls for thirteen and a half quarts."

"That's a lot, isn't it?"

"Yes, but you won't get all the oil out, and you better have a big enough pan for what you will get without slopping it on the concrete. Even if you pulled three oil plugs, you could measure how much drained out and know how much remained, because they filled it up the night before." I was beginning to think I was seeing something I missed earlier. "That would give you an idea of how soon the engine would overheat and blow. Even if two or three quarts were left in, the way he drove, the car would blow the first day."

"Would that cause a wreck? Wouldn't anyone see them working on the car?"

"Well, maybe, maybe not to both your questions. Depending where he was on the track, at those speeds a wreck could be possible. With most of the guests gone, we turned off the garage cameras. His car was sitting out because he wanted to show it off. We have a guard with a dog. His office is at the end of the garages, but his window doesn't look out over the parking lot."

Peggy scratched her chin. "You made me think of something. Would rain have any effect?"

"Rain? We get an average of four inches of rain in May. What made you think of that? "

"My dog is afraid of lightning and thunder. She'll be scratching to get in even before a storm starts. She's a better forecaster than my local TV weatherman."

"I'll be darned. So is this dog. The guard keeps him in when there's a storm. If it rained, and there was more than one person it might be possible to sabotage that car. Damn." *What's getting a little wet compared to getting half a million dollars in revenge?* Even if the car didn't wreck, a new engine, parts and labor, transportation, and all—probably worth it.

128

"What happened to the car?"

"Know what? The brother-in-law left it here. I cleaned it up, removed all the fuel, oil, and other liquids and mounted it on the wall in the Sports Lounge."

"That's the car I touched yesterday."

"For sure." Abdul's accidental death was a bonus his brother-in-law didn't expect. *Sweet!* "Let me give you a ride back to the resort and I'll buy you a drink."

I considered if I should have another talk with the Boss about Abdul's death. He wouldn't like it. It might affect my new contract—if I get one. I snickered thinking of the ingenuity used to bring down Abdul who was an embezzler or guilty of fraud at the least.

"I'll take the ride but pass on the drink. Sorry, but may I ask you one more question?"

"Sure thing."

"How did you and Boss meet and how did you end up here?"

I bent down to tie a shoelace. My face puckered up when I stood. I wasn't sure how much I wanted to admit. "I screwed up big time. I had a ride in the number one NASCAR team six years ago. I got cocky and cost the owner a lot of money. I wrecked every car he had in one season starting with The Lady in Black."

"Lady in Black? I'm not familiar…"

"Darlington Raceway in South Carolina." *After the owner fired me no one else would hire me. I coasted on my past wins and everyone I hung out with dropped me when my money ran out.* "Boss bought the team cheap, but he hired new drivers. After he won the title that year, he looked me up. I assumed he wanted to rub my nose in my mess, but he didn't. He offered me a job. This job." *He asked if I'd like to design a twenty-five-mile track in the middle of nowhere for a bunch or filthy rich assholes to play and crash half a million-dollar cars. What a waste of my time and talent.*

"I needed a job, so I took it. My contract is up this season. Don't squeal to Boss, but I got an offer to build a similar track like this in Asia. I don't see how Boss can stop me."

"Sure thing. Do you have a car available for a guest who just wants to take a spin?"

I mulled her idea over. " It could set a bad precedent to say 'yes.' So no, not at this time." I looked at Peggy. "Ready to go back?" After the gym I'm tuning up Boss's car for his end-of-season drive around the track. Then, we'll winterize it and lock it away until next year. *If there is a next year.*

****

"I was here before. Back then Boss said, 'Player Two is a beautiful, Oscar-nominated actress. Her last three films grossed over five hundred million dollars. Playing for the first time, welcome Ms. Two.' Some of that will be updated for this week's introduction."

"I'm Peggy. Could you tell me a bit about your life?"

"The studio script or the real story?"

"It's up to you."

"The real story, huh. Well, first you need to understand that actors are self-centered, attention-seeking bastards who will do anything to anyone for attention. But not me. I got ahead the old-fashioned way any gal gets ahead in a man's world. But not like you might think." *That raised Peggy's eyebrows.* "You understand me all right, but it wasn't my idea—it was my mother's. Next, the only thing real about me is my name, Lola. With a name like that I'd have to be a sexpot, right? No one's going to cast me as a scientist who cures cancer or an astronaut unless it's a comedy."

"Where were you born?"

"Near Chicago. A little town with one movie theater. That's where my mom spent a lot of her time while I was in school, watching movies and wishing she was that girl on the screen."

"When did you start in Hollywood and was it hard?"

"If I say 'stage mother' you'll understand a lot right away. I called her Roberta. Never mom or mama." *I feel sorry for kids who are cute, outgoing, and talented.* "Everything my mom was not but wanted to be. I understood at an early age that if I wanted people to love me, I had to use what I had. So it was, "…the sun will come out tomorrow…" and "…how's about cooking something up with me?" *Sexy at six.* "I think that's why I never wanted kids." *First, too much competition.* Second, as I got older, I didn't want to exploit someone as I was. "Roberta pushed me into little girl beauty pageants at six. "

"How did that impact you as a child?"

"Child? I never comprehended what it meant to be a child. My life was all about how superficial I could be. I couldn't play outside because I'd get skin damage, or get scraped up, or heaven forbid, a broken arm or nose."

"What did you do then if you didn't get to play?"

"My life was indoors learning to paint my nails, put curlers in my hair, and to use hair extensions. My birthday presents included a cosmetology mannequin head so I could practice. I was an expert by eight at applying makeup so the back row could see me even if I looked like a street walker up close."

"A mannequin head? That's clever. What were your special talents?"

"I had stage presence and I could dance. Best of all, the camera loved me. One year I wanted to learn to walk on stilts and use that as my talent in the beauty pageants. You'd have guessed I wanted to dye my teeth purple. I was the beauty queen, but Roberta was the drama queen.

"If it's not personal, what was a positive aspect of your relationship with your mother?"

"The thing I can honestly say was she never let me go into an audition or meeting alone." While some directors and producers fondled prepubescent girls or worse, I wasn't molested." *She didn't pimp me out to get a job.*

"Why? Was that an issue?"

"Read an honest actress's biography or read a newspaper and you'll understand that females of all ages are prey in this industry. At least some people are being held accountable now, but it happens everywhere."

"I get what you mean. Was your 'discovery' sudden, or not?"

"Not. By the time I was sixteen I had appeared in seven movies where I had five or more lines. That's a big deal, the five lines, because it affected my paycheck and being listed in the cast credits." I stopped for a moment. My relationship with my mom was complicated and still evolving. Peggy was the most patient interviewer I'd ever talked with. "We were on the west coast by then and Dad was moving up as an entertainment lawyer.

"That was the year Roberta got a diagnosis of pancreatic cancer. Eighteen months later she was in stage III with less than a year to live. My Dad was taking me to auditions and movie sets. As I approached twenty, some of the auditions got a bit hairy. 'Come alone,' they told me. As I was now 'of age,' I would be called a 'consenting adult' if I complained about things."

Dad had a plan, Roberta's plan really since she could see what was coming. "One night at dinner Dad explained the plan to me. In its simplest form—I needed to get married."

"Married? At twenty? How was that a plan to protect you?" Her face was turning pink.

I was touched by Peggy's show of outrage. "Let me explain. I was floored until he explained it. Everyone pigeonholed me as a single girl, and I'd be more respectable as a *married* woman. I would be off the casting couch merry-go-round because my bodyguard husband would accompany me to auditions, rehearsals, anytime I needed a chaperone. But your point is not lost on me." *Funny, isn't it?* "A single female star is damaged goods if she sleeps with too many men, even if it's not true. But a married woman—she's better protected. It's still more traditional even if she divorces and remarries." *I could see the logic to the plan and how mom was still protecting me. Thanks, Roberta.*

"The main sticking point was who would be my Prince Charming? Roberta was ready here too. She had an extensive network and a list of six guys within five years of my age. I became a media darling rotating around this list. Every other day I had a lunch date or a movie date or, horrors, a beach date—yes, even in the sun. My agent pedaled like mad to keep my face in front of Hollywood."

Peggy looked horrified at this admission. "How did you settle on a husband? It sounds like men would be lined up to date you."

Chapter 14

"In truth, and I don't think I am telling anything you don't already know, I was self-centered, as I had to be to get ahead in Hollywood. Dad and I looked for a man who could stand me as much as I could stand him, someone who understood the demands of the movie world, a business partner, and it was all right if he was closeted."

"You mean a man who was gay and *not* out of the closet?"

"That's correct. We didn't care. He had to be discreet though."

"But that seems unfair to both of you."

"Probably, but it did serve a purpose. We both accepted what that purpose was, and we had few illusions about our marriage. We helped and supported each other. He was a nice guy."

"So, what was the outcome of this little sham courtship?" Peggy had calmed down by now.

"As Etta James sang, 'At last, my love has come along,' and my most compatible swain and I ended up in the same picture. We fell in love on the set, or so our story went."

My courtship was finagled behind the scenes, but we ended up married. I said, "His name was Dean Hannigan. We cared about each either and promoted ourselves together. If I had an audition or meeting that I was uncomfortable with, my gallant hubby would all-of-a-sudden decide to drive me there and wait to take me to lunch. I'm surprised it lasted as long as it did, but five years later he met the love of his life Carlo. They moved to Europe to make wine."

"And no one caught on, Lola? You and he never…?" Peggy was asking a very personal question. *Dean deserved some respect.*

"There might have been rumors behind the scenes, but…no. The divorce was amicable. Now I was single but a respectable divorced woman."

"How did that work out for you and your career?"

"Dad was my lawyer and agent, and I got a lot of work in a short period of time. I won an Academy Award. Dad managed my money. By the time I was thirty, neither of us needed to work again."

"But I've seen you in pictures lately."

"Yes. It wasn't long before we were both bored—B-O-R-E-D. Trouble was the out-of-sight out-of-mind thing happened. I wasn't a hot commodity anymore. I got depressed. I came to Drake's and tried my luck. I guessed if I lost all my money, I would magically lose the depression too. Ha!" *I was stupid and too afraid to try suicide.* Didn't want any media photos with bandaged wrists and an oxygen tube taped up my nose. *I still had one thing going for me.* "Dad foresaw this day would come. While I had a lot of liquid assets, enough to get me in the Chairs, more were in a trust fund, and Drake's doesn't collect on those. Mom and Dad created a safety net for me, and I'll never forget it." *I made my peace with Roberta, thanks to Dad.* "I was high on something the night of the Chairs because I don't remember much of it. I remember I came in second, or as Roberta used to call it 'first loser.'"

"You lost? But I was told you..."

"...won? No, I lost. I was waiting in the Consolation Room draining a bottle of Dean's wine, which turned out to be darned good. Dex came in and asked me to step in to Boss's office. There was some commotion in the hall, and then Dex and Boss came in.

"'Lola,' Boss said, 'let me offer my apologies. For the first time we had a case of cheating tonight. No, don't ask me how, but it was caught and we are correcting it now. The winner has been disqualified. This means that you, Lola, are the winner of the Chairs.' I don't know how long I sat there but then he said, 'By way of apology, I will add two million dollars to your winnings. Congratulations, Lola.'"

"That's amazing. What did you win?"

"I didn't know what else I won but I did know I had two million bucks, enough to let me produce my own movie. Now this was the weirdest part. The fortune I won belonged to a playboy who had a lot of investments. His grandmother left him the majority share in the second most successful movie studio in California. Boss collected it and turned it over to me. That was six years ago."

"Has it been good for you?"

"I'll say. I got back into pictures with Dad at my side. We produced movies that addressed issues for people over thirty, for women, for senior citizens, and for military veterans. Did we miss anyone? I hope not. We weren't making a fortune, but we were covering our costs and providing entertainment for people who wanted more than Superheroes, car crashes, explosions, and frat boy fart jokes. I'm still vain. I try every face serum that comes along, all my teeth look like chiclets, and I'm always hungry. I never leave the house without makeup, my hair combed, slathered in sunscreen, and wearing a hat."

I date rich and powerful businessmen and listen when they talk. I avoid certain producers who have tested their slimy ways on me. I suspected one even drugged me, but I couldn't prove it. After talking to other actresses with a similar story, I arranged to have him drugged one night at a club. He woke up naked in a garbage dumpster with a new tattoo. *It made the front page. I always liked the movie about the girl with a dragon tattoo.*

"Most importantly, I have a private tutor and seventy hours of college credits towards my business and finance degree."

"That's incredible. That's why I've seen you," Peggy said. "Are you still the top billing in your films?"

"No. I'm happy to play cameo roles, and guess what? I won two more Academy Award nominations for 'Best Supporting Actress' and for 'Producing.' It's this last one I'm proudest of. Mom didn't let me get much education, so that my peers recognized me for something other than performing tickled me pink."

"It sounds like you are a real mover and shaker. How is your dad involved?"

"Dad passed away recently. He put me on the path to normalcy. He loved me just because I was his daughter. I treasure that more than you can know."

"Last question, Lola."

"Why am I back at Drake's?"

Peggy nodded.

"Not the same reason as before. I have a big idea that needs tons of cash. I don't want to spend all my time negotiating with stockholders, so I'm *really* taking a gamble this time."

"What if you lose? Do you have a plan for that?"

"I'll still have my trust fund. I could just keep on doing what I've been doing, but I think I'd like to try something new."

"And if you have to transfer?"

"I guess I won't be the first actor in Hollywood to 'come out' as transexual but I'll have all functioning equipment."

"Well, you won't have to take hormones for the rest of your life," Peggy joked.

"I already have a new career being an intimacy coach on set. Yes, now they have rules and referees for actors during intimate scenes. Oh, I think I have you to thank. I'm meeting with Rhonda right after this. It might be possible for us to collaborate whether we win, lose, or both in the Chairs. I *am* nervous. My body is like this through dieting and a personal trainer and plastic surgery. I ran into Rhonda at the beach. She's got the best body I've ever seen, and she didn't do a thing. I wonder if I could get her for my body double?"

****

I was in the interview room when the Count arrived. This guy was slick and from old money. Dex said he put up one of those exquisite Russian Easter Eggs for part of his bet. Of course, Boss made him replace the paste with the real gems before they accepted it.

"Bonjour, mademoiselle. Are *you* my interviewer?" he asked politely.

The Count was right out of central casting: slim, a full head of snow-white hair carefully coiffed, and the deepest icy blue eyes I'd ever seen. He wore the best cut suit of anyone at Drake's including Boss.

"Yes, I am Peggy." I reached for a handshake. The Count took my hand, bowed, and kissed the back of my hand. My face must have had an astonished grin, and I mumbled a gurgle of exhilaration.

"May I?" he whispered as he nodded to a chair.

I nodded back and he sat across from me. Although still handsome, the lines around his eyes gave him a tired appearance. He wore a vintage Heuer wristwatch. It's a time-only model meaning no moon phases or extraneous information. It does have a twin-time for a second time zone. Probably from the 1950s: classic, simple, expensive. There's no other jewelry that would spoil his effect.

"Lovely watch," I said.

He nodded.

I noticed it because my grandfather had one, but he left it to my cousin. My interviewee fit that old saying that if you look up "class" in the dictionary, it is a picture of the Count. "Uhm, how shall we start then? What shall I call you?" I stammered. I was a bit conflicted on how to proceed. Here is a man with one foot in the past and the requisite baggage that entailed. *What could be the reason that brought him here?*

"I am His Serenity the Count Constantine Erik Antonovich. Call me Erik. Boss has shown me how he will welcome me for the Chairs. 'Player Nine is a hereditary Russian Count with claims to estates that covers a third of Siberia. *Пожалуйста*—which is welcome in Russian—Count Nine.'"

"Erik, tell me about your family, and make yourself comfortable."

He poured a vodka that I declined. "With pleasure.

My family goes back centuries. The Tsar gifted us large tracts of land in Siberia that even today contain significant amounts of timber, furs, some gold, and even a few diamonds. I have sought the return of my ancestral lands my entire life."

"Do you live in Russia now?" He sipped his vodka with slow and obvious appreciation.

"*Nyet*. The western trends forced upon nobility landowners disturbed my grandfather, as well as restlessness in the peasants. He moved my immediate family to France in the late 19th century. He was able to transport enough of his wealth with him to sustain us to this day." *He's classy but an old-time snob*, I wrote in my notes.

"That explains your charming French accent."

He dipped his chin slightly. "Of course. Even before my family left Russia, French was the language of the royal court. My family always spoke French and Russian, and obviously some English. I don't believe the last Tsar even spoke Russian nor English. He considered Russian a peasant language. My family spoke it to communicate with the workers on our lands who only spoke Russian crudely. When I speak Russian, it is with an educated accent, and you notice I am speaking it today. It does help my claims to Russian land."

I learned from my research the Count gave private, very discreet Russian language and culture lessons in his educated Russian accent to snob-wannabees from around the globe. "Have you visited the estates you are seeking to recover?" I read of Russian expats living in France for generations.

"Unfortunately, a post-Tsarist Russian government has not allowed me to travel within the country. I have old family friends who keep me informed."

"And what do they say?"

"Sadly, the government has allowed a few oligarchs to pillage the natural resources of all of Siberia. These men care nothing for the natural beauty of the land. I fear they will not be done until it is stripped and dying."

"I am aware your bet has a very unique item in it." *This I have to hear about.*

"Indeed. You speak of the Golden Fabergé Siberia Egg I offered for my wager. It was presented to my direct ancestor around 1850 by Tsar Nicholas I."

"What did he do to earn that?" *He is fascinating.*

"It was awarded for bravery in saving the royal family's life during an anarchist's assassination attempt. Sadly, the heir was severely injured and unable to assume the throne. His brother succeeded him. I am also a direct descendent of the brother, Vasiliy."

"Also?"

"Yes. Most Russian nobility did not marry outside of Russia. As a result, many of us have an almost incestuous family tree. It is like the English queen Victoria who was related to many royal houses across Europe."

"How is it you still had this fabulous egg, Erik?"

"Ah, yes, the Siberia Egg. Fortunately, my great-great-grandfather took it with him to Paris, so it was out of the country when the Bolsheviks stole most of them."

"What did your family do in France while you pursued your claim?"

"We continued living, as everyone else did. My grandfather was a famous and prolific writer. He established a Russian diaspora community in Paris where he socialized with all the famous early twentieth-century artists, writers, intellectuals, and aristocracy. His salon was at the forefront of establishing manners in Parisienne society and promoting ideas. "We suffered greatly after the Boche—pardon, mademoiselle, the Germans— damaged France during the First World War even though Paris was spared. We did have to evacuate when they succeeded in occupying Paris during the second war. My family sponsored an avant-garde dance troupe called Les Ballets Russe starting in 1909. Although not strictly Russian, it gave us an artistic cause during troubled times. It was a cultural revolution. Ah, Nijinsky, Pavlova, Stravinsky!"

"I am a fan of the dance. Did your grandfather meet these famous artists?"

"Of course. He told me about them when I was young. They filled his salon to eat and toast the arts."

"How thrilling that all sounds." I looked away imagining Nijinsky pirouetting through the grand salon of his grandfather's apartments while Stravinsky conducted the violins in the hall. Back in the present I asked, "Did you marry, Erik? Did you have someone to share your grand life with?"

He poured another drink. "*Oui*, my charming Peggy. My wife was from the Russian diaspora. I met her in our childhood, and she was a distant cousin, but it was a love marriage. She moved in with me into my Paris apartment." He showed me a photo from his wallet. It must be from her wedding day. She was regal and dripping with jewels. "Her name was Alexandra, after the last Empress of Russia."

"The one who was…?"

"Yes, the one slaughtered with her husband and children. I believe my wife married down when she agreed to be my bride."

A snob. A high-class snob, but still a snob.

"Were there any children?"

The Count looked at me for a few moments and said, "Pardon my rudeness, but you remind me so much of our daughter. Our only child died in Paris from…most ironically, from the Russian flu. I believe it was this loss that broke Alexandra's heart and her will to live."

"I am sorry for your personal loss."

"I accept your kindness with gratitude." He flashed his polished smile, but I feel he was sincere.

"Did you never consider another marriage? Companionship seems to be agreeable to many people."

"There has been a great deal of loss in my family. We are accustomed to it. Perhaps I am the last dinosaur of my family. May we change the subject?" He produced a faint smile and flashed his bluest of eyes.

"Of course. How is your lawsuit progressing?" I hoped finances was a safer topic.

"I am *not* the only Russian in France suing to recover stolen treasures. Land is not the only possession at stake but many precious works of art are disputed. Paintings, statues, jewelry, books, religious icons, I could go on all afternoon. Starting in 1917, the Bolsheviks looted private families, museums, churches, anything they could sell to finance their revolution. They took billions of dollars' worth of objects and even more in property. Since the Bolshevik government 'privatized' everything in sight, it has been a dismal outcome in the courts for the old families. However, a painting or an emerald tiara is easily transported, hidden, and even lost. My land is still where it has always been."

How right he is. Maybe he has a chance after all. I

have to ask. "Erik, why are you gambling your potential Siberian lands in the Chairs?"

"To be brutally honest, I am near the end of my life and of my resources to continue these never-ending lawsuits. I need a change and an infusion of capital."

"What will you do if you win?"

"I am here to win enough to formally sue the present Russian Republic for the return of my family estates in Siberia. They will serve as a source of income to establish and sustain a Russian Siberia Culture Institute in the Russian Far East, after I am gone, of course." He reached into his pocket and pulled out a magnificent gold cigarette case. He opened it and offered me a French-brand cigarette.

"No thank you, but may I look at that case? It's so beautiful." He casually handed me the singularly most magnificent object I have ever held as if it were a pebble from the beach.

"Yes, of course. It was another Imperial gift that came to me. The gold, amethyst, and diamonds are of course from Siberia. Look." He pointed to a flower on the lid. "This is a purple bellflower done in amethyst." He pointed to an animal. "This, a Siberian ibex. Those curved horns are magnificent, aren't they? The horns do have those bumps in them where the small diamonds are placed." He tapped each diamond with his manicured finger. "The body is a thin layer of Siberian sunstone. Its rusty-gold color is similar to that of the animal itself. It is the last vestige of my family, so I dare not lose it."

Chapter 15

Erik's His eyes never left the case as he described it to me.

"Have you considered what you will do if you lose?" I whispered as I returned the case.

"Yes, in detail. I have friends in France who would help me, of course. I fear I shall not be a burden for many years more."

"And, if you are transferred to another person's body?" I almost apologized for asking.

The Count ran his hand over his chin and paused. "Who would want an old man's body?" he stated in a self-assured manner.

I didn't dare ask how he was so certain of the outcome.

The Count rose from his chair. He bowed, kissed my right cheek, then the left, then the right again, and left the room. I've had my hand kissed before, but usually by someone who wanted something from me. He asked for nothing. I was dumbfounded at this more intimate and outdated display. Was it simply a cordial goodbye, or will there be more to come?

I stepped into the Maze, walked to the dressing rooms, and changed my disguise.

****

"Peaches, bring me Rusty's contract."

"Yes, Boss. Do you want me to have some lunch

sent in?" Despite all the food at the cricket match turned carnival, I didn't get a chance to eat.

"Yes and ask the kitchen to put on a plate of those oatmeal raisin cookies that Rusty says remind him of home, and a pot of coffee."

My racetrack manager's contract was up for renewal. He's done a spectacular job with the track he designed and built. But I suspected he missed the limelight. Rusty usually leaves at the end of our season and goes straight to North Carolina to follow the rest of the NASCAR season. He returns in November. I'll need to make him a deal that solves all those issues and keeps me alive. He has a hot temper. How can I cool him off?

I reviewed his contract and ate my grilled scallops with red cabbage and mango slaw before he arrived. My chef prepared it just right today. I got through the contract and shad already cribbled a few ideas down before Rusty showed up. "Rusty, sit down. I'm drinking coffee. Let me get you a cup. Black with sugar, isn't it?" I poured him a cup and placed the plate of cookies where we both could reach it.

"First, good job showing the young lady around the track. It impressed her. I gathered she was a racing fan." He had his poker face on.

Rusty said, "I don't think she was that young. And I didn't get the impression she cared much about racing. She *was* real interested in the 3-D topographical map." He took a still warm cookie while I warmed him up.

"That map was genius. The accident rate went down after you required all drivers to review it before starting their cars. What was the utilization of the track this season? How much was dead time, not including maintenance?" I didn't think he expected that.

Rusty scratched his head. He took a pen and a small notepad with a calculator out of his pocket. Yes, he was a real engineer. He ran some numbers and then asked, "All year long or just in the main season?" He finished his cookie and took another. I topped off his coffee.

"Both." He made some notations and pounded on his calculator again. He sipped his coffee and looked away as if recalling information. Rusty was thorough and never gave me an answer he couldn't support. He sat back taking another cookie. After a bite he said, "I'd say about forty-five percent during the season, twenty percent during the rest of the year."

"Not too bad, but I think we could do better. Don't you?" I picked up my coffee and waited.

"Well, yes, if you're seriously asking." His face shifted gears. He had something in mind. "We could put in five-mile and ten-mile running tracks. We could do short tracks over the mountain for folks training for long distance running or marathons. I've gotten inquiries."

Wow. That's ambitious. He didn't just think that up while eating a cookie. *Okay, Rusty. Let's dance.* "Can we hold a training camp, off-season? Use the crew quarters?"

He leaned forward. "I hadn't studied it, but maybe."

I upped my ante." *Step up. Break step, break step.* "How about a race team? Is Drake's too far to come for training or development?"

Rusty's hand jerked and spilled coffee on his lap, but he never missed a beat. "It's pretty far, but way out of the public eye. With the right marketing, I don't see why not."

I proceeded as if I expected him to renew his contract rather than knock me off. *One two, cha, cha,*

cha. "Okay. Let's switch gears." I leaned forward and looked him in the eye.

"I'm considering starting a new division of Drake Inc., a division that designs and builds custom tracks around the world. We'll use ours as a showcase but do tracks of all sizes." Rusty straighten up in his seat. His cookie stopped six inches from his mouth. "Do you think there's enough business for that?"

His eyes got bigger as his breathing changed. *Turn left, cha, cha, cha.* "By 'enough business' you mean?" His eyes held mine.

"Follow the money. Start in the US, then Asia, then South American, then Europe." *Turn right, cha, cha, cha.*

"I'm thinking the answer is yes." His eyes never moved from mine.

Here comes the spin. "In that case, do you want the job?"

"Define the job." Rusty was barely breathing by now.

It was my turn to jump in feet first. "Help me plan the company. Be the face of the company. Head the design team at first, then supervise. Travel looking for new sites and customers anywhere and everywhere. Travel to races around the world promoting our brand. Hell, we could even sponsor our own team, but not the first three years until we get established." I have him hooked. Now I need to reel him in. *Second spin, other direction.* "Set up a stateside corporate office you'd run as corporate VP. Make our targets in five years and you'll be a corporate president. You might want to keep the fun part and let some other stiff be President and sit in all the meetings and get an ulcer over budgets." By now he was drooling all over my desk.

"And compensation?" He barely got the whispered question out.

I took in a breath while taking the measure of the man and what I just promised him. "Start at three times your current salary at signing a new contract. Reviews at six-month intervals. Benefits same as now but with stateside extras including a new corporate car of your choice— every year. Did I miss anything?" *Last spin.*

"Corporate frequent flyer miles. Mine or yours?" he rasped.

"Yours." *I'm done.*

Rusty stood up in an aggressive manner. *Did I just insult him?* He moved towards me, and I stood to protect myself. I put my left hand in my pocket on my taser.

He shoved his right hand towards me. "Deal. When do I start?" *Dip, and dance over! Take a bow.* It's fortunate I never flinched. The meeting ended with me owning a new company, but I also owned the confidence that I neutralized Rusty as far as a threat to my life. What did that leave? More importantly, *who did that leave?* Talk about leaving. I'm beginning to question why I ever left Oklahoma.

Senior year went by so fast. Then it was my senior prom. "I didn't know if you'd be here," I said.

"I came with a group of girls, but would you take me home?"

We had our only picture together taken at the prom. Then it was off to the Army for me because it would help pay for college. I wanted to follow my dad into law and that was pricey. Rosalie planned to be a nurse and work in a family practice. We had a long-term plan, but in five years we would be married. We wrote back and forth ever week. The Army sent me to Africa and Albania evacuating Americans.

I still had the letters. I should read them again.

****

"Miss. Are you looking for me?" I was eating my first breakfast as Peggy walked by.

"Yes, Dex. Could I ask you a few more questions?" She sat across from me in the shade.

"Sure. You don't mind if I eat while we talk, do you?" I waved for a waiter who brought her a menu and me another cup o' coffee. I gobbled down my breakfast eggs and ham, but I took my time with the lemon Danish. I was trying to guess how old she was.

"Dex, what are day trippers?" Peggy asked as she put on tortoiseshell sunglasses.

"Where did you hear that?" *Now what?*

"It was a term they used at the desk when I asked about accommodations. In case I want to come back for a vacation."

Her? A guest? No way. "We don't get but a couple o' year. They're guests who are here for less than 24 hours." *We're both wearing sunglasses, only hers covers a lot more territory.*

"Really? People come to Drake's just for one day. Why?" She looked down so I couldn't see her face.

"I guess they got other stuff to do. See, for some people Drake's is like a fancy restaurant but it's a long way from home. If you got a big boat or your own plane, you could still work while you're getting here. Or you can drop in if you're on a cruise already."

"I see. Do you get many?" She looked up as she talked but the wind was blowing. The sun kept shining in my eyes as the palm trees waved around making shadows and sunlight all mix together.

"No too many. It's a long way to come." I finished my eggs before they got cold. I still got pie coming to eat after the Danish.

"Could you tell me about your most memorable Gizmo transfers then?"

I looked towards the pool. *That's a funny question.* I guessed I usually remembered the Players who win big or lose even bigger. But I'd have to say…"The twins— for sure. We had identical twins named Rob and Bob Jones. O' course that's not their real names. Twins don't look so much alike when they get older, but these guys never seemed to change."

"How long ago was this, Dex?"

"They first came the year we opened. They'd inherited a fortune from their folks, so they split it into two companies. Each was the president o' one of the companies and each did a bang-up job. They only got richer."

"Why did they come here to Drake's?"

I don't usually get to talk to a woman who don't expect to be paid for it, so I agreed to tell her the story. "Naw. They came for a regular vacation. See, they each married a gorgeous dame and were happy and in love. They'd come on vacations together, but a funny thing happened. I noticed that Rob's wife liked to do the things Bob did, so they'd go fishing together, they'd scuba dive together, they'd go parasailing together, anything like a sport, they'd try it out. Except golf, and the brothers did that together. Most likely to talk a little business since they promised their wives they wouldn't while they were here. Anyways, while Bob and his sister-in-law were out enjoying the sportier things, the other two, meaning Rob and his sister-in-law, were playing bridge with some hoity-toity Grand Master, or taking cooking lessons from a celebrity chef, or sitting in a lecture by some hot writer whose latest book was topping the *New York Time's* list of books, uh, maybe that's a list of books that people are buying fast. I don't know what cha call it."

"The best seller list. What were these people like?" Now the sun was just starting to creep into our shady spot, so Peggy gets out a hat, and puts it on. *Spoil sport!*

"That's probably it. I finally made a rule for myself. I couldn't tell the men apart, but the ladies were different. Rob's wife was a natural brunette and a natural athlete who liked a little adventure and danger. She saved a guest's life once."

"What? That sounds like a real story. What happened?" *Now she looks up.*

"Uh-huh. You got me right. You know we got a scuba boat trip going out every day it ain't raining, right? One morning when they was done diving, a shark grabbed o' hold of this other guy by the leg when he was waiting to climb back in the boat. She jumped off the boat on top of the shark and started scratching its eyes. That shark let go o' the guy and took off." *That cured me o' taking scuba lessons.* "He didn't go wading at the beach for the rest o' his stay. He didn't even get in the pool." *That part was still funny.*

"And was she hurt?"

"A little scraped up 'cause shark skin is kind o' like sandpaper, but she climbed back on the boat laughing. She went out diving again after lunch."

"How would you describe the other wife?"

Why am I even talking to this dame? She's real nosy. "Bob's wife was thin but not a natural blonde. She was quiet and really smart and pretty, not movie-star pretty but classy. More like Bacall with Bogart in *To Have and To Have Not.* She wore glasses and didn't care what people said about her. But now I remember, she liked to talk to people about what they did and what they supported about stuff like trade and the economy— business stuff. If she was alone, she was in the library reading. Boss has some first editions in there, I hear. I heard someone call her doctor once, but she never wore a white coat here at Drake's."

"What was your rule…?"

"My rule?" *What rule?*

"How did you tell the brothers apart?"

"Oh—so my rule was the men were with their wives at dinner and the rest of the night. The rest of the day they were with their sister-in-law. Did I mention they came every year? No? Well, they did. Now Boss and I would discuss these couples because it seemed to us that they was hooked up to the wrong spouses, but it wasn't none of our business. But something must of happened."

"What happened to the twins?" Peggy said as she wrote at ambulance speed.

"This is where it gets real interesting. The fourth year they had a big blow up the second night. They had adjoining suites, but the noise was loud, and someone complained. It was sad because these were all nice people and family to boot. Boss and I went over there 'cause that's part of the job, and we kind of felt like we wanted to help them out. First thing Boss did was put each of them into a separate room to cool off. Then he went in and talked to them alone kind of like a priest. He promised not to repeat what anybody told him. It was real hostile in those rooms. I made sure they had drinks, but no booze, and some conch fritters to nibble on 'cause conch fritters is one fish dish I enjoy myself."

"I'll try the fritters. How long did this go on for?"

"Almost two hours. The women were crying. I could see the muscles in the guy's jaws were all clenched up like they was ready to go at it." I planned to use my boxing skills if one of the guys came at me. *Boss might of fired me over that.* Boss told me about it later, but not every detail I'm guessing. "He started out by asking what was the problem? Every one of them started out complaining about their spouse. Then it was 'why couldn't he be more like his brother or 'why couldn't she be more like the sister-in-law?'"

"Finally Boss called them together again. He said, 'Look, listen, and wait until I'm finished before asking questions. Dex and I see you when you come every year.' I nodded real hard when he said that 'cause I agreed. 'Frankly, it seems to us you are mismatched, but not during the daytime. We think that's when you are most relaxed and enjoying yourselves. It's in the evenings that you seem more distant.'"

"That was a bold move," Peggy said.

"Yeah, it was. Boss has a lot of guts. So, each one of them started eyeballing their own wife and then their brother's wife. The ladies did the same thing, only, you know it was the men they looked at. Boss said, 'I don't know if that has occurred to any of you, or if you've acted upon it. May I be allowed to offer a candid opinion and a possible solution?'

"The folks looked around the room and started nodding a little." I was wound up, so I waved at the waitress to refill my cup and bring my pie. "Boss went straight for the kill. 'I believe you should switch spouses.

I know that sounds complicated, but maybe not. And the decision will never be known outside of this group of people.' Nobody said nothin,' but I was getting an idea of what Boss was driving at.

"He said, 'I know you're thinking about all the problems of divorces, property settlements, splitting up the businesses, publicity. At least you don't have any children to get hurt. Correct?' Everyone agreed to that statement. That was a good sign. 'Suppose that I could offer you a solution wherein none of those were issues? Would you want to hear about it?' The couples had guilty looks on their faces but every one of them shook their head in favor.

" Boss said, 'All right. Do any of you know about the Gizmo?' Three of them raised their hands. 'Let me explain. The Gizmo exchanges the minds, memories, and mental processes of two people. In this case, Rob would get all the memories and mental processes of Bob, and Bob would get Rob's. You take your old memories with you in the process.'

"The Boss stopped so's they could chew that over for a minute. By now no one was looking at nothin' but the floor or the ceiling. 'Now, ladies…,' Boss said to the wives, '…the physical person you married would be the same—the same body with all its scars and moles that you've made love to. That's what the law recognizes in a marriage or a divorce, when you come down to it.' Boss stopped to let that sink in and catch his breath. He made a good point."

"I never connected that angle about marriage and divorce. That was clever," Peggy said as she wrote.

Chapter 16

"'Your husband will have the same DNA and fingerprints as he has now. But when he remembers, or when he speaks, it's a different mind working. When your husband kisses you or makes love to you, he will be making a new memory of you.' Then he said, 'One benefit I think you all will see is that these new couples will be much more compatible and fun.'"

"Bob raised his hand. 'If we *did* do this, people who know us would notice something was different.'"

"Boss nodded 'cause he agreed but said, 'Just tell your friends you went to couple's therapy and worked out a few wrinkles.' All o' their heads started to nod a little. Then Boss said, 'As you can see, there's no need for a divorce, nor a property settlement, nor a company breakup. No public scandal, no bad publicity.' You could hear a pin drop by then, miss. Then Boss spilled his plan. 'Rob and Bob, you'd exchange which company you manage, and nobody will notice a thing. You won't even have to buy new wardrobes unless you have different fashion tastes, and it all would start the instant you transfer.' He added, 'I'll even offer you a family discount.' Then he nodded towards the door to me. 'We're going now. If you decide to use the Gizmo, see me in the morning.' Me and Boss left at that point. I'm telling you—those folks was quiet when we left."

My pie arrived and I dug right in. "Someone said

later that they started out by discussing the change first with the person who would be their new spouse, so to say, to see if that was good for both of them. No use to ask a girl to the prom if she don't want to dance. It seems everyone was of the same opinion, in all honesty. Miss, you should try this pie. Chocolate coconut cream. I'll sure miss my pie after the season ends this week. Anyways, they talked to Boss in the morning. We warmed up the Gizmo in time for Bob and his new wife to go out on the afternoon scuba trip. Personally, the way they was all laughing and smiling at breakfast, I think they gave it a tryout the night before and everyone was happy."

Peggy shook her head. "That was an ingenious conclusion to an unusual love story, I must say."

"Yeah, I think Boss and I both agree that was one of the most satisfying transfers we did. They came back the next year as day trippers just to thank us. Both o' the wives was pregnant and glowing, and the future daddies was grinning ear to ear. That was the last time they were here since we ain't a family resort. I wouldn't be surprised if they show up again when they need a break. Nice people, all of them."

I had a question for her. "Say, are you having any trouble going through the Maze? No one's seen you or stopped you?" I couldn't see through her sunglasses. *She could be my old Navy boxing coach for all knew.*

"No, I don't think so, but I appreciate your concern."

"That's good. But you have my number, right?"

"I'd say I *do* have your number. Do you think I'm in danger?"

"Not that I know of but if you think you are, let me know pronto," I said. "What's next?"

157

"What about the worst Gizmo transfer?" Peggy asked.

I had to think about this. I sure don't wanna talk about…."Hmm, how about one o' the saddest? Honestly, this one makes me wanna cry when I think of it." I refilled our cups as Peggy turned to a new page. She was a real good listener. She was wearing the scarf around her neck I gave her. She must like it. "We had this young married couple who came here the second year. Both of them were really smart, full o' piss and vinegar. They made a fortune and lost it, made another fortune, and came here. This was a first at Drake's 'cause they wanted to switch themselves. Boss said it sounded like a social experiment, whatever that means, but that their money was good no matter who was who."

"A social experiment? What did he mean by that?"

"I don't know. Maybe you could tell me when I get done. The husband wanted to know what life was like for a woman and she wanted to try out being a man to see if that would make her more successful in business." Peggy snickered so I guess she got what Boss meant. "They spent a week here and had a great time. Then they transferred in the Gizmo and spent another week. It was pretty funny for a while." I took a minute to drink my coffee. I needed to think what to say 'cause it ain't pretty.

"I think he had a harder time than she did on the physical stuff. He-now-she used to sit like a man at the pool with his legs all spread apart, and she-now-he would remind her to keep them together. He-now-she smacked the first guy who made a pass and pinched his-now-her butt. She-now-he had to stop him-now-her from opening the door first. I'm getting confused just talking about it." I couldn't help myself and we both laughed. "Two days later the most hilarious thing happened. She seemed real cranky and puffed up at lunch. I guess I had a look on my face and the now husband leaned over to me and said, 'It's that time of the month.' Then he laughed this big ol' horse laugh. So far, I believed the new husband got the best end o' the deal, but I waited until I got into the Maze to laugh until honest-to-god tears came to my eyes. I bet he never stopped to think of that before they switched."

"Is that it? Story over?"

I wagged my head. "Not by a longshot. Four years go by. The new husband was real successful in business and jacked up their fortune 300 percent. See, he was still thinking like always, and was probably right, that as a female she had been kept back because of her sex. "

"So even though he increased their fortune, she wasn't satisfied?" Peggy asked.

"I don't think so. The new wife was for sure the one having trouble. She could never fit in where she wanted to be. She hated being told to go 'join the girls' at times while her husband made deals and chatted with the guys. She hated being judged by how she looked. See, she never got the hang of putting on lipstick so she didn't look drunk, and mascara—fuhgeddaboudit. She always looked like she had at least one black eye. Because she usually forgot, or refused, to wear a bra, men imagined she was a hooker or something." *The old wife's life got much better, the new wife's life got worse, and the marriage went to hell in a handbasket.*

"They separated and the husband supported her moneywise. They lost touch for a while, got back together for a while, again and again. I think they needed to be together because they couldn't tell anyone what they'd done, but that didn't change anything else between them. After a year of this the wife got a surprise that changed her life for real. The husband offered to transfer back. She agreed without even asking why. They called Boss that day and flew in the next. They weren't back together and had separate suites as far apart as possible. They went out of their way to avoid each other." I finished my pie and pushed the plate away. "All the piss and vinegar was gone but they both had a sour taste in their mouths from the looks of them. Both looked old and tired. We did the transfer, and they didn't even say goodbye. They just opened the doors and left. By noon, the next day both of them were gone. That was last time we spoke with either one of them."

"What happened to them, do you know?"

"Yeah, and that's the saddest part. He died a month later of small cell lung cancer." *It made me glad I never started smoking in the first place.* "She died later that year from cancer in her female parts. They never told the other they was sick. I guess both of them believed they'd pull a fast one and be their old healthy self again. The way I look at it today is they would of been better off just getting some shrink to talk to instead of transferring. I bet when they got sick, the other would of stayed by their side. We don't do transfers between husbands and wives because of them." I had things to do, and I didn't want to talk to her any more than I had to, so I stood up before she could ask to see my tat again.

"It's odd that your most memorable transfers aren't Players," she says.

I'm trying to cut her off. "Those stories are for another time. If we're done, I'll let you in the door from the pool to the Maze. Where do you want to go?" Peggy gave me a coordinate in the Maze. *She's no chorus girl.*

Who can tell any broad's age anymore? "You sure? Okay, turn left though the door, then right, then third door on the right and you'll be there. Just be real careful opening the door, miss. It's a men's toilet."

****

"Peggy, I believe Boss may be flummoxed at introducing me. I picked number twelve. It was my NFL jersey number and Crusher was my nickname. The coaches were always, 'Crusher, get the second wide receiver,' or sometimes, 'Crusher, flatten the tight end.' I played Sam Linebacker, so I was fast and versatile. I like to say I am still 'versatile,' if you catch my drift." I stood and made a slow pirouette, so she got the full treatment. At least I got a reaction from her. "I've made some changes since then. I might be the biggest woman in the room Saturday night. I'm off steroids and I'm on a diet and below 225 pounds." *But I pitied anyone who tried to elbow me away from a Chair.*

"Yes, indeed. Do you know how Boss will introduce you for the Chairs?" Peggy grinned as she asked me, but I might have imagined it.

"I'm thinking it will be like 'Player Twelve is a retired professional athlete who didn't squander her money. Welcome, Ms. Twelve.' If he says that, I expect quite a buzz. There will be some who are disgusted, but I ignore them. They have more problems than I do." *Along with taking my daily hormones, I attend a support group for transsexuals and have a regular weekly session with my shrink.* I was confident I had my mental health in shape.

"Do you mind if I ask the obvious questions?"

"Shoot. Did I always want to be a girl?"

Peggy's mouth pursed as she nodded. "It took me a

161

while, so not always. It was a girlfriend who suggested the problems we were having could be my sexuality. She recommended a doctor, and that got me on the road to who I am today. Happier and more confident than I've ever been. What else?" That was a *gorgeous* Hermès scarf Peggy was wearing. *Did she get that here?*

"Do you have a close relationship with your parents?" *Obvious question.*

"You know I really do—now. They miss their little boy, but they've looked beyond that and see that I still have the basic family values they taught me. They see me as the good person I try to be." I opened my purse and pulled out a photo of me at seven: big for my age, buck teeth, and a cowlick in the front.

"Classic kid photo," Peggy offered. "Do they know what you are doing here?"

I nodded slowly, remembering the conversations about it. *You must be mental. You're throwing your life away.* My sister called the cops on them. "They did discourage me from coming. They've been through stuff with my gambling in the past. I promised them this was my last bet. I don't break my promises to them, ever."

"What do you want out of this new life you've found?"

She is digging so deeply into my psyche I feel it in my heart of hearts. "Great question." I stopped to gather my courage. "What I really want out of life is children." *Whew. She didn't laugh. This is a safe space.* "I haven't quite figured that part out yet, but I have a healthy trust fund set up for them, so if I lose tonight, they'll be taken care of—when I get them. My folks will be over the moon when that happens. I imagine my kids won't have to worry about bullies." I flexed my still muscular biceps. Peggy rolled her eyes in mock terror. "I still have my NFL sweats and I'll be wearing them and ready to rumble. I also have boots with heels that bring me up to seven foot tall, so all I have to do is stand there. The first time I show up at school or knock on a bully's door and the dad answers, the problem is already solved. I can't help but giggle just thinking about it."

"That picture is hilarious. Call me if that happens. I want to see it. Do you wear your Superbowl ring?"

"Do I wear it? Of course, I wear it, honey. I worked hard for it and how many people have a Super Bowl ring? I had mine sized. My hands are still big, so yeah, I have it and I wear it proudly. Even if some guy is looking down his nose at me, he still wants to try on my ring. Then we talk football, then he's buying me a drink. No Pink Ladies, either. I still like twelve-year old scotch." I left my ring with a buddy who was here with me. *It's mine even if everything else changes this week.* He was in on what to do if things went badly for me. *That's not all I left behind.* I've got a hefty sample of sperm in a cryogenics locker if I find a suitable surrogate. "Confidentially, wearing my ring is almost like wearing brass knuckles. Ask Lenny Bigstrom how he got that scar over his eye. My name will come up. My given name. I changed it from Oliver to Livy."

Peggy looked like she was dithering about asking her next question. "If you don't mind me asking, how did you know?" she asked in a tentative voice.

"How did I know... Oh, that. Confidentially, I think I was always a bisexual, or is that pansexual? I get confused at all the terms today. I just know I've always been attracted to people because of their intelligence, sense of humor, and a belief in 'justice for all.' Notice that gender was not mentioned. I just don't want to be told what I can't do, or what type of relationships I shouldn't have with people based upon the junk in their trunk."

"If you've made it through so much, why risk that now? Why are you taking such a big gamble with the Chairs?" *That sounded like real concern in her voice.*

"I won at sports. I won at finding out who I am and being happy. As a former gambler I know things come in threes. I just don't know how that will apply to me, but it's my last bet."

"How do you think you'll do in the Chairs?"

"I'm a numbers gal. I see that of the twelve of us in the Chairs, half are women. In theory I stand a fifty-fifty chance of leaving here tonight female. I did pay a fortune for what I've got. I'd hate to do that all over again. But heck, I could end up with a fully functional vagina and start on those kids I was talking about." *And use my own sperm. Wow! Momma and daddy.* "Besides, if you were trying to avoid people noticing you, being a six-foot five-inch-tall woman with—well I won't say what my bustline is, but's it's noticeable—and wearing seven-inch spike heels and platinum hair, well I would *not* be your first pick for a body transfer, would I?"

Peggy shrugged. "So far everyone I've interviewed seems to think that same thing."

"Well, if I'm still in this body I can get a coaching job at a high school or college. I might try announcing on ESPN. Wouldn't that cause a commotion when I walked into a locker room?"

"And if you win?"

"If I win, what do I…? Oh, if I win, I plan to expand my support for the public schools in my hometown.

Teachers are underpaid. I'll sponsor more teacher aides in the classroom. I want to see more equitable facilities across the whole school district. I want to know that every child has a breakfast before starting the school day, and on the weekends too. Did I mention I have a master's degree in education? No? I am very proud of that. I did it off-season."

"Do you support athletics in the schools?"

I sip on the scotch I brought in with me as I form my answer. "Athletics? Sorry about repeating your questions but football has left me slightly deaf. In the schools? Yes, I do support them. Exercise is an important outlet for burning off energy, socialization and for brain development. However, I hope to live long enough to see football removed from the schools. Surprised?"

"Well, yes and no."

I offered Peggy a scotch. I was surprised when she accepted. "It's too dangerous for growing brains. In number terms, the costs outweigh the benefits. My hope has already earned me some enemies from parents, but how am I more concerned about their kids than they are?"

Peggy nodded in response to her first sip. "Do you suppose you'll ever come back to Drake's?"

"I doubt it. Tonight, I'm weaning myself off gambling. Wish me luck." I refilled our glasses that we clinked together in a toast. "Could I have a hug? You've been so sweet interviewing me and all. You made me very comfortable, unlike some others I've had." My interviewer agreed to a hug. I tried not to squeeze her too tight. "May I say something girl to girl, Peggy, is it? Wear that Hermès as a neck scarf. It will hide your

Adam's apple. Or get it shaved down. And don't be ashamed of who you are, sweetie. Keep the scotch."

Chapter 17

"You ask me how I am called, señorita. My name is Geraldo Juan Jesus Fernández de Garcia, but my friends call me Chuy. You may call me Your Majesty when we meet for the first time—that is now, and after that Señor Fernández. Since I will be changing my name tomorrow, I do not mind giving it now. I have been here before but not in the Chairs, so I am confident Boss will introduce me with 'Player Three is the beloved hereditary ruler of a gold producing country in South America. Welcome, Señor Three.'"

"Please tell me about your background, Your Majesty," the interviewer said.

She is quite lovely. I do have a weakness for golden hair. "Gladly. I am the sixth hereditary King of Merida. My fourth great grandfather saved the life of the hero El Libertador, Simón Bolívar, at the Battle of Boyaca. For this he was awarded land in the Cordillera de Merida, mountains that cross Venezuela and Colombia: the Kingdom of Merida. You must have seen our flag out front, the yellow flag with a gold pan and shovel on it." She nodded. *My pedigree was impressing her. I will be caressing her hair before tomorrow.* "By the grace of God, we discovered gold in our mountains. It financed our country for 200 years." I moved my chair closer.

"How is your gold supply holding out. Have you found any new sources?"

She writes everything down. Why does she sit so far away? She wants to know about my money. Perhaps later we will have a more private talk. Women will do anything for money. "I believe our gold supply has hardly been touched. It will last for generations. However, in recent months we have been searching for a source of emeralds." *Her eyes light up at the mention of jewelry.*

"That sounds exciting. What led to that?"

I imagined how she looked in a swimming costume. "Surely you know of the Spanish treasure ships from South America…"

"Yes, as a matter of fact…"

"…part of the treasures were emeralds from Colombia, but a part that is very near to Merida. I feel that mother nature must have extended that source into my own land."

"And if you don't find emeralds?"

"I suspect the emerald that one of the Players in the Chairs has been wearing was actually from Merida, so I am optimistic others will be found."

"Tell me about the people in Merida, Señor Fernández."

I will touch her heart. I leaned in and lowered my voice. "My people love me. The men stop and bow as I drive by. The women kiss my cheek as I walk through the marketplace. Small children kiss my feet for a blessing. And my enemies fear me." *I must also appeal to her sense of strength.*

"What enemies would you have, sir?"

Perhaps she does not see me here. "There are rumors of rebels in the mountain passes who want to bring in so called modern ideas. They are few and disorganized. Nothing to worry about if you should wish to visit, as my guest." *My opening invitation.*

"Very kind. What products do you export besides gold?"

She may not have heard my offer. I raised my voice lightly. "The women produce shawls and embroidered clothing. I must have one of our alpaca shawls sent to you. Can you give me your personal address?" She was hiding her smile. *How modest.*

"Again that's kind of you but I am allergic to animal products. How long have you been King?"

Allergic? What is there that will persuade her? "Such a pity. Alpaca is very soft. My family has lived in Merida for generations. I myself have been King since I was twenty-five. I was crowned after my older brother drowned while fishing. Would you like to have a necklace made from Merida gold? It would be lovely around your neck. I will place it there myself." I lightly touched her neck, but she recoiled.

"I was asking about your sister, Marina Julieta. Tell me about her."

She must not hear well. Gold gets everyone's attention. "Who said to ask about my sister? It is unfortunate but there have been several assassinations attempts upon my person." *Do I have a traitor near me?* I moved my chair away. "My older sister Marina would have inherited the throne but for the sad fact she was killed instead of me in a car bombing. I changed cars with her at the last moment since I had all my children with me and needed the larger limo. Perhaps that is why I brought my own limo here. It makes me sad to travel in cars someone else has used."

"How many children *do* you have?"

She does not sneer as she asked this of me. Does she not love niños? "*Seis.* That is six. A handsome family. I am very virile, you see. In fact, I love children. The more there are, the happier I am."

Peggy nodded politely. "Do they go to your public schools?"

Nada. "Schools? No there are no public schools in Merida. The church conducts lessons for my people's children. My own children have private tutors as befitting a king's family."

"What kind of jobs are they prepared for, the peasants' children, Señor Fernández?"

"Why the mines, of course. The farms so we all can eat. And they produce certain exports such as…uh, crafts, as I said." *Why is she not looking at me now?*

"What do you do for excitement personally? As king you must have many choices?"

She must be impressed with sport. "I am a well-known fisherman in South America. We have a rare breed of mountain trout that I cultivate and catch in a private lake. What else? Oh, as the head judge of my country, I have a unique method of dispensing justice. I am a humanitarian at heart. I do not like to see criminals in cages."

"A humanitarian. I am gratified to hear those words, *señor.*"

"*Muchas graçias, senorita.* You will understand if a man is found guilty of a crime that would result in prison, I have an alternative. I give him thirty-minutes to flee. Then my hunting guides and I try to find him. If he can make it to the border, good for him, he is free." *I see the smile has gone from her eyes.*

"Doesn't that violate international human rights?"

"*¡No estoy de acuerdo!* I disagree! The concept of 'human rights' is a new one. There is no universal agreement on the definition which rights should be accorded. For me as for my father and his father before him, *I* am the law in Merida. *I* decide what my people need."

"Yes, of course. Why are you playing the Chairs? Why are you risking your kingdom?"

"I am playing so I may retire from public life. I need a long vacation to relax and write my memoir. I'm sure it will be a best seller, even an important film." She did not seem impressed. *Perhaps my accent is too refined for her.*

"Who will become the new ruler of Merida when you retire?"

"My children are young but one day my oldest son will succeed me. Until that day, I will be regent from afar." *She must love children.*

"Is that why you plan to change your name? To become anonymous?"

"What other reason could I have?"

She shook her head. "I don't have an answer to that. What will you do if you lose? What if you exchange bodies and end up as a woman?"

"Lose? I do not understand what you are asking me. Losing is a concept very foreign to me. I always *win* in my country and this island is even smaller than Merida. Why should I lose? Is there another king playing? I think not. As a king, I deserve it and I outrank the other Players."

"And Drake's has agreed to this outcome?"

Now she is rude! She is no lady. "I see no reason to address the issue. I am a frequent guest. I am sure Boss is eager to show his gratitude. As to your last question, it is so preposterous it does not deserve an answer. Me a woman. Besides that, I have never been in a situation where my bodyguards have not triumphed. They will give their life for me."

The interviewer closed her notebook. "Thank you, Señor Fernández. I wish you luck. May you get everything you deserve."

So she is attracted to me.

####

****

"Just call me Vic, Peggy. I am the *de facto* manager of security for Drake's. Who doesn't dream of having a movie-star-gorgeous companion on their arm? Here at Drake's, we provide them." *I've seen her a lot this week.* She was everywhere on the security tapes.

"You provide a security detail for each Player?"

For our security, not theirs. "That's one way to put it. You might notice in the Chairs that each Player has an escort during and after the game. The Player knows they will have an escort and they choose if that escort is a man or a woman." I picked an outdoor meeting spot for our interview. It got a little bit close being inside, but out here I can see the sky.

"Does it matter if they pick an escort of the same sex?"

I noticed she has questions written down and she was right-handed. "No, it doesn't matter which they choose, but it can't be their own bodyguard or guest. No judgements are made."

"Do escorts work all season? It would seem to present a potential problem." She looked up as I answered.

"No. These escorts only work during the Chairs, so only once a year. We have some specific requirements for escorts. Because there is always a certain level of danger involved, perhaps even death, they are very well paid and insured." *Supply and demand in action.*

"What danger specifically? And what requirement?"

I noticed she turned her left ear towards me when I talked. "What requirements? You're right to ask. First, every one of them is someone you would pick a fight with only if you were insane. Sure, they clean up and look dashing in a tux or evening gown, but that's because we don't let them wear their black belts or Seal or Ranger patches to work."

This amused Peggy. She shook her head but smiled. "And the danger part?" She held her gaze at my eyes.

Ah, she noticed I skipped that part of her question. "Some Players don't play fair. Some are poor losers. Some I wouldn't want to meet in a dark alley."

"I can only imagine. How do you select the Escorts?"

She's digging below the surface here. I need to be careful. "We hold interviews in Florida. There's a set of tests. Each escort is an expert in some form of close-in fighting, but we look for charm and restraint too. Being tactful is an important part of the job."

"I can see that. Honey before vinegar, really."

"Very apt analogy. We set up a mugger to surprise them in the parking lot. We only want them to disarm the attacker, not to kill them. We want bodyguards not assassins, at least as Escorts. Each one can handle weapons and disarm the people holding them." *It's a different story for our Security people.* "Each and every escort can put you in a choke hold and, whether you decide to play nice or not, can render you unconscious or dead—your choice. You can wake up in a bed or in a body bag, which FYI, only comes in black."

Peggy laughed at my FYI. "Very slimming, they say."

I liked her sense of humor. I nodded at her comeback. "So they say. Our Security people have to walk a fine line. They don't suffer fools lightly, but that describes a few—very few—of our Guests. Some Guests have their own security, and their people and our people sometimes cross swords. So far, all issues that have arisen here have been resolved here."

Her eyebrows rose slightly. *Why did that get her attention?* "How did you meet Dex? He mentioned that you two go way back."

Pure curiosity or more? I made her to be 5' 9" without the heels. Tall for a woman. "Way back is correct. I met Dex at a boxing gym. I was the first guy who could take his beating but wouldn't go down. A couple of those scars on his face came from me. Eventually I became his alter ego. He was the cool guy running the poker game." *I was what happened if you cheated or tried to welch on a bet.*

"So his muscle? How did you get into that line of work? You hardly fit the stereotype of an enforcer." She gave me the quick once-over.

My dad was a caporegime, or capo, in a crime family. His job was to head up the soldiers. I listened and learned from him about his work, even though what I wanted was to go to college. "I was born in Philly," is all I said.

My father's guys taught me to fight and to set booby

174

traps, to shoot, and use a knife. They gifted me with my first set of brass knuckles. Now I wear heavy men's rings on both hands. They looked flashy and added character to Drake's, but they worked just as well as brass knuckles. *If I need a quick getaway, they're portable and quite valuable.* "My uncle was a cop at one time and of the old school. I picked up a trick or two from him. He taught me to box to make a man of me."

Crime family and cops—*there's a lot in common there. One day I deliberately screwed up a hit on another family.* No big deal, just the guy took a lot longer to die and my father's soldiers had to hang around, which was dangerous, to make sure he was done. *My dad got the message.* "I got into a college in New York where I majored in history and languages. I loved Latin and added to my already passable Italian. I taught Latin but I got tired of the hours, the whiney kids, the school politics. I was lucky I had a skill set I could fall back on. Security."

"College. I'm not surprised. Did you ever study abroad?"

Lady, I've added new pages twice to my current passport. "Yeah. I still go to Europe each summer to study and brush up. Never know when I'll need to teach again." *Mostly I brush up on Russian and Latin, so I combine business and pleasure.* "Then I met Dex. End of story." *Did that satisfy her? What I really like about this job is I have plenty of time to work on my translations of Cicero.* He had a lot to say that cost him his life.

"But again, you don't…I mean you look more like a teacher than…" She was searching for a word, but I didn't want to mention I'd been through the Gizmo.

"I went on a diet. Doc's orders. I still work out in the gym."

"Thanks. I didn't mean to pry."

"That's your job, isn't it?" *Don't blow it, Vic.*

"Well, I suppose you could put it that way. So, you are planning on coming back next year?" I see her put her pen in her purse.

"Sure," I answered. *Why not.*

"I take it you are not one of the managers who are up for contract renewal." I shook my head. *What's she fishing for?* "Ever been married?" At least she didn't laugh when she asked it.

"Take a good look at me. I don't exactly make women's heart flutter. I'm too old for the staff and too poor for the guests, so, no. No wife, no kids." *The single life satisfies me. No loose ends.*

"Okay. But I think you are selling some of my sisters short. An intelligent guy who travels and speaks multiple languages? I got a couple of friends who would jump at the chance for a dinner date."

My eyebrows twitched. *Not that I've ever noticed, signorina. Was she pulling my leg?*

"Enough of the personal questions. Have you had any deaths at Drake's?"

"A couple of heart attacks, a stroke or two. One drowning at the beach. All guests."

"Any others? None of your staff? Nothing more recent?"

Does she know about Mr. Stewart? "Except for a scuba accident this week that is still under investigation, so I can't talk about it, I'd have to review the records. But I'm confident that the only graves you'll find on the island are those of the residents." *That even made me laugh.*

Chapter 18

"Vic, I've noticed cameras around the grounds. I've been through the Maze a bit. Are you able to tell me a little more about the island security?"

"Sure. We have a local island police force to handle local security. That includes poaching for fish, seafood, some of the native fruits and plants. The usual local stuff. Most of the island is a national park, and Boss takes that seriously."

She's sipped juice from locally grown mangoes. "That's good to hear. It's so easy to go the exploitation route for natural resources. Anything else to add?"

"I will say this. Our guests are high dollar people. I am grateful we don't allow them to bring their kids. The prospect of kidnapping would keep me awake at night." *I wouldn't lose sleep over a few of our Guests getting kidnapped.* Money, enemies, egos, and opportunity abound here. Sometimes I feel like I'm back on the streets of Philly. *Kids, on the other hand, what could they have done to deserve that?*

####

****

"Good afternoon. Do you mind if I sit?" I asked. *She is attractive for a foreigner.*

The interviewer, already in the room, nodded. "Please. My name is Peggy."

I sat down in what I perceived to be a lucky chair. I

178

took out my cigarette case. "Do you mind?"

"Not at all. That case is beautiful. May I look at it?"

I slid the cigarettes across the table. "Be my guest." She lightly ran her brightly lacquered nails across the carved lacquer surface.

"Cinnabar red over black. I've never seen an object this small before. Breathtaking."

"Early Ming, most likely to hold opium for use as an aphrodisiac."

"How did you determine that?" She turned the box over to look at the obverse side.

"The rearing dragon, a sign of virility and masculinity. Of course, I have repurposed it for a modern addiction of tobacco."

"Shall we start?"

I nodded.

"Is this your first time to Drake's?" She wrote as quickly as I spoke. She was using a script I didn't recognize. *Arabic perhaps?*

I had the skill of reading upside down. It saved time in meetings and negotiations. I was ruffled that I couldn't read what she wrote about me. "I visited Drake's and observed the Chairs. I was quite drawn to the risk involved and the variability in the expected payoffs." *What was she writing?* I rested my elbows on the table and leaned forward.

"But you gambled when you were here before?"

I looked up. "Of course. What man of my culture doesn't? Money is a thing easily replaced." *Was that amusement her eyes betrayed?*

"What prompted you to play the Chairs?"

I glanced down as if contemplating my answer. *It just looked like scribbling—is that a six or a zero?* "I asked my astrologer to cast my fortune months ago. By sheer coincidence—or was it—the date of the Chairs is a fortuitous day for me. I asked for my lucky Kua number as my player number."

She leaned back a few degrees and pulled her pad closer. "Kwa number? What is that?" She wrote more odd characters.

What is that? "Kua number. K-U-A, in English. It is a lucky feng shui number based on my birth date and gender." I leaned part way across the table and reached for an ashtray near her.

"But why here? Why Drake's?" At least she wrote 'kua' correctly.

"Do you mind if we turn on a light? All the better to see you, my dear." I came around to the lamp on her side and switched it on. I paused to look at her notes not more than a meter away. *It is not any more recognizable from this side!* "You see, I believe that wind and water elements can bring me luck and prosperity. What casino is better located than Drake's Key for wind and water? It is here that they surround me. And the payoffs are astronomical. Look out the window for yourself."

She nodded at my last comment and glanced out the window. "How do you think Boss will introduce you for the Chairs?"

"My expectation is Boss will follow his usual pattern and say, 'Player Four is a dealer in Asian antiquities. He says he's played in a previous life but it's his first time in the Chairs in this life. Welcome Mr. Four.' Or perhaps he will call me Chiang Xin, but I doubt it. So many people find Mandarin unlearnable." *I was irritated.* Was I losing control of this interview? She was using a code right under my nose. "There may be some slight variation, but my fortune teller assures me I am in an excellent position to not lose, and in an even better position to win." I stubbed out my cigarette and looked around the room.

"Have you met any of the other Players?"

"No." *And I have not planned for others to see me here. Too risky.* "Do you mind if I order a drink? May I order for you?"

"Shall we take a short break?" she asked.

I nodded and ordered a *Sanhuajiu*—110 proof and just what I needed at this moment, and an island iced tea for the lady. We sat for a few moments until there was a knock at the door.

We stood as we held our drinks. She walked over to look out the window. I moved closer to enjoy the calming water view.

"Are you enjoying the rest of the resort?" she asked.

Such insipid topics. "I'm not here for the sybaritic life of the West. I brought my own diversions with me." *I was here strictly for the treasure.* She was taller than I expected. "Boss has been most accommodating in assigning me a suite decorated to my taste and arranged according to feng shui requirements. My lucky direction is east." I checked my watch and pointed in what I calculated was east. "That way."

She nodded in agreement. "You should see the array of lucky objects in that section of my room I brought. This room could use some feng shui arranging. It is very unlucky."

"The food here *is* amazing though, don't you agree?" she gushed.

"Yes. While I like to experience foreign foods and delicacies, Drake's has done a superb job in supplying my Asian favorites as well."

"How did you get into the antiques business?" She sat down and started writing again.

I looked out to the sky. *How did I get started?*

Now for some fun. She asked a logical question about how I started my business. "My father was a professor of history. As such he had access to the national museum and their tempting collection of priceless treasures." *Greed. Pure greed.* That's what tempted him, corrupted him, and that is my heritage. *And no one is greedier than I am.* I walked to the other side of the room. "One could say I followed my father into his business: antiquities." Does she even follow what that meant. She wrote more squiggles on her notepad. "This baijiu is nicely complex. I must compliment Boss," I said as the sunlight penetrated my drink.

"I read about that field quite a bit. Is it as lucrative as I think?"

She has no idea. I could only offer a cryptic expression and say, "I am here, am I not?" I refilled my glass.

"Of course. Well then, could you describe your education to me?"

Yes, I must maintain some semblance of legitimacy. I started to pace the room always keeping her in view. "My father made sure I had an international education. I speak several languages, and I carry multiple passports." I have dual citizenships. *I may need them after the Chairs especially since Boss holds my Chinese passport.* "I majored in art history and antique ceramics. My father taught me all his knowledge regarding antiquities. He passed away unexpectedly on a field trip to Mongolia."

"Outer or Inner Mongolia?" she asked completely

oblivious to the large crack she just exposed in her own knowledge.

Outer Mongolia is Mongolia. I turned my back as I turned the corner to keep her from seeing my smirk. "There is no Inner Mongolia. The People's Republic of China swallowed it up some time ago. Of course, the people there are still Mongolians." *Really. What kind of an education did you have, miss?*

"I see. I apologize for my ignorance. Why are you here to participate in this year's Chairs?" Peggy shook her hand up and down. *Now what?*

"Why am I in the Chairs? Such an obvious question. To please my honored mother. She's ninety-four. Her greatest wish is to see me restored to my rightful place as Emperor of China. I shall restore China to its glorious place as the Center of the World. That's what the Chinese characters for China mean—Center of the World." *I wanted a fortune or two even if I didn't want to be emperor.*

She sipped her tea a moment, and then looked to me. "That's quite an ambitious plan. You certainly need a fortune to do that."

I'll let my inscrutable face tell her nothing, or perhaps everything. I returned my glass to the tray as I must not appear to be foolish to this woman. I walked slowly to the other end of the room.

"Are you traveling alone on this trip? I haven't noticed you in the restaurants or nightclub."

Really? As if she is paying attention to me—or is she? Quite unexpectedly Peggy stood. I did not think the interview was yet over so…"Unfortunately, my wife and traveling companion could not be here." *In fact, they may not be anywhere.* They took our older yacht to Macau to shop and gamble while the yacht was getting an engine overhaul. I'm told it's overdue in port. Not to worry. *Wives and mistresses are easy to come by.*

Peggy walked to the tray and poured more tea.

Why am I jumpy at this moment while she seems so serene?

"And children? I suppose the government mandated number?" she inquired.

I simpered, I lied, I shrugged. My wives have given me a dozen children, some of whom I've never met. "I am a responsible parent. They go to English boarding school at age six. As I did."

"Do you know any of the Players already?"

This is unexpected. She may have seen me lunching with one of the them. *Is she trying to catch me in a lie? How do I throw her off?* She sat again and picked up her pen and it gave me an idea. "I noticed King Three leaving as I approached the door. He gave you that story about his grandfather saving Simón Bolívar, didn't he?" Bahahaha. *I see she is surprised at this. Good.* "That man doesn't even know who his own father is. Yes, he has exported a lot of gold but that was quickly depleted. He's exploiting a different natural resource now—his peasants, or the women, more precisely."

Her eyebrows shot up as she looked from her paper. "How's that? He exploits women in his kingdom?"

"Babies. That what he exports. Babies and children. I have obtained a dozen of them for household slaves." *He disposes of all my children by my mistresses too.* We had a mutual relationship that benefited us both. There was a limit to how many English boarding schools I could support.

She stopped writing those infernal squiggles. "This

is shocking. Why are you letting me interview you?"

Now the threat. "I might as well confess my duplicitous behavior. You see, several of the Players have bet whether you make it off the island alive or not. As such, we raised the stakes between ourselves." I took a step towards her. "Some of us are telling you our most despicable secrets. Some of us might even be lying. However, it's up to us as individuals to decide. Some may decide to tell the truth. Some Players aren't even aware of this private betting pool." She was serious in her demeanor. I took another step.

"Are you saying you took out a contract on me, or that one of you may just decide to kill me if you can?"

I must say the lady is unfazed at this declaration of mine. *How can that be?* "We don't know if you can be trusted. One of us might have buyer's remorse and have you removed from the equation, is all I'm saying." Again quite unexpectedly she rose and quickly walked to her bag. I noticed she was fumbling in her purse. *Does she carry a weapon?* Now what do I do?

Peggy faced me. I suspected she had something in her clenched hand. She sat again in front of her notepad. From her hand she drew out a new pen and continued writing. *False alarm.*

"Let me expand upon my business. Just how many temples do you honestly believe there are in Asia that have antiquities worth stealing and fencing? Much easier to manufacture them." I paced across the room again, always in her eyeline. "What really sells is the opium. That's my cash cow. Opium and weapons grade nuclear materials."

She stopped and stared at me.

"Don't be shocked! Do you remember that

explosion in Beirut a short time ago? My stuff. Just covered up to keep the people from panicking." Her mouth dropped open. *Good. I wanted her scared.* I walked nearer to the table.

She regained her composure by half and said, "How are such goods transported around the world?"

Bold move. Puzzling, but bold. "Transportation? Haven't you figured that out yet? What kind of a journalist are you? Antiquities are shipped all over the world. Draw your own conclusions." I see no way for her to summon help if I should choose to—

In rapid turn she asked, "What about your family. Are they involved?" She drew more symbols quickly.

"My mother is still alive, that part is true. Some of my daughters would have their feet bound, if *mamâ* had her way. She has dementia. We don't let her make any decisions. She just thinks she does." *Chew on that, Miss Peggy.*

"If you have such a great deal going, why are you playing the Chairs?" *She is the proverbial cat consumed by curiosity.* "Ah. I am playing in the Chairs because I have money hidden so deeply that even I have forgotten it. That in of itself is as high a status as anyone can obtain, isn't it*?" I was the present-day equivalent of Chinese royalty.* My opportunity arrived . I started towards her.

There was a rapid knock on the door. A waiter opened it apologizing profusely. "Anything else?" He looked to her rather than to me.

An accomplice? I stepped towards the door to leave. "The real beauty of me telling you this is if you publish, it's the poor suckers who ended up as someone else who will pay the price."

"What if *you* switch bod—"

"Delicious, isn't it? I can't wait to read your book if you make it out alive. At that, I shall take my leave as this interview is over."

****

I crossed the pool area where Peggy sat at the bar. I nodded as she spoke up. We didn't have an appointment, but we were always polite to—well, everyone here.

"Vic. May I ask you a question?"

"Of course. For the book?"

"Yes. There was a young couple here yesterday who seemed to be carrying someone's ashes. I'd like to approach them today, but they have vanished into thin air."

I sipped my coffee evaluating what card to play in this little game. She was observant. I had an idea it was a couple I cared for and I wanted to protect their privacy. Peggy had an itch that needed to be scratched. "Do you remember what the container looked like?" I could feign ignorance if she didn't get my trip up questions right.

"Yes, a small treasure chest with three gold coins on the top." The description was spot on. This lady was good with details.

"And the lady carrying it, was she a tall woman with curly auburn hair?"

"Blonde, not a redhead. She kept calling the treasure chest 'Tom.'" Peggy looked bewildered, but she hit the description dead on.

Tom's name took this to another level. I opted to give Peggy enough to satisfy her curiosity. "No, you're not imagining anything. Would you like something to drink?"

We sat at the end of the bar under shady palm trees.

A slight breeze shifted past rattling the palm fronds. "We have guests we refer to as 'day trippers' because they only come for a twenty-four-hour period or less. The people you described were Beryl and Curtis. Tom's ashes were in the chest."

"Dex told me about day trippers. Beryl and Curtis are given names. You sound like you know them. Are they friends?"

I pondered how best to temper my reply. "I do know them, and we are friends. But, Peggy, I would greatly appreciate it if you tread lightly here." *I was not threatening her.*

Peggy's expression turned intense. In a flat tone she said, "I can promise you that."

I believed her. *Trust is not something I give casually.* "I'll hold you to that." I hoped that sounded more like a request. *Now where to start?* "Tom and Curtis—sons born into a wealthy family. Tom headed up the family business. Curtis and several other siblings worked in it." *In a very authentic way, Tom is still the head of the business.*

"The two men came here our first year. The stress of their business made a vacation a necessity. They came for three weeks. Their third day they fell in love with Beryl. She was the perfect combination of beauty and brains. Beryl was our original accountant. She set up all our financial accounts and books. I saw Beryl as simply beautiful in every aspect. Her appropriate name came from the Latin *beryllus* meaning a stone of the green-blue color of the sea." Peggy took notes in Teeline shorthand. *Clever and efficient.*

Chapter 19

Vic said, "Tom and Curtis were at the lagoon snorkeling when they encountered Beryl. She walked out of the water wearing a blue bikini, a knife strapped on her hip, and a milk conch in her hand. They described her as looking like Ursula Andress in *Dr. No.*"

Peggy shook her head and laughed. *I realized I've picked up Dex's practice of movie references and haven't even noticed.*

"Why did she have a conch and what is it?"

She really wants to know everything, doesn't she? I needed to be careful around her. "The conch? It's a mollusk that's quite edible and exceedingly popular with our guests. She collected her own lunch that day, a unique perk Boss allowed her." Beryl loved the sea. *She was the closest thing to a sea nymph I'd ever seen.*

"Are they on the menu here? I'd like to try it."

"We serve conch we farm ourselves, not taken from the wild. To continue, they introduced themselves to her, and the guys were smitten. After that, they made sure to be on the beach at the same time as she was. Personally, I think it started with the men thinking she could be an interesting 'diversion' for them, especially when she left to go back to work. They assumed she danced as a show girl—rightly so—but as hard as they looked, they never found her in the floor show." I pulled a bowl of macadamia nuts between us.

Peggy said, "Did she notice them?" as she popped a nut into her mouth.

"Yes and no. She became used to male guests, and even female guests, coming on to her. She was polite but ignored them. The brothers looked for her but failed. They received a message from their home office that required accounting advice. Boss sent them to Beryl, only she wasn't in a bikini. Passing an afternoon with Beryl gave the brothers a new respect for her. By the end of their vacation, they were in love." Boss enforced a strict no fraternization policy, but even he could see what was between them was real, so he looked the other way. "The problem arose that each brother fell for Beryl, and she was in love with both of them. Honestly and truly. She couldn't bear to pick one and lose the other. Neither of the men wanted to lose Beryl. What they did all want was to continue as they were."

"Are you telling me there existed a ménage à trois for love? Everyone was okay with that?"

I granted her a rare laugh. "Exactly. They put their heads together and drew up a plan to defeat family opposition. Beryl gave Boss her notice through the end of the season, while agreeing to be an on-call consultant. Next, the guys hired Beryl into their company as comptroller for a new division they recently created." *She was qualified and came with a great recommendation from Boss.*

"Since neither guy was married, they agreed to live together quietly back home. When their vacation ended, Tom went back and found a large, secluded, and private mansion that suited their needs. Curtis stayed here. After three weeks the men switched places. They were commuting back and forth from home to Drake's."

Every once in a while, Tom and Curtis were both here, and Beryl worked her day job.

"How long did that go?"

I held up my forefinger to indicate she should be patient. "At the end of the season, Beryl moved into the mansion. The three were incredibly happy. Unfortunately, the guys' other family members did not share that feeling. They did everything they could to embarrass our happy trio. Then a strange coincidence happened. Beryl discovered she was pregnant. Birth control failed and *voila*, a baby was on the way, Curtis's baby."

"Babies change everything," Peggy commented.

And indeed, she was correct. Although not a part of their original plan, it made the plan better. "Next, something happened that all companies dread. A court found them criminally liable for a flaw in their product that cost six people their lives. The contractor who designed the product was also held liable, but since the family made and sold the product, they were held liable financially. They had the deep pockets lawyers look for."

"Do you remember what the product was?"

I lied to Peggy, "No. Unfortunately, one of our guests brought one here though and was one of the fatalities. We airlifted her to St. Croix, and then home to Frankfurt. She was hospitalized but, well…"

"That's a shame every way you look at it." She chewed on a chocolate covered nut as she mulled this plot point.

"As CEO, Tom was sentenced to jail for several years, leaving Curtis to manage both companies. Curtis got it that he wasn't the man for the job. He'd gotten into trouble when he was younger. Tom found him and brought him home to rehab and a stable life. If Tom went to prison the whole family would be ruined including Beryl and their baby."

"Did the rest of the family know about this situation?"

"Not at first. Tom, Curtis, and Beryl came up with a new plan. First, Curtis and Beryl married. They held a small wedding when Beryl was five months pregnant. Boss and Peaches attended. This legitimized their baby. They came here for their honeymoon. Tom came as a day tripper. Curtis and Tom went through the Gizmo and transferred. In that way, Tom ran the companies, but everyone acknowledged Curtis as the company head and as Beryl's husband. The honeymoon couple stayed for a few more weeks, while 'Tom'—Curtis's mind in Tom's body—went to prison."

"Why did Curtis agree to the switch?" She looked genuinely confused as she shook her right hand. *Writing cramps.*

"His idea really. He loved his wife and brother. They planned to switch back once he got out of jail. He owed his brother this favor since Tom saved his life."

"I can't imagine doing that for anyone," she said rubbing her wrist.

I can. "But there's more. Tom received a seven-year sentence, but in a bizarre twist, he left a sample in a sperm bank in case he didn't make it back. He remembered it while in Curtis's body. About a year after Beryl's first baby arrived, she used Tom's sample to become pregnant again."

"That seems awfully soon to have another baby," Peggy said.

I noticed that Peggy was using an expensive

Waterman pen. "That's a very nice *man's* pen you have there, Peggy," I said fishing for an explanation.

"Uh, thank you." She added, "My father is one of those eccentrics who collect fountain pens. I can't seem to write with one without smudging the ink. He gifted me this Christmas a year ago. So, another baby…?"

Nice save, young lady. "Yes, quite soon. They told the family they agreed before Tom went to prison for Beryl to bear his child." They wanted to be double sure the relatives couldn't bellyache over it all.

"That seems complicated by design. Why?" *She doesn't miss a thing.*

"Very astute. DNA proved that Curtis was the father of Beryl's first baby, a baby boy. DNA also proved that Tom was the father of her second baby, a little girl. Finally, DNA proved Beryl was the biological mother of both babies."

"Now that's clever." Peggy grinned at this twist on a family plot.

We clinked glasses in acknowledgement of a plan well-conceived and delivered. "That was their plan to protect Beryl against the family in case anything happened to them both. They took both babies to show Curtis, now Tom, in prison."

"I suppose that was the best expected outcome for everyone." Peggy took the last macadamia nut, examined it closely, placed it in her perfect red mouth, and crushed it.

"Well, not really. Curtis got the see his own child that would be raised by his wife and brother because a month later, he was killed in a prison riot." *His death affected all of us here.* "They were guests we looked forward to seeing."

Peggy said, "Biologically speaking, it's even possible that more babies for both brothers could show up. In a strange way, Vic, I find this solution very satisfying and definitely ingenious."

More babies? "That would be their business, but ever since then, Beryl and Curtis with Tom's mind, bring the ashes of Tom, who died with Curtis's mind, back to Drake's as day trippers." *They have a standing reservation for that day for as long as Drake's is in business.* "So, you see, they've already left. You could come back next year but I doubt they would have time for you. The three of them make a full day of it and we want to respect their time." That's all I intended to say about these friends and family of Drake's.

She then said, "*Amor vincit omnia.*" There was more to Peggy than met the eye.

I answered, "Exactly. Love conquers all."

****

"Good morning, miss. I'm—"

"Peggy. I know. I also know some people call me Dr. Jane the Brain. No, it doesn't bother me. In fact, I take pride in it. I know you have a lot of questions, some that I won't answer. Here's how it's going to go. I'll talk. You listen. Ready?" *If anything, I was impatient.* I hated interviews so I only do them on my terms. In this case, as a favor to Boss. Peggy turned on a recorder. *Good. Maybe she won't interrupt.* "With a Nobel Prize I can write my own ticket. I don't know where that ticket's going yet. Maybe rehab. *I* know I'm a serious adrenaline junkie. I imagine Boss's intro for me will go like this: 'A world-class research chemist, Player Six holds a Nobel Prize and five of the world's top patents in biotechnology. Playing for the third time, Dr. Six.' That barely scratches the surface."

"About the—"

I cut her off. "Don't get excited by any of that. Those all come through challenging work. Understand I've got this brain that never shuts down. My father asked me once if it ever stopped working and the answer was no—never."

She raised her pen. "By never you mean—"

"—I mean the key thing you should ask is why am I here at Drake's a third time? I won both times before. The answer is *winning bores me.* It's the stress, the suspense, the mystery that pumps out the adrenaline I crave."

Her eyes widened. "Were you always—"

"—hyper? Yes, always. Growing up I was the kid who climbed the highest tree. I jumped off the cliff into the lake. I rode my bike faster and took the curbs higher. Yes, I was a regular in the ER, and there was always a next time."

"Even in high—"

Peggy was twitching, but I didn't care. I intended to get this over ASAP. "—school? No. It got worse but in unusual ways. With the highest average in the Honor Society that my folks made me join, I was restless, always searching. I wasn't a bad kid, and I didn't know why I did things. I just had to. What I didn't know was that the physiological response was brought on by the stress I craved that turned on the *adrenaline*. I was hooked on how exciting the high was."

"It must have—"

I held up both hand; rude, but effective. "I tried driving too fast—note the small scar across my left eyebrow." I turned my face so she could inspect the scar.

"I excelled at dangerous sports like snowboarding and motocross—again, see scar over right ear." I pulled back my hair to expose this last scar. "I jumped into risky and unprotected sex, until mom had birth control installed that I couldn't remove. Then it wasn't stressful, just fun." I know now I dodged the bullet on that one. *I should thank them for that sometime.*

"Anything illegal or—"

Now it was my turn to start twitching. "—criminal? I tried stealing one time. Spent three nights in juvenile detention. Sitting in jail for any amount of time slowed me down with no adrenaline payoff, so I stopped. Still graduated at the top of my class." *High school must have scared the crap out of my parents. I regret that now.*

"College must have—" Peggy was speaking at a slower pace.

I'm wearing her down. "Not really. I channeled my energy into academics. I got a full ride to Johns Hopkins in Baltimore. Everything—tuition, room and board, books, lab fees, student fees—for seven years. Again, graduated top of my class for my bachelors in three years, and MD/PhD degrees four years later. It wasn't hard for me, but I expected the technical and intellectual challenges and credentials might pay off." *They have big time.*

"Sometimes I think it's really my brain's life and I'm just a convenient hell-on-wheels vessel for it to get from here to there." I stood and did a couple of jumping jacks to loosen up.

"But as a doctor—"

This interviewer stinks at taking instructions. "—I must have been gratified. No. Not for me. For a while I was afraid I really screwed up. It didn't take me long to learn I didn't want to stand around a hospital all day. Where's the fun in that? Well, okay, a patient having a seizure or a stroke or a heart attack in the ER—that did get my heart rate up." *That got old fast.*

"So how did you decide—"

I see she is watching my mouth. Must think she can sneak in a question when I close my mouth. *Clever.* "—to leave medicine and go into biotech? I had a chance to do some independent research to take up my spare time in med school. I got a grant from the National Institute of Health. Six months later I had a new drug in field trials." I jogged in place.

"For?" Peggy slipped in.

I have to give her kudos for perseverance. "It's a once-a-month tablet that prevents the buildup in the brain of abnormal proteins called beta amyloids. It may prevent Alzheimer's disease. It will be on the market next year starting as a recommended preventive treatment at age sixty or sooner." I took a sip of water as I paced.

"That's remarkable. My mother—Where do you get your ideas," Peggy asked as I finished the water.

"Where do my ideas come from? I have no fricking idea. If I did I could sell it and teach everyone else. Some of them just appear." I caught my breath, but not long enough to let her slip in another question. This is now a game, a game I always win. "Sometimes I think my brain just takes in just so much information, and then it slinks off into some dark corner of my subconscious where it percolates and calculates combinations and permutations until bam!"

Peggy jumped at this point.

Yea. "Then it pops through to my consciousness and

I go huh, I hear a voice, and I think what's that all about?
"

"Do drugs affect your—?"

"No, I don't do drugs, especially hallucinogens. I have to be in control, so I don't even do alcohol or weed." The interviewer 's eyes gave me a quick once over. "You are thinking I don't look like my resume, aren't you? *What* should I look like? Because of people like you, people who look like me have a tough time. Maybe my brown eyes should be darker rather than the gold-flecked they are. Maybe this body should be different, this body that I take to the gym and work until it's in a pool of sweat and my muscles scream. This body gets me to the front of the line. Especially when I see a guy who could turn me on, and I need a diversion for a few minutes." Peggy blushed. *Caught you, didn't I.* "So again, what should I look like? Would you even be interviewing me if I looked like you? I've got this thing I say to myself now. It's my body they come for but it's my brain that makes them stay or run screaming away."

Peggy sipped from her cup. "So, as far as relationships go—"

"I've seen that same look of contempt that's on your face many times before. Relationships? What's that? I must be the most exhausting woman in the world. I like men, maybe I even love men. But I haven't found one yet who loves me just like this. I haven't found one yet who can take my highs and lows and be happy for me. I haven't found a man I can slow down for, for even an hour much less a lifetime. I haven't found one who doesn't want to compete with me and beat me, and then stay around when they realize that's never going to happen." I started on my squats.

"No marriage or kids in—"

"—my future. Not based upon what I know so far. It'll be too late by the time I slow down enough to focus on it." She must be running out of questions. *What else is there?*

"The Chairs are very soon. What will you do if—"

I held up my hands again; it worked before. "If I win, I'm still rich and I'll still have this brain. If I only lose my fortune, no sweat. I can do what I always do. But if I lose and I trade bodies—now that's got me on edge. This idea that you take your unchanged memories and mental processes with you is *unproven,* and I think, highly unlikely." I leaned in towards Peggy. "There's your physical brain and how it's 'wired' is unique to you. The memories and ideas it's created and stored through my experiences and 'talents' might not have been the same with a different brain. Does the brain build the process, or does the process build the brain? Am I at the peak of my mental powers right at this moment and wasting them talking to you? Will my next brain be even more powerful or totally incompatible or meh, the same? My stress level is at an all-time high. I can't even think—" and then she *actually* interrupted me.

"What did you mean when you mentioned rehab?"

She checked her recorder quickly, so I checked my watch.

"Rehab? That's always the next question."

"If you'd rather not…"

"I'd *rather* not be late to my date with a parasailing pro in half an hour. Rehab? That might be in the cards.

Chapter 20

Dr. Brain said, I've read it's too late to completely change my behavior, but I might be able to moderate it. I do know that deep breathing and yoga and meditating are a waste of my time. Didn't work, any of it. I do know I'm not going to be taking any meds. See, I love my brain. Where it goes, I go." My watch alarm beeped. "Time's up. In case you ever interview me again don't ask me a question unless I haven't already answered it. Don't listen to my answer, and then say, 'How do you know?' If I bothered to give you an answer, trust me I know. If I don't know, I'll say so. Otherwise, the interview is over."

"Whew. I'm glad I had the recorder on," Peggy said. "I think I need a drink before this next one." She called the bar next door as I left.

****

I was reviewing tax documents as Peaches peeked in and said, "Boss, you're needed at the clinic. There's been a stabbing, lovie." She looked concerned.

I've made more than the average number of trips to the clinic this week. I knocked on the door to be let in. Doc kept it locked because of the drugs that might tempt someone who assumed they were part of their resort package. I straightened up when I spotted Rhonda— AKA Captain Ten—sitting by the desk in a two-piece bathing suit. "Are you all right, Captain?" I asked with genuine concern. Out of the corner of my eye I noticed Vic standing in back of a strange man.

Rhonda nodded towards the man all in black the Doc was bandaging. "I've never seen that man until tonight," she stated.

He was a stranger to me too, one of my latest fears. *What does this man have to do with Rhonda?* "Vic, do you know who he is?"

"No. He said he's one of the new temps, one of the grounds crew."

"Have you verified that yet? Where's his Drake's ID?"

"Working on it. No ID of any kind on him. Kellie's reviewing all the photos and

work permits as we speak."

I stepped on a bloody rag on the floor next to Doc. "Did you get his fingerprints?"

"We'll get what we can. So far, it looks like they've been burned off."

Red flag! "Did you get his story?"

Vic nodded.

"And Rhonda's?"

Vic nodded again.

I took a chair by Rhonda. I smiled. "Can I get you anything? A drink? Coffee…?" Noticing she was wet I added, "…a towel?"

"No, very kind but nothing." She was cool and calm for someone who just stabbed a shady looking guy missing all his fingerprints.

"Would you tell me what happened?"

Her hair dribbled water into her eyes, so I offered my handkerchief. She wiped her face and looked me in the eye. "Not at all. I was down at the beach for a moonlight swim. It was deserted. I took a wrong turn coming out of the surf and got lost. There was a small statue of a woman and child reading a book. I stopped there to check the resort layout app on my watch. I tried to get my bearings. I spotted a red door and hoped it might bring me into the main complex.

"That man stepped from behind the oleanders, out into the dim light startling me. 'Where are you going? This is forbidden area,' he told me. "I didn't like his looks. I opted to take my chances with the door. As I reached for the doorknob, he grabbed my arm. I never let *anyone* manhandle me. I reached under the towel wrapped around my waist, drew the knife I always wear, and stabbed him. I tried to cut across his wrist to sever the tendons to disabled his hand. It was dark and he wore dark clothing, so my aim was off. He was thrown off by the injury I inflicted, so I grabbed him and executed a quick foot sweep to take him down. I held him on the ground while I yelled for help." Rhonda stopped and asked, "Do you know where that statue is?"

"Yes, I do." *Twenty steps from my apartment door.* I glance at Vic who nodded that he'd already taken a look at the camera footage. *I owe this lady a thank you, and maybe my life.*

"Doc, how'd she do?"

"She got a couple of tendons. The top two flexor muscles are damaged. This guy needs hand surgery but may never get full use again. He'll need to go to St. Thomas."

I scratched my chin and turned to Vic. "Notify St. Thomas and the St. Croix police. Let

them know what happened, See if they can identify him. Get my plane ready. St. Croix might be best. Have our police take him into custody. Send two security people along but warn them to be careful. Use cuffs. Get a victim statement." I nodded towards Rhonda. "Doc, send any relevant info with this guy for the hospital."

I turned to Rhonda. "I am sorry this happened. I doubt you will be charged with anything, but the police will want to interview you tomorrow. Why don't you go to bed? Don't lose any sleep over this guy."

She stood and walked to the man in black. "Just so you know, you got off easy tonight. I killed the last man who grabbed me like that." She turned to me. "Boss, I won't be losing any sleep. Just point me towards the Lizard Lounge." She headed for the door. As she passed Vic he leaned in and whispered in her ear. She nodded and left.

Vic and I moved out of earshot of the prisoner. "Make sure he doesn't escape. He may be a pro. It's odd he used the word 'forbidden,' isn't it. Just out of curiosity, what did you say to her. Something in Latin?"

Vic grinned slightly. "Hardly, I told her she was rusty and need to practice her knife skills, and that the lounge was to the left."

I cocked my head and let out a deep sigh. "They were outside of my apartment. Since she was there accidently, he might have been waiting for me."

"You're right. We took a knife off him and a garotte. Not your typical yard tools, are they?"

"No, at least not on my island."

"You know what this means? *Alea iacta est.*"

"Mr. Stewart might be a coincidence, but Captain Ten—not. Yes. The die *is* cast."

****

"I'm famous for saying the Chairs is more

predictable than the stock market. I'm Player number Seven because this is my seventh time here. I'm a regular, but this time I'm taking the plunge. What's your name?"

"Peggy is fine, Mr. Twitchell."

Seems appropriate. Why do female writers dress so plain? Her hair style is old-style.

"How did you become wealthy on Wall Street, Mr. Seven? Any hints I might use?"

As if she'd understand. "No hints. It's complicated and predicated on years of experience. To back up a bit, I built my portfolio by being safe rather than sorry. Dad gifted me ten million dollars when I graduated from Yale. I did take a flyer or two. I bought Apple when they introduced the iPod. A 'friend' told me in advance about it." *We're on a tropical island and she is covered from head to toe. At least wear a low-cut blouse, lady.* "I realized I was buying the same music over and over. As a kid I bought vinyl records that needed a record player, and it wasn't portable. Then the cassette players came out." *Amazingly enough she is taking notes.*

"I had to buy the same music but on tape, and with a different player. Those players were more portable, but they tended to *eat* the tape. Then the CD came out. I'm buying the same Beatles songs on a CD using a different player. Finally digital came along. Yes, another player but one that could carry all the music. No more records, no more cassettes, no more tapes."

She started to interrupt but I flashed my "talk to the hand" signal. "I had private listening through headphones on a device that held more than I could listen to on a single charge and fit in my pocket. That's why I invested in Apple. Your turn."

"What investments attracts you now?"

She wasn't so young but not unattractive. *But still, I have her attention.* "My dear, the last big flyer I took was on Tesla, and I don't mean Nikola. Both seemed to be geniuses, but I think they both spread themselves out too thin. I rode in one of those cars. I'm keeping my Rolls. That back seat is large and comfortable." I suppressed a belly laugh imagining her in the back seat of *my* Rolls. *Not a chance.*

"You must have quite a portfolio by now. Any advice for a girl saving for her retirement?"

A girl? Hardly. She's flirting with me though. "Most of my portfolio is in diversified stocks and real estate. I don't really know my total worth. Ask my ex-wives. Their lawyers have a better—and imaginary—number than I do."

"How many ex-wives and children do you have? Are you currently in a relationship?"

"I'm not sure but I am paying my alimony and child support. Every healthy man needs a companion, doesn't he?" *How could I be blamed for being a man?*

"Sir, you appear to be the oldest Player in the Chairs. Why take such a risk at this point in life? There has been news in the press that you're being investigated for bank fraud. Would you comment on that?"

Did she just call me "sir"? "Bank fraud? Yes, I know what the federal government is alleging. I've read they mentioned Russians and Saudi Princes, but I'm innocent until proven guilty.*" I pay my lawyers better than my former wives.* "Besides, I'm an exceptionally large contributor to the political party that just loves Wall Street. That's my insurance, you see. I'd rather have one tiny little White House pardon than my usual Christmas card." *I sensed disapproval at the mention of a pardon.*

"You look remarkably fit. What do you do for exercise? Have you played a round on the course here?"

"Do I play what? Of course, I play around. I'm a wealthy and rich eligible bachelor in my prime who—"

"I'm referring to golf."

"Oh, golf. The course here is nice. I play the senior back nine every day while my uhm, niece, takes a spa treatment."

"Who do you think will win the Chairs?"

I needed to adjust my hearing aid. *Time for the casual scratch of my ear diversion.* "Who do I what? Oh, …win? Me, of course. Why play now? I think it's because of the flu I had. I learned life is unpredictable. I like my odds better here."

"What if you lose? Do you have a backup plan?"

"A man with my knowledge can easily author a 'how to' book." *Books sold to millions of schnooks who can't do the math.* "Besides, I have contacts at several prestigious business schools and would enhance any faculty."

"And if your body is switched?"

"If my body is—?" I already hedged my bet on that when I realized I've never been told of announcements about transfers for past winners. *That's when I sabotaged the Gizmo, but just enough that it won't be operable this week. Did they fix it? Crap.* "I'm running late. I'm trying out a new 'rejuvenation' treatment. I'm not sure how it works but I am expecting 'big' results today. I better cancel my golf game."

I got out fast, took a Xanax, and headed to the Boss's office. I signed all the papers, but is it too late to withdraw? I've seen the other Players. *I refuse to be in any of those skins.*

####

I rushed into the office where Peaches sat opening mail. "Where's Boss? I've got to talk to him." My shirt was soaked.

"Good afternoon to you, Max," she said. "How is Marie today?"

"Peaches!" I was frantic. She buzzed the Boss. I was embarrassed as she caught me shaking and on the verge of tears.

"Sit down, Max," the Boss said as he poured out a glass of water for me. "What's the matter?"

I shivered. "I'm so sorry. She didn't know, I didn't know she—"

"Stop and catch your breath." Boss was beginning to sweat along his own brow line. "Tell me from the start."

"It's Marie. I didn't know she was slipping so fast. If I hadn't been so busy with work and my damned lizards, I might have…"

"Focus, please. What about Marie?"

"She's worse, much worse. She got this idea…I'm sorry."

"We go back a long way. What could Marie possibly have done?"

"She got this idea that our oldest kid is yours and that you were going to take him away from us. I know I'm his father in every way."

The Boss nodded. "I know. You are his father."

"I *know* that. I love my kids more than my own life."

"Everyone here knows that. What is so important right now?"

"I was afraid if she wanted to test the kids' DNA,

and who knows what it could lead to."

"Max, you are his father. I can't have children."

My head snapped up. "What do you mean you can't?"

"I had a vasectomy before I met Marie. I have it checked every year," Boss admitted.

"But sometimes those fail, don't they?"

"And I use a condom. Always have, always will."

The Boss relaxed in his chair but I slumped in mine. "That makes it worse."

"There's more?" Boss's shirt showed sweat circles under his arms.

"Yeah. Marie got it into her head that you'd—you know— and she made up her mind to stop you. She took a vial of venom to poison you with." I held my head in my hands.

"How? I never see Marie. When was she planning on poisoning me?"

"She finally realized that, so she gave it to someone else to do it for her," I cried.

"Who was it? Someone here, or don't you know?" I wiped my handkerchief over my face.

"That's the thing. She can't remember. I checked my lab. There is a vial missing. The stuff is odorless. I don't know if it has a taste though. Boss, I'm sorry."

"Yeah. Me too. I'm sorry for Marie. This poison would be odorless in coffee, wouldn't you guess? Or in a decompression chamber?" Boss dabbed at his upper lip with a monogrammed handkerchief. "Or most anything else, for that matter?"

****

"Welcome, mademoiselle Peggy. I am Yvette, the casino manager. Tonight is the next to last night at the

Casino. The room is decorated as a 1940s New York nightclub. Very amusing."

Peggy nodded. A flashbulb went Pop! nearby and she was nearly blinded.

"The people who come to be in the Chairs, or just to watch, will be here." *Because bigger bets are placed, and bigger payoffs are paid off.* "There is a dress code, so many will come from the Starlight after dinner."

"How did you get this job as casino manager?" Peggy asked as she looked everywhere at once as the afternoon gamblers crowded around the roulette wheels, the twenty-one tables, and the craps tables.

"Place your bets, ladies," the croupier said to a group of giggling women rattling chips.

"Monaco, *ma chérie.* I worked my way up until I mastered every job in the casinos. No one could do more than I did, so what choice did they have? We have a poker table off to the side by appointment only. Last year we tried Punta Banco, but there was little interest. We change it according to who our guests are."

"Champagne, madame?" asked a hat check girl. In the background a champagne cork popped and people laughed.

"And baccarat?" Peggy asked as people always did.

The James Bond theme was playing so I pointed up to the speaker. "On occasion but guaranteed when James Bond is a guest." I even laughed at this jest. *I grew up in Belgium, so I am faking the Parisians accent.* I was the top student in math at my secondary school and in college. I can walk around the casino for ten minutes every hour and estimate within half a million dollars what the house will earn that night. I handed Peggy a package. "A small souvenir for you, Peggy."

"Merci beaucoup. Shall I open it now?"

"But of course. Do you speak French, *chérie*?"

She slipped the gold-colored ribbon off and unfolded the gold-speckled burgundy paper. In her hand was a pack of casino cards. There was a photo of one of the Chairs, of course, on the backs.

"Cards! Now this is something I can really use." She put them into her purse.

I was surprised. *Truly, she will use these?*

"Thank you for thinking of me. These will keep me busy during my flight home. And no, you already know the French I speak. Yvette, you are the only woman I've seen in a management position. Can you explain that?"

"Surely you have been told of the fabulous Marie, the wife of Max. She designs all the costumes and makes them too. She makes all my dresses. She has a—what is the woman shape a dressmaker has?"

"A dressmaker mannequin?" Dice were rattled and rolled onto the table next to us.

"The same in French. Marie has a mannequin of me she uses to fit my gowns perfectly. She even tailors my nightgowns. Marie is one who suggested I get solid gold frames for my glasses. Many people asked where I got them." I noticed Peggy's clothes look tailor-made. *Very chic. Classic.* "Drake's chief accountant is Sylvia, the head chef is Olga, and the head of marketing is Damini. Even the chief pilot Mike is a woman. The assistant pro and manager at the golf course is Yoko. I think you are only looking in a few departments. We are here, but perhaps behind the scenes making things run. One thing I much appreciated about Boss was his advanced belief that a women could do a job as well as men."

Chapter 21

Peggy smiled at this confession of mine. *Perhaps she agreed with me.* "Because of this view, I very much enjoy working here for part of the year, and I spend the rest at home with my son. My mama cares for him in Mons, Belgium."

"Next shooter," was announced from the nearby craps table.

"I see. What's something special Drake's did for this week?"

"Every year Boss finds something unique. Guests who lose or win over a million dollars get a coin from their country equivalent to $1000 U.S. set into a key fob. The ladies receive the same but have the option of having it as set as a pendant." *Mine is a key ring so I always have spending money near.* "Then, he has something everyone can enjoy. Last year we had a licensed Japanese fugu chef who sliced those deadly fish. Only the real thrill seekers ate it. Tonight it's the champagne."

"Thank goodness. Raw fish does not agree with me, but champagne? What's the label?"

I refilled Peggy's champagne flute. "Boss bought a famous champagne label, *Sabrage*. Incredibly old, very exclusive. It is what we are sipping now." *Dex tried it. It was not to his taste.* He was still a 'beer guy' as he so charmingly puts it, and we stocked only the best.

"The Chairs have been on display for three nights.

Boss had the idea to take pictures of guests sitting in them for souvenirs. It is *très* popular. Some asked me to pose beside them. Here. Sit. Let's have our own photo taken." We sat and a flashbulb went POP! in the Graflex Speed Graphic camera. Boss insisted on this camera. *"It was good for a large tip, so why not?"* Same for the servers. They made *beaucoup* tips this week. Tomorrow too if they play their part.

"When may I have my souvenir photo, Yvette?"

"It will be delivered to your room, *ma chérie*. What else do you wish to know?"

"What is something about a casino that people may not think of?"

"*Eh bien.* A casino is tricky. You want the music to be just the right tempo—not too slow, but not too fast. Not too loud, but where you can hear it during a break in the action and so dealers can hear the bets. The sounds of the voices and the shuffle of cards, a spin of the wheel, the rattle of dice are all unique to a casino. It helps create the ambiance our players expect. Listen." We sipped our delicious wine and listened to the sounds. "Marcel," I called to the nearest croupier. "A spin, *s'il vous plaît*. Now listen. First the click of the little wheel: •click•click•click. Now he throws the ball in the other direction. Now wait. Did you hear the bounce of the ball? Yes? Good. We win. We are a casino in the traditional sense."

"All true. I never considered all those aspects. It's a multisensory experience."

I turned to a less desirable aspect of a casino. " We do not have the noisy video gambling machines where a player puts a credit card into a slot. There are *no* dealers, *no* actual cards you can feel and arrange, *no* dice you can shuffle in your hand before you throw them, and *no* reaction from other players by your side. Those machines vacuum money out of your pocket as you are hypnotized by the flashing loud screens. Those machines are for tourists. It is an addiction not a game of chance."

Peggy pulled her scarf up under her chin and I was reminded of something else. "Because the messieurs wear tuxes on a tropical island we need a lot of air conditioning, but not too much because the mademoiselles are showing off their tans and décolleté, uhm what is the ...?" I ran my hand across the top of my breasts.

Peggy offered, "Cleavage."

"Cleavage? *Ah, oui.* As I was saying, the temperature is tricky."

"I am a little chilly, but if the room were full, I probably wouldn't notice. What do *you* do when the Casino is closed?" Peggy asked.

"Pass wins," was announced from another table. Squeals emanated from female guests.

"I am the casino manager so have things I must do. I schedule my dealers and their breaks. I make that the arrangements are proper for each player in my Casino, their line of credit is arranged, and the dealers know what it is. I manage the repair and maintenance of the equipment. It would not do to have the roulette wheel to stop turning, or the music to stop. I am the face of the Casino so I must make a losing guest to calm down, and a winning guest to realize Drake's policy on the size of a bet *does* apply to him."

"You are one busy lady. Everyone I've seen here works long, hard hours."

"Of course. Boss has many times said, 'If you want

real pay, you must do real work,' and we do."

"And the pay?"

"Very real, mademoiselle, *trés magnifique.* Thank you for noticing. I also train the personnel who work here, so I am checking on them as I walk around. I look for cheats in the personnel and the guests. I draft reports about the cash flow, the income, the operating expenses, and I make suggestions on how to improve profitability."

A deep voice exclaimed, "Baby needs a new pair of shoes!" and Peggy's eyes darted to the craps table.

"Cheats? What happens when you catch one?"

"I alert *monsieur* Dex and *monsieur* Vic. They quietly escort them from the casino. The cameras and security who circulate in disguise have all the evidence."

"What happens to them, to the cheats?"

"I was told legitimate guests leave the island within an hour."

"And if they are not guests?"

"I cannot say. I never see or hear about them again."

"How would they leave the island?"

"I cannot say. I have never concerned myself with this. Perhaps Dex or Vic could answer that for you."

Peggy said, "I think you may be the most important manager Boss has. And you have such as perfect disguise."

"*Merci, chérie,* but what do you mean?" I noticed her own thick mink eyelashes.

"I mean the guests think you are a charming hostess wearing a sexy dress on your sexy body, when you are a shrewd capitalist watching through your gold glasses making sure the business is running like a top."

My interviewer perfectly understood the points I tried to make. The harder I worked the better Boss does, and the bigger my bonus. I winked at the interviewer. "You are too kind, *chérie*. More champagne?" *Disguise indeed. How funny coming from her.*

Dex came back into the casino. He was gone while I talked with the interviewer. He looked worried. Will I see him later? And for how long?

****

"Mr. Dex, will you authorize this bet," a croupier asked me. Usually that's Yvette's job, but I had the authority too. I circulated in the Casino in the evenings, doing the meet and greet thing. Of course Yvette was there too, but I hoped she don't notice when I stepped out for few minutes.

Lau and Velasco waited for me outside. They came on the *Night Song*, a 150-foot yacht of a Panamanian guest, but their names ain't on its passenger list. They sent one of their bodyguards to "invite" me to a negotiation. I already had their money in my Cayman account. They were scheduled to do a walk-in transfer after the Chairs. Of course, Boss don't know nothing about it, and they know it.

"Mr. Dex," Velasco said. "We must complete the transfer tonight."

"We agreed after the Chairs," I said looking over my shoulder. "Someone might see you. Go back to your boat." I started to leave but a hand stopped me. *Put a hand on me, and you'll regret it.*

"Mr. Dex," Lau said in his girly voice. "We have to conduct our business now. If that is not possible, we will be forced to appeal to your Boss. I suspect he will be disappointed in your conduct."

His pukey smirk pissed me off. *Blackmail? Now?* I raised my right hand to point my finger into his face and snarled, "Blackmail will get you into serious trouble here, Lau. You are in my territory now." and I jabbed my finger in his face.

His puny bodyguard blocked my right hand. He had a knife or a razor 'cause I felt something sharp cut across the top of that hand, and it stung. I had thirty-five pounds of muscle on the guy, and I was a southpaw. When that sting smarted, I drew back and threw a left hook to his glass jaw, he folded, fell to the cement, and was out for the count.

Lau and Velasco went pale, immediately shut up, and stepped back. I snatched Lau's handkerchief from his pocket and wrapped it around my bleeding cut. The two "gentlemen" picked up the bodyguard and melted into the dark. Even so, I kept looking over my shoulder. Twenty-four more hours and they'd be gone. I didn't need no chicken-shit distractions so close to the end of the season. I got bigger fish to fry.

####

Rosalie's letters stopped in February of her senior year but I figured they would catch up to me once I returned from deployment. What I got was my last letter from Rosalie, a letter from her mother, and a letter from my dad. Rosalie wrote, "I can't wait to see you in your uniform. You must be so handsome and proud." She wrote how our love made her happy, as it did me.

Her mother wrote saying, "… our beloved Rosalie died in an accident." She enclosed the Promise ring I gave Rosalie for Christmas my senior year.

My dad wrote, "…there is little for you in this town. Mom and I will understand if you start a new life elsewhere after the army." If ever I needed them, I had their address and could find them.

****

I've got more money and more property than God. *Why am I still at it?* Building up Drake's was a challenge based on luck that Dex and I stumbled across each other's path. He had the Gizmo; I had the island. The Gizmo gave us an edge. The island was remote but under U.S. law. It was big enough to spread out and offer the most attractions. Dex was the brawn, but it was my brains that created and ran it. Even so, he was the one I had to keep ahead of.

I'm burned out, a kid with rotten teeth from too much time in the candy store. *What comes next?* This question gnawed at my gut. I had quietly cross examined my records over the last three months. My financials were heavily encrypted so I was confident that my assets were safe. I made sure that Forbes couldn't put me on that wretched billionaire list. There was a constant nagging feeling that I missed something, something that would jump up and tear my throat out after I got that note: "Boss, you will die before sunrise on Sunday."

Earlier today I came across a folder from the Gizmo I had forgotten about. It looked like an instruction manual the professor wrote. I remembered that Dex found it in a drawer under the control panel when we first set the Gizmo up. "What's this," Dex said. "Probably just some of the professor's notes." He threw them in the trash. I pulled the papers out and guessed without these notes the Gizmo was likely useless to us. I kept them.

The manual included a schematic of the panel. It's deceptively simple and showed where everything went and what it's called. I must have read this sometime when we started the transfers, but I don't recall when. *It was scary how simple the control panel was compared to the technology that must be in there.*

The line drawing of the clock was well drafted and detailed. The thing that everyone noticed was the clock. *Where did he get that clock?* It was very ornate with a Latin inscription. I believed it was brass. I don't think anyone realized the numbers were Roman numerals. People just stared as the secondhand swept through two complete circles, and then looked for the yellow lights on the booths to indicate the doors were closed and locked. *At least that's what I did.* Push the green button and the Gizmo started up. *Yep.* The red button showed the transfer was finished, and voila! *The deal was done.* I noticed something on the panel that I'd never noticed before. It was labeled "Countdown Meter." *That didn't tell me a thing.*

The professor must have been an engineer as his paperwork was meticulous. There was an index in the back like in a textbook. The Countdown Meter was referenced on pages eleven, thirty-seven, fifty-five and in the Glossary. Page eleven was the picture of the Control Panel with labelled arrows pointing to each control. Page thirty-seven gave a description of the wiring and installation procedure for the meter. Page fifty-five described the function of the meter as being to track and count down the number of cycles. *Cycles of what?* Whatever that meter did, I didn't remember noticing it before. *I had a sinking feeling this was what might bite me in the butt.*

We didn't understand the reason for this meter earlier as it didn't seem to control anything. The Glossary just repeated what was on page fifty-five. This was when a photo fell out of the file that was taken just after we assembled the Gizmo here. Using a magnifying glass, the meter read "L." Having never seen a meter that didn't read in Latin numbers, I wasn't sure how to phrase my question to Chet. It's my lunchtime. I put the file away and headed out to my table by the seaside pool. I enjoyed my grilled grouper and pineapple and made a mental note to visit the engineering plant later.

My physical plant manager Chet was something I was not: an engineer. Since we have so much equipment behind the scenes and potted palms, we needed an entire staff of engineers and technicians to keep everything up and running.

"Rosalie Warner Smith" and her "uncle" walked past and sat at the table next to mine. I greeted them, "Mr. and Ms. Fitche, join me, please," as I waved them over. Every guest recognized me, and it would be unseemly to refuse an invitation. Sometimes guests "accidently" come through and invite themselves, usually an attempt to bribe me or make a pass. Truth be known, I'm worth more than any of the Players. I asked the uncle about his plane, but behind my sunglasses I was looking at his niece. They say everyone has a doppelganger somewhere.

She asked, "What are you drinking?"

"Hibiscus tea, Ms. Fitche. It's nonalcoholic. It has a slight cranberry flavor but needs a little sugar."

"Sounds perfect," she said smiling at me from behind her mystery. "Call me Janet." She looked at the birds in the trees. "Are those the famous Drake's Dandies?"

"Yes. Are you a bird watcher?"

"Only on vacation. I took the eco tour this morning, but even with binoculars I didn't get close enough to see them like this. I did see the orchids though. You named them well, sir. They look good enough to eat."

"Did they mention that a group of parrots is called a 'company of parrots' or a 'pandemonium of parrots?'"

"Yes. I prefer the latter. More typical I think since they never seem to be quiet."

Ms. Janet Fitche doesn't seem like most of the female guests we get here. I already know a lot about her because of the background checks we make for every guest before we allow them on the island. She's quiet, but in a self-possessed way. I have a feeling that I may know more than she thinks. After the Fitches left, I impulsively pocketed Janet's glass and her uncle's and took them to the Doc. He could conduct a DNA test in his lab in less than an hour.

****

I had an urgent message from Vic. I hurried to his office. On entering I saw a young man dressed as a cook talking to Vic. I didn't recognize his face, but I recognized a French accent. It confused me because he looked African.

"Boss, this is Idrissa. He's one of our temps this week. He's from the Congo and works in the kitchen."

I extended my hand to Idrissa. "How is it you speak French?"

"Many people in Congo speak French. It was my first language and English is my second."

"I see. How did you get this job?"

"I registered with the agency you use. I jumped at a chance to work with chef Jules. He is a *Meilleur Ouvrier de France* and I aspire to be one before I die." He referred to my head pastry chef who wears a blue-white-red stripe on the collar of his chef's jacket.

I hired Jules because he was an MOF and word-famous for his desserts and treats. Saying someone is "best in France" for anything means they went through a soul crushing ordeal. He earned those stripes. "Good luck on that," I sincerely offered. If the agency sent this young man here, then they had conducted the required security check. I relaxed a moment until I noticed he held a knife. I glanced at Vic and then at the knife. I had mentioned the death threat in the note to Vic earlier. I put my hand in my pocket and fingered my switchblade. *I had knife skills of my own.*

"Idrissa, do you mind leaving your knife on my desk?" Vic said.

"*Ah, pardon*! I did not realize I brought it with me. You see it is my own knife and expensive for me. Do you understand?" He quickly put his knife on Vic's desk and stood back, his hands in sight.

I well understood the importance of knives to my chefs, but I know what kind of knife skills they possessed. If Idrissa was here to kill me, I didn't want to make it easy.

Vic said, "Boss. He was working near the station where your coffee tray was. He overheard something. Tell Boss what that was."

"*Oui.* For a moment I was entranced by a beautiful lady who was holding her head. She ordered a café au lait. She had an authentic French accent. She say she had a head...hurt. Then she stepped back, and I didn't see her, but I could tell she was waiting."

"A headache," Vic prompted.

Chapter 22

"*Oui, merci.* A headache. Then there was a man's voice. He was an *Americaine* from his accent. I think he did not know I was around the corner because he said how pretty her mouth was, and what color was that, and she said kiss me and guess. I think they were kissing. Then he said why are you drinking coffee and she said she wasn't, that it was for Boss. She said she was waiting for her order."

"Is that all," I asked. "There had to be more."

" Yes. She said she had a headache and she needed to get cured. He said take this. If you see Boss give it to him. He has a headache too, and he takes his medicine in his coffee. Then he said, 'Oh, why not put it in his cup now? It's strong and works fast. Try it yourself.' I think he left. I never looked at his face."

Vic glanced to me and I said, "Thank you, Idrissa. Good luck again on your career." He picked up his knife and left. I didn't let my breath out until the door closed.

"I think Yvette was played by a player we know well, Boss."

"I think so too. But she may have some feeling for him so let's not inform her just yet. If you need me, I'm on my way to see Chet."

"I'm on my way to see Marie," Vic answered back. "I may sew this up soon."

****

222

Chet didn't know much about the Gizmo . He wasn't here when we installed it, and it hasn't needed any maintenance. Just cosmetic repairs to the replica Twitchell damaged. I showed him the photo of the meter. "What do you think this meter is for?"

"I'm not sure. My best guess is it measures some type of function in the Gizmo. Usually a meter like this measures something that needs to be repaired or replaced. But none of that has ever been done, correct?"

I nodded with rueful jerks of my head.

He showed me a meter that kept track of the hours a generator runs. "It starts at zero and when it reaches 525 hours of total service, I shut it down and do maintenance. Then it goes back into service. The Gizmo meter doesn't seem to be like that." Next, he showed me a meter that measured the rotations a generator shaft makes. "This has a limit before it needs repair or replacement too. The Gizmo meter seems to be more like this one." Quite suddenly he added a final idea. "Or as a worst-case scenario, it might signal a sudden event to occur."

"An event? Like what?" *Cripes.*

"A breakdown or even a self-destruct event." *Strange. Chet didn't seem fazed.*

"Like an explosion?" I was worried for my guests' and staff's safety. This could be a disaster I didn't see coming. *What's worse? I have no idea what to do next.*

Chet shook his head quickly. "I can't say for sure without more information. Maybe it just stops and doesn't work anymore."

"That was a best-case scenario at this point," I guessed.

He scratched his head. "Does the manual say anything about the number of cycles the Gizmo can handle?"

"Nothing. And I don't remember that the inventor mentioned it to Dex either."

"Is it too late to call him?"

With a bullet through his brain, I'm guessing yes. "He's out of business," I mumbled.

"Boss, all equipment experiences wear and tear, and much of it is designed to operate for a limited time. It's called built in obsolescence, or regular wear."

I heard the "limited time" part. "What happens after you reach the limited time?" I asked trying to maintain my cool.

"Something could break down and the machine would be finished."

He said "finished" and I started to sweat on my upper lip and I left. Now I had an incentive to figure out what comes next. Tonight marked the end of Dex's contract. I figured he's either going to leave with his pay-off or he's going to kill me. Either way, can I beat him to the punch if the Gizmo doesn't beat us all?

****

I stopped by the deserted casino, slipped down the hall, and unlocked the Gizmo room. I glared at the control panel when Dex walked in.

"Everything okay, Boss?"

I forced myself to smile. "Reminiscing. Just thinking how the time has gone by fast. What are your plans for the summer?"

"Uh. The usual, I guess. The track mostly. You know I can't keep away from the ponies."

I remembered we had two "walk-in" transferences for tonight after the Chairs. "Walk-in" transfers are what we call two people who want to pay to transfer between bodies. It's a very discreet service we carry out about twice a year. "How many times have we used this thing? How many transfers did you do before we started Drake's?"

He scratched his head. "I expected you was counting. You do all the financials, so…I'm guessing for the Chairs maybe two out of three transfer?" Then he added, "And about one or two walk-ins a year. Don't forget we got two of those later."

Those numbers sounded high to me for the transfers. I couldn't help myself, but I asked, "If you understood back then what you know now, would you still do it?"

His eyes lit up. "I'd do it again just to know how it feels," he said. "Would you?" Dex's biggest dream is to get his old self back so I just nodded, snuck a glance at the meter, and walked to the door.

"Maybe that's why you work out with me every day. Keeping the real estate in shape." We laughed like it was a big joke. "Lock it up as you leave, Dex." My hope was to put the idea in his head that I'm worth more to him alive than dead.

At my office, I rechecked the meter photo. Yes, the meter read "L." During my quick last glance at it minutes ago I read III. The meter was keeping track of something, maybe even transfers. If it's counting shouldn't there be two numbers to compare? Apples to apples kind of thing? I had hours to figure this out.

Max's revelation that his wife Marie planned to poison me shook me to my bones. She had a diagnosis of early-stage dementia but she could manage the sewing and costuming. I hired an assistant to help with the costuming but also to report on Marie.

There was a knock on my door. I was expecting

Max. I hesitated in case it was someone I didn't want to see. "Come in." I relaxed as my impresario open the door. "Max. You and Marie have been a part of Drake's since the first year. You both are key players here. Now let's figure out what comes next for you."

"Boss, I can't thank you enough. We—" I stopped him. It was becoming personal, and I didn't like that. We spent part of an hour planning next steps and finding a place for Marie. " I can arrange a residential placement in a leading facility in New York near your apartment." Max's eyes glistened, but I looked away. "You'll be able to live and work from home and see Marie every day. Can we try that as a start?"

"I want to—"

"No need, Max. You both worked for this."

"No, I want to say I'll close down my lab and release all my reptiles in the rain forest. I can't just kill them…" I nodded, "…and I can't keep them in the apartment in New York even if I wanted to.

"I have an idea for a replacement for Marie. There's a local lady who has been working for Marie here who might do for a while. Her work is impeccable. I'll look for a designer in New York and send down a couple of designs and materials she can tackle as a trial. Thanks again. You do not know how much this means to us both. I hope keeping Marie busy will keep her alive."

I've known them for a long time. *This arrangement pleases me as well.* "Have you made plans with our chief pilot to take you and your luggage home in our corporate jet? Oh, if you need anything for Marie or the new designer for designing or sewing supplies, charge it to me."

"Sure and, yes, I called Mike, and we are all set.

We'll wait a day or two until things settle down."

"You could hire a nurse to accompany Marie. It could be easier and might protect her dignity. Ask Peaches. She knows someone." We debated hiring a new impresario but deferred the decision until Marie's situation was clearer.

I pay well and take care of my employees, even if they plot to kill me. I still do *not* know who has the poison Marie meant for me. *And will they use it?*

****

I waved at Livy, or Player Twelve, across the pool where she was getting a lot of attention. "Hey, Boss, come on over," she yelled. I waved her off and kept on walking. She is one of my most memorable guests. I could safely say she had a generous heart of gold and nothing that happens tonight can take that away.

I identified another guest, Player Eight AKA Diamond, amid the crowd of men around Livy. Now that had to be a lively group. I picked up my pace before she spotted me. Most of tonight's Players had private bungalows with pools, so it was rare to see one at the common pools.

I walked around the grounds every day to loosen up and get a little authentic sunlight on my face. I also did this so guests could see me and perhaps pass along a comment or two. I was *trying* to make sense of the events of these last few days, but I couldn't get my head around to sorting it all out. Tiny and Bobby took turns shadowing me.

I passed the shady part of the beach and spied two Players together: Lola, the Hollywood actress, and Khan, the Bollywood actor. I stopped and caught a few words of their conversation.

"…and Roberta would never let me come out in the sun like this. The only time I wore a bathing suit was in the promo shots and the movie," Lola exclaimed.

Khan countered with, "I was six before I could identify my mom on sight. She looked like all the other…"

Ah, fond childhood reminiscence. I should have known. Every actor I ever met talked about themselves incessantly.

At the far end of the pool, deep in the shade, I spotted Rosalie, or whatever her name was and her "uncle" sitting with a lady and a man I didn't recognize. They ate, drank, and talked. The lady made an occasional notation on a lined pad but closed it as I approached. I identified the lady as Peggy but she looked different. Her hair was darker, and she had huge sunglasses.

"Mr. and Ms. Fitche. I hope you've enjoyed your stay with us." It was hard to look away from my imagined Rosalie as I turned to the others. "I'm Boss, but I'm sorry to say I don't think I've had the pleasure of meeting you, unless you are in disguise." I grinned as if I had told a clever joke.

The now dark-haired lady said, "I'm your book interviewer, Boss." She winked at me to let me know she got my jest. "I met these lovely people just a few minutes ago, and they agreed to be interviewed for my book. I hope you don't mind." She looked very different from when we spoke before, but many of our guests change their clothes and hair during the day.

"I don't mind if they don't mind."

The other man stood, extended his hand, and introduced himself with, "Bringing up the rear here, I'm Jack Bollar, Jamie Justice's manager."

I do know about him. "Yes, Max mentioned you and your talented star. Thank you for booking at the last minute. Does everyone have all they need? Any refills?"

Ms. Fiche asked, "Do you have mango milkshakes?" I had the distinct feeling she was watching *me from* behind *her* dark glasses.

"The bartender at the pool bar will be happy to whip one up. I'll just let your waiter know on my way out. Will you all be at the Chairs tonight? It's our last hurrah for the season." Everyone nodded and smiled. No one said a thing until I left. The conversation pick up as I moved away.

A man died instead of me from snake venom in a cup of coffee. I had to call his brother and sister to notify them. Pure, dumb luck averted another death from that same venom. A second man was stabbed and was in custody in a hospital. He was lurking in a place just steps from my bedroom, and in possession of items usually reserved for assassination.

I was sliding into paranoia. The hair on the back of my neck stood up. I have the distinct feeling the people I just left were talking about me. And to top it all off, I just had lunch with the love of my life who died a quarter century ago. I never did need my family after those last letters I received. I made sure of that. Grief ripped my heart from my chest. The wound never healed. Gutted, I lost my ability to love and to be loved.

Never looking back, I went to the best law school I could afford and studied relentlessly, graduating at the top of my class. That attracted very lucrative and dangerous offers. None were as good as the personal lawyer to a crime family. I took it and was as ruthless as they were, without breaking the law. It was easy without a heart. I never went back to my town nor called my family. Now I'm questioning if that was a mistake.

****

The first limo of the night pulled up. Vic opened the door and out stepped a gorgeous dame like you never seen before and like you ain't never gonna see again. She was a Spectator here with one of the Players who wanted to spin the wheel and shake some sticks before the Chairs. "She follows the money, so I bet if she'll be leaving in the same car or not," I told Peggy.

"Do you size up everyone in the Chairs, Dex?"

"Every single one. Good evening, Miss Fleur." She shot me a smirk as she passed by. *Not tonight, Miss Fleur. I'm busy.*

"Do people bring their own cars on vacation?"

Some of the priciest reservations will get you what was a private estate. "Some guests bring their own car *and* driver. We have a private ferry to bring cars over with cargo if you didn't bring it on your yacht.

"Here comes Señor Fernandez, Player Three." His bodyguards escorted him in and surrounded him. "He sneers likes a snake, but his shiny face shows he sweats like a pig."

"You may have to wring him out like a dishrag?" Peggy said. "He gave me the impressions this was a sure thing."

"Yeah, well, he's not the only one. Watch for Mr. Xin, Player Four. See how many times he reaches in his pockets."

"What's in his pockets?"

"Only every Chinese rabbit's foot and lucky charm he could cram in."

Vic opened the door and I said, "Mrs. and Mr. Bo.

Welcome back. Your usual table?" She nodded and he winked as he slipped a fat tip in my pocket.

Cars backed up: Rolls, Bentleys, or custom Lincolns, but a few hypercars owned by new money showing off. "We only allow an exclusive clientele, and I know them all by name." They always slipped a wad of C-notes or two in my pocket for a good table. I'll have to move the bills to another pocket soon 'cause it fills up fast.

"Good evening, Mr. Smythe," I said, as I signaled for a table, or "Gorgeous like always, Princess Jones." *At this rate I'll have a stash again before I'm too old to enjoy it. 'Course even if I win it won't be like before.* Boss, he don't play no more. "I make sure the caviar and champagne keep coming or whatever anyone wants. The band takes requests and I know our regulars' favorites."

Lola, Player Two and Player Ten, Rhonda sashayed past me arm-in-arm. They were *knockouts.* Honey tans, emerald-colored floor-length gowns, expensive jewelry, long evening gloves. Every eyeball in the place was on them.

Peggy whispered, "Wow."

Only *I* know one o' them is carrying a knife. I hope she don't use it tonight. "I check the birthday list again; regulars get cakes and presents."

"What kind of presents? What do you give someone who has everything?" Peggy asked as she looked over boxes wrapped in paper and ribbons and cakes the same colors as the Chairs.

"Uh, we personalize it for each guest." I moved away to greet the bigshots. I checked on Player escorts. Before an hour went by, most of the Big Players had arrived. I've made a few bets with myself and a couple with Vic. I don't know if the Players bet between themselves.

"I'm curious if Boss tries to guess the winners. Of course, it don't matter much; any way you cut it, he wins big."

"I bet he does. In a way he's in the Chairs too, isn't he?" Peggy said.

"I don't get...Good evening, Mr. Xin. Good luck tonight." Xin had two gorgeous China dolls by his side, but his hands were in his pockets.

"I know he picked his number himself. Uh—I don't get what you mean about the Boss."

"I see what you mean about Xin. He hasn't had his hand out for more than ten seconds. I mean, Boss doesn't even play the game but he's the biggest winner, isn't he?"

Yeah, she's right. Boss wins any way you cut it with no risk. "I suppose so. I never counted it that way. Anyway, a few of the Players met with Boss in his office earlier. The superstitious ones like to pick their own number, which is their right considering how much is on the line. The rest draw from a box."

I checked out the floor action. "Lots of winners tonight, miss. Drake's pays better than any other place. Because of the cut from the Chairs, Drake's can afford to give the customers better odds. It's almost time for the floorshow and then it's the Chairs. "I got my eye on one of them dames in the chorus. She's the one on the end— no, the other end. Yeah, the brunette. Merlene. She works here at the last half of the season putting herself through dental school on her tips. She takes classes on the Internet and gives private dance lesson. Me, I can't imagine spending your life with wrinkled fingers in someone's wet mouth."

Chapter 23

I spotted the Lottery Queen dancing alongside the chorus girls. I waved to her Escort. That lady is dancing like there's no tomorrow. I don't want her to pass out like she did at the cricket match.

"The girl singer's a knockout. She used to be a Player. Couldn't take the new life though and went broke inside a year. Sure, she won herself a great looking package though. Package? Boss calls it that; I just say body. You know—body, plastic surgery, caps, all that stuff. You didn't think that was all original equipment, did you? Hold up a minute, would you? This song's my favorite." *Five minutes to go.*

"That redhead over there made a pile in biotech something or another since she was here last. Some o' the Players are new money types. They either struck it rich or swindled their stockholders." The redhead was off or something. *She hasn't moved in the last hour.* I've never seen her when she wasn't moving or twitching. I signaled her escort to check for a pulse.

"We don't get many Players from old money, or the oil families. I guess they wouldn't take that big a chance, not knowing where they'd end up. Maybe I should suggest to Boss we do a special game for Old Money without transfers. We get them in here. They just don't play the Chairs."

"Could you point out someone to me who is old

money?" Peggy was scanning the room like a narc at the border.

I looked around as in walked Mr. and Mrs. Rockaway. I pointed to them. "That couple. Their money goes back a hundred-fifty years. Her family were some o' the first in the oil business. His made money in railroads. They don't need fancy clothes and giant jewelry. Everybody knows who they are." *The Russian!* "Oh, we actually have a Player who is old old money. A real Russian Count, remember him?" I pointed to the Count sitting alone at the bar flipping a swanky gold cigarette case back and forth in his hands. I would swear Peggy was blushing but it must just be the excitement and the crowd.

"Miss, look around the Chairs. I place the personal Escorts near the circle. Each Player is assigned someone to bird dog them, and to escort them to a Payoff Room, or a Consolation Room afterwards. Everything is aboveboard in the Chairs. Once in a while, we get someone who tries to sneak out without waiting or transferring bodies, but since we started with the Escorts the problems have been small ones 'cause they know their job." We had a few extras walking the floor—kinda like air marshals, looking for trouble. *We had Doc in the back with an x-ray machine for any "unfortunate" accidents.*

I noticed the Greek shipping heiress was missing. Vic signaled me pointing towards the patio door. It's almost time for the Chairs. I found her with a dance instructor laying on a deck chair in the shadows. I couldn't touch her but he was mine. I jerked him up by the collar. "Don't you have a costume to get into? This ain't a *Dirty Dancing* sequel." I pushed him so hard from the patio he fell down the steps. If he'd given me any lip I'd of smashed his pretty face.

I extended my elbow. "May I escort you to the Chairs, Player Six?"

She gave me the evil eye. "Idiot. I am Player Five."

A movement out the side of my eye got my attention and I raised my arm. Her slap missed and landed on my shoulder. "Shall we?" I laid my boxer's hand on the small of her back and shoved her. She was all composed when we broke through the curtains to the casino.

I stood next to Peggy again. "When that clock strikes eleven the Chairs begins. Here comes Boss."

The lights dimmed except on the Boss. "Ladies and Gentlemen, Spectators and Players. It's time to begin the Chairs. This is what you've all come to see and to enjoy."

Boss always did the intro up big. I don't know if I could do that.

"First, let me review the rules. This game is simplicity itself, a version of the children's game Musical Chairs. We put chairs in the circle, one for each Player. When the music starts the Players circle around, but before they start, we remove one chair at random. When the music stops, everyone sits in a chair. The Player without a chair is eliminated. We continue until six players are left. Then the Chairs ends. As I said, simplicity itself." Boss paused for effect. *He's got it down real good.*

"The Payoff for this game can be determined in several ways…"

"See, miss, if you're one of those six who don't get a chair, you already lost your bet and any chance of a payoff. All your current assets, and maybe more, gone."

Boss goes on, "However, the Payoff tonight will be

random. This means the final six Players will receive the prize assigned to the number of their chair they find themselves in at the end of the game. Transference of physical persons will take place at the winners' discretion."

"Peggy, This last part always gets people rolling their eyes, thinking if they'd do it or not if they won big."

She said, "That really is random. What if —"

I stopped her so I could hear Boss.

"The six chairs removed from the circle are selected at random. The six prizes not selected by the winners are retained by the house. If one of the last six players ends up with their own number, they keep their bet and their body. Lastly, this is a genteel game. No rough play is allowed. Anyone not abiding by the rules is automatically disqualified and removed. Any questions?"

Newbies shook their heads in amazement. *It sounded so unbelievable.*

The Boss said, "Now our Players for tonight. No real names are used. Player One is a South African diamond king in the Chairs for the first time. Those cuff links and shirt studs are the real things, ladies, and gentlemen. Welcome Mr. One." His face was shiny and his smile forced as he stepped into the center of the Chairs.

"I've seen this guy around. He was kicked out of his country last year for selling blood diamonds. Maybe that's why he needed to play now," I told Peggy.

Her eyes popped wide open. "He seemed so decent in his interview."

That was part of his con, lady.

"Player Two is a beautiful, Oscar-winning actress, producer, and director. Her last three films grossed over two billion dollars. Playing for the second time, welcome Ms. Two." Still patting her hair, Lola flashed her brilliant camera-ready smile and joined Player One.

You'd recognize this dame on any movie screen in the country. "She wanted to be a producer; not too many roles coming' her way since the bloom is off the rose. She got lucky last time in the Chairs. Yeah, you didn't think she got all that dough by flashing skin and private body parts, did you?" I looked around for Vic.

"Player Three is the hereditary ruler of a gold producing country in South America, also playing for the first time. Welcome, Señor Three." The Player waved and swaggered into the circle, stopping to bow and kiss Lola's hand.

"We had to disarm a couple o' his bodyguards. He doesn't know it yet, but that bulletproof limo of his *ain't* parked at the side door." We discovered it's not gold he traffics all over the world but kids, other people's kids. Vic signaled all of Player Three's bodyguards had been detained. Señor Three's jacket had growing pit stains.

"Player Four is a dealer in Asian temple antiquities. He said he's played in a previous life. By our reckoning, it's his first time in the Chairs. Welcome, Mr. Four."

Peggy looked nervous as this Player brushed by her on his way to the Chairs, and she moved closer to me. *That was weird.*

Mr. Xin ignored Players Three and One and stood close to Lola. A ripple of laughter passed through the crowd as Xin made an attempt to peek down her cleavage as his hands stayed in his pockets.

"Peggy, don't let that inscrutable smirk fool you. He won't try anything here."

"Don't be so sure, Dex," she whispered.

What did she mean by that?

Boss announced, "Player Five is the young widow of a Greek tycoon. She says ocean travel makes her seasick. Welcome, Ms. Five."

The Player kissed a baccarat dealer and stepped into the circle of Chairs. A murmur rippled through the crowd that stretched their necks towards the baccarat table. She ignored the Players and the crowd.

Peggy moved away from my side a little to watch the Greek heiress. *Seasick—right.* She was here before with the husband. I think it was *him* who made her sick. "I feel bad for her, but she got real lucky not to be on the yacht when it went down last summer, if you—."

Peggy nodded quickly and squished her lips together.

"Player Six is a research chemist who holds a Nobel Prize and five of the world's top biotechnology patents. Playing for the third time at Drake's, welcome, Dr. Six."

Dr. Six was cool as a cucumber but had to be blazing inside. Her face almost matched her fire-engine red dress. She's been too lucky too long. "She's due for a fall. I bet against her big time." The thing is Drake's would never get her biggest asset—her brain.

Boss stopped and looked around the room. "These are our first six contestants. Players, select a chair and be seated." These folks were dressed swell, tuxedos and long swishy dresses, diamonds, and plenty of platinum. For some of them, that's all they'll take out with them when they leave—that, two hundred-fifty thousand bucks, and a ticket to any place in the world, maybe a new passport, and maybe a different body.

I caught my breath. *So far so good.* There was a loud commotion by the door. Someone screamed. I pushed my way over to the crowd around the lady on the floor. I didn't recognize her but she looked dead.

Vic and I moved the casino crowd back so Doc could work.

Boss signaled the band to play. "Ladies and gentlemen. Nothing to worry about. Our medical team is already at work. If you've been here before you know how exciting the Chairs can be even to the audience."

The lady sat in a wheelchair. Doc pushed her towards the clinic. She said in a loud, hysterical voice, "You've got to stop the Chairs. I see my husband is going to be in it and I didn't know…" It's not the first time a spouse has claimed that. I gave Boss the 'okay' sign.

"Now before I introduce our last six Players," said Boss, building up the crowd, "may I ask you to fill up your glasses and pick a spot. Once we start the music, we ask that you not move around and distract the Players. After all, it's their life at stake, not yours!"

"Boss always chuckles when he says that." *Someone always laughed, but not me. Too close to home.* I slipped back to the Transference Room and checked the Gizmo. Then I checked each Escort, to make sure they can identify their Player and aren't more than two feet from them.

The waiters circulated filling glasses and looking for trouble. Never can be too careful when the stakes are this high. Nervous voices rose up as side bets were made as the Plyers were announced.

Boss started again. "Let's meet our final six Players to fill out our field. Let me introduce Player Seven. He's a Wall Street Wizard playing for his first time, Welcome Mr. Seven."

"Twitchell doesn't look too good. Maybe he got

word of an arrest warrant coming his way," Peggy said.

"Player Eight hit two giant lotteries in one year and she says she's on a roll. Welcome, Ms. Eight," Boss announced.

Diamond pushed her way through. "That's me. That's me." She tripped over to stand by Player Four and twerked against his tux.

Xin moved aside with a sneer and said something in Chinese as the crowd laughed, before he glared towards Boss.

"Yeah, her eight kids could use something better than new cars and a mamma who's a Player." Peggy nodded to that.

"Player Nine is a Russian Count with claims to estates covering a third of Siberia. Welcome, Count Nine"

This guy is slick and from old money. He walks in like he's done this every day o' his life. "He put up one of those fancy Russian Easter Eggs for his bet. I never seen nothin' like that before."

"Player Ten is a dare devil oceanic salvor. She recovered a Spanish treasure from the sea. Now she's mining for gold on dry land. Welcome, Captain Ten." Rhonda swirled into the circle and stood by Lola. They exchanged shaky laughs and held hands like beauty pageant contestants.

"Check out that emerald the size of a pigeon egg hanging around her neck. You better believe it's real. She's a real gutsy lady." *I'd want her in my corner if I was in a jam. I knew she could swing a mean shiv and not spill her drink.*

"The next Player is a classic actor from Bollywood. He's a third-generation star that has ladies swooning all over the globe. Welcome, Player Eleven." Khan walked in playing to the crowd. His cousin hugged him as he passed and whispered in his ear.

"Miss, this guy has so much he is sick of it. I can't even think o' what he would do if he wins. He sure got the attention from the ladies since he's been here."

"And finally, our last Player of this evening. Player Twelve is a retired professional athlete who called the right plays with her investments. Welcome, Ms. Twelve." Livy looked a little shaky in stilettos. She flipped her hair back and adjusted her dress. She held hands with Diamond.

Now that is an odd couple if there ever was one. I lean in towards Peggy. "It's pretty funny that she's number twelve. That was her number when she was a he and an NFL linemen. She's really a sweet dame, but still competitive."

"It takes all kinds, Dex," Peggy said.

I guess she would know since she met all o' them. Boss pulled out his fancy pocket watch and opened it. He had a picture inside but I didn't get a good look at it yet.

"Players, all rise." Boss looked to the orchestra. "At my signal, the orchestra will start playing and continue until I signal to stop. At this point each Player will sit in the nearest chair. Anyone sitting before the music stops will be disqualified." Boss turned to me. "Dexter, remove the first chair." *Game on!*

I moved to the circle and took a chair, the one the redhead was sitting on. I bet Vic a ten spot she's going down. I put the chair by the wall and handed Boss the envelope.

The music began. The Players started moving in a circle. Their eyes jumped from chair to chair, slowing down as they got even with it, then faster as they moved on. Boss checked his watch and let the music go a good four minutes, then he pushed a secret button in his pocket. The music stopped. There's a swish of lace and silk and the Count was left standing. *I didn't imagine he was ever gonna get that chunk o' Russia back.* He kept his cool and stood back with no fuss. He was whiter than a sheet, so his Escort took his arm to hold him up.

The Players rose and I took another chair out from the other side, and the music started. Everyone was jumpy and expected a short waltz around, but no. Boss kept it up for almost another four minutes before he stopped the show. The actress tripped on her skin-tight dress and missed a seat; no one offered her theirs. *Looks like she's in shock. She might get to keep her body if I pulled her chair.*

The Players rose and I went to work again. Ten Players and nine chairs. The music started in a new tempo to throw the Players off. They move to it easy like, faster than before, when it stopped. Number Four reached towards the elbow o' the lady in front o' him. I got ready to nab him. No bumping other Players. He didn't and I pulled back. Two other Players bumped, but it was number Three left standing. He slicked back his hair and flashed his pearly whites in the direction he last saw his bodyguards. He backed smoothly away from the center and turned into the crowd. His Escort took his arm before he got to the door. He'll be diverted to a Consolation Room. *He'll find out the hardware he carried was missing.* Player Three made a fist. When he tried his knuckles on his Escort, he learned how she got her job. Doc will put a cast on his broken wrist.

I took another chair. Sweat was poppin' out on some

o' the Players. The music started. Boss let it go longer. Some players tried to tell when he'll stop the music. He just looked at his watch. When the dust settled it was Mr. Wall Street who stood alone; his fancy footwork was done on paper, not on his feet. He cracked a thin smile like it was a secret joke. *Maybe he wanted to lose; that happens sometimes. The last player who did that died of something expensive a few months later.*

Another chair, another change in tempo. I caught the Bollywood star wink at the Lottery Queen who grinned back so's her grill sparkled. Whadda ya think? Maybe a fix? He seemed to relax a bit and repositioned his tie. When the music stopped, he's standing and she ain't. He scowled at her but regained his movie star smile. He headed for the bar, his Escort nearby.

Boss announced, "Ladies and Gentlemen. This is the decisive round. After this there'll be a thirty-minute break, after which I'll formally announce the winners and details of the next big Chairs. Don't go away! Music, please." The room was dead silent. We had six chairs and seven Players. The music played forever. There was always a fake start or two for a Chair, but they caught themselves. Luck's in the air tonight. No one was thrown outta the game. It's better, cleaner that way. *No questions to answer later to the police or the coroner.* Finally, the music stopped and the final rush for seats was over.

Yes. I knew it! The redhead's number finally came up. Vic owes me ten grand. The six Players left with nervous grins that said they're winners. Even if they didn't know what the prize was yet, they didn't lose it all.

Chapter 24

"Miss. Are you curious what happens after the Chairs? I'll let you in a couple o' secrets. Keep them to yourself though. Wait. Boss makes one more announcement."

"Players, stand by your Chair while Mr. Dexter determines your numbers."

I went from chair to chair, removing the envelope with their number and handing it to the Player. When I was done, they walked towards the Payoff Rooms. Their Escorts slipped their arm through the Player's in case anyone bolted, and to make sure they didn't switch envelopes.

"Now it was Vic's job to discreetly get the losers to the Consolation Rooms and hold them. We may not be finished with them yet," I told Peggy.

The gold exporter sipped his favorite scotch and nursed a broken finger and wrist. "We'll stop by the doctor's office first and get you fixed up, sweetie. I've got a special treat I've been saving for you," his escort cooed as she leaned in giving him a peek down her cleavage. "Here, let's get you a refill," she said as she poured him a Mickey Finn.

"I am the rightful winner. I am a King!" His escort patted his hand, and kept his drink filled. He didn't know it's a special blend for him. He'll go out the back door to a real special payoff, but I can't tell you about it."

"Here comes the Count," Peggy said and he nodded to her as he passed.

"The Count might be for real. He showed real class when his Escort slipped her arm though his and walked him towards the back."

I heard the Count say, "What is your name, *devushka*? Would you care to join me for dinner? We'll start with Ossetra sturgeon caviar, of course." *Always the aristocrat.*

"The actress grimaced like she lost the Academy Award to her worst enemy, didn't she? See how she leaned her chest against her Escort's arm and whispered in his ear. 'Would you like my autograph and a very personal, deep kiss you'll never forget?'"

Peggy laughed, "How did you know?"

"He's been made better offers; the storage closet she expects will be the Consolation Room where he'll kiss her hand and leave with, "Some other time, some other place.""

Our Bollywood star finished off almost a quart o' his private stock earlier and yet he walked back on his own. "Now what? Is it over yet? Where is my cousin? His escort is asking, 'Can I get you another cup o' your reserve coffee with a shot?' on the way back. She'll leave out the shot."

"Who's next?" she asked.

I pointed to the Redhead who scratched something on a cocktail napkin and put it in her pocket. I bet our cameras will show it's a chemical formula. *Her next patent, I figure.* Her escort flattered her, "I look to you as a role model. I know I'll see you in here again. Oh, and I love your gown!" she gushed.

"The winners are escorted with fanfare to the Payoff

Room, miss. Each one goes in alone to see the Boss, opens their envelope, and decides."

"Mr. Gogo, congratulations. Open your envelope." Boss had a professional smile on his face when he handed a blunted letter opener to the former Diamond King. Peaches shined up Tiny and Bobby tonight and they stood behind Boss wearing tuxes.

"This document says I win the Bollywood actor's assets. What does that mean? What did I win?"

"Mr. Gogo, here is a list of the assets you now own and instructions. It includes a part interest in an Indian movie studio and a very profitable bus company. Our estimate of your win is approximately two hundred-fifty-seven million dollars."

The African grinned from ear to ear. "Not to sound greedy," Gogo said, "but, anything else?"

Boss nodded. "That's up to you. Do you wish to trade bodies?"

Gogo sat still. "Is this man a good man?"

"This man has been spoiled his whole life. He often mistreats people but has never killed anyone. You can make him into anyone you wish."

"A new start then. I do wish to trade. A transition to a brown skin would be easier than to a white skin."

Boss asked, "To make sure you understand the process, you, a Black South African male will come out as an East Indian male movie star. Is that what you are deciding?"

"Yes, you may be my salvation in this life. Thank you."

"You're welcome. Step this way to sign papers. After the winners make their decisions, we will transfer you." Mr. Gogo was led away by a clerk from the legal office.

Mr. Xin came in.

"Mr. Xin, congratulations. Open your envelope." Boss handed the Antiquities dealer the letter opener.

"This document states I win the biotechnologist's fortune. What is that?"

"Here is a list of the assets you now own and pertinent information. It is primarily licensing income from four patents in use worldwide. It is worth today close to four hundred million dollars a year."

"I see. Not what my fortune teller predicted but still respectable. Didn't she have more than that? You said five patents in her introduction."

"True. One paid for her upfront costs."

"I see. Is there anything else?"

"Do you wish to transfer bodies?"

Mr. Xin burst out laughing. "Only an Occidental would ask that. You must be joking. Become a weak, mewling woman? I hardly think so. Anything else?" He had a smirk on his face that wouldn't quit.

"One more thing. You were charged an extra security fee to protect Miss Peggy that I initiated after you leveled a threat at her."

That smirk fell from Xin's face. "That was only a joke. You know how hysterical women get. I only wanted a little fun at someone else's expense."

"Ironic, isn't it, that I have already collected the five million security fee from your winnings. Good evening, Mr. Xin. Go with this gentleman to sign final papers. And Mr. Xin, you are permanently banned from Drake's."

"What? Impossible. Do you know who I am?" His face was purple.

"What's more important is I know what you are, and I cannot allow you to threaten anyone on my island again." Boss was implacable.

Xin's face got even darker and he spit out, "You will regret this, Drake." He pulled a business card from his jacket. With a big show he wrote something Chinese on the back and threw it down on Boss's desk. "Death is in *your* cards now." Boss didn't correct Xin when he called him by the wrong name.

Vic escorted Mr. Xin out as Peaches showed the Greek widow in. "Mrs. Pappas, congratulations, Open your envelope." She took the letter opener and stabbed the envelope, finally ripping it open with her fingernails.

"I win the assets of the Professional Athlete's life. What is that?"

"This list names all of those assets. A large part is half ownership in both a U.S. professional football team and a professional baseball team. Your total assets are approximately one billion dollars." Her eyebrows flew up. Her deer in the headlights expression transformed into a let's eat Bambi for dinner leer. "Do you wish to transfer bodies?"

Her head started shaking. "No, I stay like this. I'm winning a team, yes? No, two teams of young *men*, yes? I stay the same."

"Any other questions?"

"Where do I sign?" she said with a satisfied look. The first clerk escorted her out.

Diamond, the Lottery Queen who came in with Peaches and sat down was shaking. "Miss Peaches, could you bring me a Jack and Coke?"

Boss nodded to his assistant. "Miss Diamond, open your envelope." He handed her the letter opener.

"Don't need that, Boss I already looked. I done won money from the Greek Widow. What's she got anyway?"

"Here is a list and instructions, Miss Diamond. Mostly it's stock in a Greek shipping company and two hundred-ten million dollars in cash.

"Cash? That'll keep me warm at night. What else do I do?"

"There is a funny rule we have at Drake's. Since the Greek widow didn't chose to transfer bodies—you will get the one she turned down if you want it."

"Well, who is it?"

"If you chose this it will be the former NFL football player, who is a transexual."

"What's that sexual thingie?"

"It means she was born a man and…"

"…had his junk cut off. I got it. I seen her around. She tall and beautiful. I want that, Boss."

"You are *sure*?" Boss was surprised.

"Yeah, but can you tell me who gets my kids? I wanna know they's gonna be okay."

"The Game isn't over yet, Diamond. I'll see what I can do."

After she left, the Professional Athlete was escorted in.

"Miss—"

"Livy, Boss." She had her legs crossed as she bounced up and down. "I'm about to pee my pants waiting to see what comes next." She sat and kept her legs crossed.

"Then open your envelope." She had the top torn off before Boss stopped speaking.

"Lottery Queen. Diamond? I won *her* fortune. Not

too shabby."

"Yes, not too shabby. The fortune is mostly in cash as she took a lumpsum payout. Have
you made a decision to transfer bodies or not?"

"Wait. Does she have all her parts if you know what I mean?"

"Uh, yes. She has a fully functioning uterus. But there is another stipulation if you chose to transfer. Her children are included in your winnings." Livy shot up from her chair.

"Yes, yes, a million times yes. Kids and a uterus is the *jackpot*." Livy pumped the Boss's hand and then put something in it. "Here, Boss. Display it in good health."

Boss looked down. In the palm of his hand was Livy's Superbowl Ring. "Really? This is too much."

"No, Boss, what I won is too much." Then she hugged Boss until his eyeballs popped.

The Salvor was the final winner. She won the Actresses' life. She took her assets but not her body. "No, I got plans like this. One question though."

"What's that?"

"If I wanted to come here to film underwater sequences and beach scenes for a movie, would you be open to that?"

"Only if I'm an investor in the film."

Her mouth fell open in surprised shock. "I'll be in touch. Thanks, Boss."

"Rhonda, the man you stabbed is on his way to prison. I owe *you* one."

####

"Peggy, the winners and losers whose packages are transferred are taken back to the Gizmo. I'm still always amazed by that thing. You put two people in two things

251

like phone booths, someone pushes some buttons and things go POP! FIZZLE!!, and out you come in the other person's body. Of course, you still know the same stuff as before. And as I remember, it don't even hurt," I admitted.

"I know the real winner is Drake's. The House gets the current assets of Mr. Diamond King, the Asian Antiquities Dealer, the Gold Exporter, the Count, and the Salvor. We even get the assets that the Players hid away. See, Boss used to be a lawyer, so's he knows how to think like that, and he's got lots o' connections. O' course, he's legit now." *No need to be crooked when you own Drake's.* I used to try and guess what Boss was worth, but I quit. I don't know any numbers that go that high. *I do think what I'd do with all that though.* "I can't tell you who changed bodies. That's confidential."

"I understand," Peggy said while sipping a glass of champagne.

When the dust cleared, it was pretty interesting. The Diamond King was now the Bollywood actor who still might have a career. *Will his cousin take him home?* The Asian Antiquities Dealer didn't switched bodies with the female chemist. I bet with his contacts he'll corner the world drug market. We'll track him for the future—*wait. Boss kicked him out.*

The Count, the Actress, the Wall Street Wizard, Dr. Brain, the Captain, and the Greek widow kept their own bodies. The Wall Street Wizard wanted a ticket to someplace without extradition to the U.S.. Since he kept his own body, it'll be him the government tracks down for insider trading. "I wouldn't be surprised if a couple of the Players buddy up to start something new. It's happened before, miss."

The Redhead left with a ticket to California, her formula in her pocket, and her greatest asset: her brain. She'll be back in the biotech game by morning. I hear there's a hot new thing in speeding up cures and vaccines. She'll make a fortune. It'll be interesting to see what a Greek widow does with half ownership in a football and a baseball team. *I hope those young guys have lots of stamina.* The old Lottery Queen took a ticket to Greece. She's dumping her kids. I think they'll be better off with the former Pro as their mom. She already said she wanted kids. *Now she's got a whole team.*

The Salvor talked with the Actress. They're cooking up a deal to do a picture about the Salvor's life starring the Actress. The Actress got to keep her own body and she ain't shy about wearing a bikini or a wet T-shirt. *I'll have to watch that flick.* They left together with tickets to Hollywood. I bet the actress gets a chance to produce or direct or both and the salvor does the underwater stuff. The old Bollywood actor approached them and they all seem happy to see each other. I smell a new flick in the making, maybe even a new studio. "Here comes Boss, miss."

Boss pulled me aside. "Good game tonight. Let's wrap it up."

We headed for the Chairs. The orchestra spotted us coming and played a fanfare. The spotlight fell on Boss, and the noise died down. "Ladies and Gentlemen. Before I announce the outcome of the Chairs for tonight, I'd like to tell you about the Winner Takes Three Chairs next season which promises to be one of our most exciting and thrilling games. We will have an as yet unknown number of Players. However, they will play until only three chairs remain. This means there will be only three winners but what wonderfully exciting prizes they will claim." The orchestra played a drumroll. "First, all envelopes are put into a hat. The Third Place Winner selects one envelope. The Second Place Winner selects two envelopes, and the First Place Winner selects three envelopes—yes—three envelopes." There was a lot of noise and clapping from the Spectators.

"The First Place Winner keeps all of the assets from the three *and* will select from any of the three for transference." There were gasps from the crowd, then applause.

Now that is a Chairs worth getting into. "Just between us, that big game only happens if we get twelve players. Here's what folks really want to know coming up."

"Now we don't announce names," the Boss said. "We respect the confidentiality of the Players. Let me just indicate the results as this: the winners, by their original introductions are the South African Diamond Mine Owner, the Asian Antiquities Dealer, the Greek Shipping Magnate, the Giant Lottery Winner, the daring Ocean Salvor, and our Professional Athlete." There's a rousing round of applause. "I cannot tell you what they won, nor if they elected transference. We'll just keep that between us here at Drake's. As always, any deals you struck with the Players before the Chairs are subject to further negotiation. We thank you all for coming to Drake's. The night is still young, so enjoy yourselves." The spotlight shut off, the band played, and the roulette wheel started spinning.

"The confidentiality part is important, miss. After all, there are people in the crowd who played before or who might play again." Boss stopped to chat with Peggy and I headed back to the kitchen for a break. All of tonight's Players left the casino except the Count. He sat and ate our top Russian caviar and drank our most champagne with his escort. Me…I wanted a little Dutch courage.

****

Time's a wasting. The Chairs was over, and the transfers were next. We never know how many Players will transfer. You'd be surprised how much of an impulse decision it is. Tonight we only have two transfers. I would have bet at least one other winner was headed for a transfer, and I'd have lost. Tonight we made a quick behind-the-scenes correction. We diverted Señor Three to a special Consolation Room minus his bodyguards. After he lost, we substituted one of the other losers' packages for his as he is headed for a just and fitting future. I met Dex at the Gizmo.

Vic brought in Mr. Gogo who kept wiping his hands on his pants as he stared at the Gizmo. Mr. Khan's escort led him in. She cut off his booze long before the Chairs started and pumped him full of black coffee. We never transfer anyone who was not cognizant of the process. We once had a Player pass out while playing the Chairs, and obviously lost. I waited until the next day and he could pass a breathalyzer test before I warmed up the Gizmo.

Chapter 25

"Mr. Khan?" He didn't answer. "Mr. Khan, can I get you something?" His knees were trembling.

"This is a real thing? You do know who I am, don't you?" His mouth hung open as he took in the Gizmo while Mr. Gogo was as still as a stone, but his eyes were everywhere.

"Yes, sir. This is real. And I do know you have an iron-clad contract with Drake's that we are about to fulfill."

"I see. Mr. Gogo, I must—"

"Mr. Khan, wait until after—"

Khan cut me off. "Boss, please." His knees were knocking so hard I could hear them. "Mr. Gogo. I fear if my family realizes that we switched bodies, they will shun you. But you still own my assets which include movies royalties, and my fans will love you. Treasure the fans or your life will end up as mine did: lonely because my family shuns me too. My cousin is here, and he is not a bad a guy. Give him time. He plays cricket. Good luck." He turned and walked into a booth.

I nodded to Mr. Gogo. He entered the second booth. What an interesting life experience these men will have, as they truly walk in another man's shoes. The years have taught me how to efficiently push the buttons and listen for the bell as the Gizmo casts its technological spell, and transforms the futures of live, breathing humans.

The new Mr. Gogo stared at his black hands and the enormous diamonds he was now wearing. He slowly turned his head to the other booth to the new Mr. Khan who stared at his own hands. As the men exited their booths new Mr. Gogo blurted out, "Well, this ought to cure my gambling habit," and he actually laughed. He took the other man's arm. "Come on, Mr. Khan. Let me introduce you to your cousin, Sanjay. I hope you like field hockey and curry." He looked to me and said, "Don't worry about me, Boss. I got a date with two beautiful ladies." The new Mr. Khan looked stunned and was led away.

The last transfer was left and even as a gambler I would never have bet on this pair: the Lottery Queen and the former NFL player.

Dex brought in Diamond but stayed out of her reach while Vic showed Livy in. The women came in giggling. Diamond acted as if she was entering a Halloween fun house and looked from Livy to the Gizmo and back. Livy grinned from ear to ear like it was Christmas morning and the mall Santa made some bigtime promises.

"Diamond—" Livy said but I stopped her. She glared and Vic moved closer to me.

"Ladies let's complete the transfer first. You can spend all night chatting. If you each will enter a booth and close your door, I promise this will be quick and painless." Each entered the closest booth. "Ready?" I asked and nodded to each in turn. *This may be my last time pushing these buttons.* I pushed them as I always have. Ding! I kept my eyes glued to the clock. The hands ticked off the seconds with excruciating slowness as sweat dribbled down my throat. I ran my finger between my shirt and neck.

Ding! I jumped at the sound. The doors opened, and Livy and Diamond burst out. Before I could speak, they rushed me. *Oh god, this is it!* Old Livy alone could crush me, so Diamond was just the accomplice? Diamond had her arms around my chest and Livy's were around my neck. I was being squeezed so hard I couldn't reach my taser or my knife. They squealed as they pulled their arms from around me and embraced each other. I sucked in air and faked a relieved expression while sliding my hand over my shiv.

"Boss, thank you so, so much," screamed new Diamond as they jumped up and down. Livy twerked her hips and almost fell off her seven-inch heels. Diamond consciously cupped her hands under her now natural breasts and stared at them.

"Yeah, Boss, I never 'spected this at all," squealed new Livy. She turned to her old self, "Livy, girl…I mean Diamond girl, you gotta promise me you'll take care of my kids."

Diamond looked up from her new breasts into her old eyes and said "They are my hearts' desire, girlfriend. I love them already." The women held hands and walked out laughing and crying.

The transfers were over. Now to save my own skin.
####

I had an unadvertised special once a year, an "arrangement" with Uncle Sam. If we got a Player on Uncle or Interpol's list of most wanted, well, no one was any the wiser if that Player disappeared after the Chairs.

Dex and Vic kept Señor Three's glass full, doctored with a sedative. After Doc patched him up, he went out the back door to a waiting limo. Since he never looked his help, he was oblivious to the fact his bodyguards and driver were strangers. But not to worry. Señor Three was in safe hands: the U.S. Marshal's Office only hired the best.

The airstrip out front was for guests, but we had a second airstrip a few miles away for cargo planes. This way guests didn't circle the resort waiting for a load of pineapples and bananas to land. Señor Three will never notice the difference until he is loaded in his own special compartment and wearing cuffs connected to his waist and legs. *Adiós, Your Majesty. Don't forget your seat belt.*

Right now, I had a more immediate problem. Most of the staff and all the guests will be leaving tomorrow for several months while we have R and R meaning rest and redecorating. The yearly hurricane season will be upon us, but there's always a skeleton crew here that Peaches oversees. We found caves under the resort and outfitted them as storm shelters. I've worked in them through five tropical storms and hurricanes myself.

I buzzed Peaches. "Well, Boss, as you like to say, 'we survived another one.'"

"Yes, so far." I handed her an envelope that she pocketed.

"Aren't you going to open it?"

"You always pay me too much, but I thank you and bless you. The town thanks you for their new emergency power plant."

"But I didn't…"

"If anyone asks, you did. Clear, lovie? I don't need every soul on the island trying to borrow money."

"I've got to get out of here. As soon as Dex shows, send him in. Be safe, Peaches."

"Dex? Be careful yourself. I'll be right out here."
She left the door ajar.

I needed to settle with Dex. His contract was up. My
belief was he planned to kill me in the next hour, if not
minutes. I was tap dancing as fast as I could to create my
Plan B. I had the one thing Dex wanted more than
anything else in the world. *Five minutes ago, the motive
to give it to him showed up.*

We still had two "walk-in" transfers. If I know Dex,
he booked another on top that's not on the books; he's
gotten greedy. I caught a glimpse earlier tonight of two
previous Players who aren't on the register as guests. I
stepped back into a shadow as they passed,

"We must show Mr. Dex our gratitude for doubling
his price. Any ideas?" Mr. Velasco said.

To which Mr. Lau answered, "My 'bodyguard' is
warming up as we speak."

And the cherry on the top? I puzzled out what the
deal was with the Gizmo's Countdown Meter. I put a few
important things in a leather portfolio including my
current passport and my passport from seven years ago.
I was ready to jump as soon as I figured out when. My
plane stood by the resort terminal with engines running—
I just got my plan B.

Opportunity knocked on my door. "Come in, Dex.
Great job as usual." I strained to maintain my
composure.

"Yeah. We still got, uh, two 'walk-ins' yet, Boss,
but pretty smooth don't you think?"

I reached for a cut glass bottle of a special whiskey
Dex gifted me earlier. "Drink, Dex?"

"Uh, Boss, you go ahead. I'll take a rain check."

That sealed the deal. Marie's poison was his plan,

Boss was his man. Not his usual *modus operandi*. "Here, Dex. There's a little bonus in there." I handed him his envelope.

"Thanks, Boss." He stuffed it in this pocket, as usual.

"No, Dex. Open it now." He cut his glance to me but ripped the envelope open.

"Boss. It's the assets of the Wall Street Wizard, made out to me, Duncan Dexter Drake. It finally happened! I'm back in the game!"

"Did you forget the seven years were up today?" My voice was low and slow. It's my turn to sucker a gambler. "Make good use of it…Dex, up for one more bet?"

"What's that, Boss?" He could not have expected me to say that.

I took dice out of my desk. "One roll. If I win, I get that back," I said pointing at the envelope. "If you win, you get the rest of your package back. One-time offer, for old time's sake." Dex's eyes were huge, but he paused. *Is he on to me? Is he thinking this is better than knocking me out, dragging me to the Gizmo, and transferring?*

After my offer to transfer, Dex smirked. "My pleasure."

Now I was one hundred percent convinced he planned to kill me.

He laid the envelope down, picked up the dice, and blew on them. He held them by his ear to hear them rattle. There was total silence for seconds as they rolled out on my desk and reality set in.

"Twelve. Twelve! I win. I get my face back."

I picked up my phone and asked Peaches to have Vic meet us. I put my loaded dice back in the drawer. Dex picked up his envelope but he didn't mention a new contract.

We walked down the hall. "Dex, do you mind handling the 'walk-ins' tonight?"

"Sure, good idea. Make everything look normal," he replied as a grin split his face.

"Then come by my office after and we'll have that drink."

"Uh, yeah, sure. It's a deal."

I took one last look at Dex. *That'll be me again in a few minutes.*

We stepped into the Transference Room where Vic waited. *Vic came with Dex when we started up Drake's. None of us remember why we called it after Dex. Maybe we cut my cards. Maybe we rolled my dice.* Vic peered at us with an odd look. *Oh yeah. Vic pushed the buttons when we transferred before.* Maybe that was a sense of déjà vu I caught on his face. I asked him to hold an envelope for me.

I flipped the Gizmo power switch on. The humming started and the hair on my neck rose as always. "Dex, you won. Pick a side."

He went to the right. I went to the left. The yellow lights came on. The Countdown Clock ticked while the Gizmo warmed up. Dex was so excited he couldn't stop grinning. Me, I couldn't afford to be excited. I'm not quite sure how it's all going to work out, but this is the first step. Ding!

Vic said, "Here we go again," and pushed the green button.

My eyes were glued to the clock. Sometimes a second seems so fast, but right now each second crawled. I worried Dex slipped me something, but his eyes were glued to the clock too. He couldn't have been expecting this change of heart on my part. I hoped he kept busy with the "walk-ins" so I could walk out the back door to my plane. I patted my pocket. *Damn! I forgot to take my pocket watch out. Rosalie's picture is still in it.* I watched the second hand finish its second sweep. Five – four – three – two – one. Ding!

I opened the door and looked over at Dex. That's the mug I faced in the mirror for the last seven years. He pushed up his right sleeve and rubbed the dice I'd worn for him.

"Well," I shrugged. "I'm getting out of this tux. See you later?"

Dex put his hand in the pocket of his tux—my tux until a moment ago—and he recognized my watch, but he didn't cough it up. I steeled myself not to ask for it. It could cost me my life.

Vic answered his phone and said, "Boss, we got a small problem. The Count is dead. Looks like suicide."

I'm stymied. This could ruin my escape. "What happened?" I acted as if it's just another night at Drake's.

"He ordered caviar and champagne after he lost. The next thing his Escort realized he collapsed on the floor. The Doc thinks the Count slipped a cyanide capsule into some caviar when she looked away. She called security."

I looked at Dex. It's still his job to clean up messes like this, and it would keep him even busier while I slipped away. "According to his paperwork, he doesn't have a next of kin or anyone named to be notified in case of an emergency. Dex?"

"Sure, Boss. Me and Vic, we'll take care of it as usual. I got something I need to do first. Vic, I'll meet you at the clinic in fifteen minutes." Dex left in a hurry.

Vic said, "Boss, I emptied the Count's pockets to avoid temptation. Here's what he had." He handed me the count's wallet, which was devoid of cash and plastic. He handed me the Count's cigarette case; it was exquisite and expensive. Vic's eyes shone as he handed me the Count's watch. Also classy and expensive, just like its owner.

I opened the cigarette case. There was an inscription. I examined it for a moment when Vic offered, "Presented to Count Victor Ivanovich Antonovich by his Imperial Majesty Tsar Alexander Nikolaevich Romanov, 1857, with gratitude."

"You read Russian?" I asked and Vic shrugged. I handed him the watch and the corners of his mouth twitched, a high display of emotion for him. The cigarette case was a family heirloom. I'll have to figure out the appropriate place for it. I was not about to ship it back to the Kremlin. I asked him to open the envelope he was holding, an envelope with a two hundred-fifty-thousand-dollar bonus in it. "Vic, you've always done a great job for me over the years. Got any plans?"

"Thanks, Boss. Yeah, I think Dex and I will go fishing tomorrow."

"Do you still have that IOU from him?"

Vic dipped his head to the side and shrugged.

"*Carpe diem.*"

"*Carpe diem,*" he repeated. He showed a remnant of his previous twitch and said, "Boss, I envy you. When the professor killed himself, he killed me too. I used to have better hair." We laughed at that remark. That was true back then; it was still true today.

"Use my boat and take whatever you want from the kitchen and bar."

"Thanks, Boss. I usually do," he said and I realized every job must have some perks.

"One more thing, Boss. I'm going to tell Yvette about the venom when I show her the tape tomorrow." He handed me a note. "Read it later."

I slipped it into my pocket and shook his hand. I glanced at the Gizmo as I left and noted the setting on the Countdown Meter. It confirmed what I suspected.

I walked quickly to my office and locked the door. Picking up my portfolio and slipped in Vic's note and the Count's cigarette case. I took a quick look around and headed to my apartment. I hung up my tux, really Dex's tux, and made a discovery. He'd left his envelope in his pocket with the Wall Street Wizard's assets. I added that to my portfolio making a mental note to have Beryl divert it to me again. I slipped into something more casual, the fit a little off, picked up a wristwatch, and grabbed my alpaca topcoat and portfolio. I'll buy what I need when I get to wherever I was going.

Chapter 26

My plane waited in full view. I sweated as it seemed a million miles away. To walk past all those eyes seemed very careless, *as if I'm inviting the world to my own murder*. I carried my knife and taser in my pockets. I stepped out of my private entrance and locked the door. I turned to check if the coast was clear and there stood U.S. Marshal Bennett and "Rosalie," AKA the Fitches. The last person who waited around here came to kill me. Was *this* it? *Was Rosalie a decoy to distract me? Could I take them or should I make a run for it?* I paused just long enough.

Bennett said, "Mr. Warren, please come with me."

Vic's voice was in my head saying *"leap fidei"* and I understood that moment what a leap of faith entailed. I took it and followed them. *This was unexpected but I had chosen to believe I was safer with them.*

They had a dark limo. "Would you like a ride?" he said casually. I sat in the back with my imagined Rosalie, while he sat up front with the driver. The limo headed towards the cargo runway.

Marshall Bennett asked, "May we see your right forearm, sir?"

I knew more than anyone what the Marshals were looking for. I unbuttoned my shirt cuff and pushed my sleeve up to my elbow. There was nothing to see.

"Just double-checking."

"That's quite all right. I don't blame you for being thorough."

He sighed with a tinge of relief. "Señor Three is in custody. We have appreciated your cooperation. On this trip we identified someone of high interest to Interpol thanks to you. We also got wind of a possible attempt upon your life. Were you aware of it?"

"Yes. I became aware on Tuesday through an anonymous note that said I would be dead…." I glanced at my wristwatch, "…by today. I had reasons to believe Dex was behind it."

"Tuesday? And yet here you are."

"Not for a lack of trying, Mr. Bennett. I have one dead guest who should have been me. One anonymous assassin in custody who just missed me. And a third person only alive because of stupidity. And today, I called in a bet you might say. How did you know who I was?"

"We were informed about the Gizmo. We learned you and Drake transferred seven years ago. We didn't know about the switch tonight. We did see your airplane warming up and figured you were making a run for it. We waited for whomever came out that door…and you answered to your name immediately. Frankly, sir, Dexter Drake couldn't fake your manner for two seconds. The lack of the dice tattoo was the clincher. You look like your old photos again, and Dexter looks like his old mug shots. We'll arrest him in the morning." He showed a satisfied smile, like one does after a hard job was done.

I relaxed for the first time all day. "Don't be in too much of a hurry. You might not have to."

His expression changed in a snap. "How's that? What happened?" He leaned in as if to insure he caught every word.

"You could say Dexter Drake got greedy and Ledger Warren got smart. I was thinking to close Drake's and to try something else. While reviewing all my accounts and assets, this turned up." I took the Gizmo instruction manual out and handed it forward.

He flipped through the pages.

"Look at page eleven, the control panel. See the small display labelled Countdown Meter? We didn't know its function."

Mr. Bennett opened the page and ran his finger to the meter.

"The professor put it there to keep track of how many transfers were left. I never noticed it until reading that manual. The fool professor designed the meter with Roman Numerals." *Who does that? I was damned lucky today.* "Less than half our winners choose to transfer, but we never remembered to keep track of how many we did. Dex didn't know how many he did before we became partners. Naïve, I know, but we sure didn't know there was a limit. I saw that meter in this photo taken the first day…," I passed it forward, "… and it read *L*. I assumed it might be a serial number. Tonight, after we finished transfers the meter read *III*. I read it as one hundred eleven, so no sweat. We still had two 'walk-ins' to transfer, and I think Dex is doing transfers off-the-books."

Bennett nodded. "Yes, he has according to our information."

"I noticed the Countdown Clock and realized fully that it has Roman Numerals on it. *III* isn't one hundred eleven, it's three. I expected Dex to kill me because his seven-year contract was up. I paid him off with one of the loser's fortune. I was afraid he'd decided why should he settle for that when he could take mine."

The Marshal listened intently.

Dex never knew his limitations, as Dirty Harry would say. He might escape his walk-ins, but his IOU was way past due with Vic. I still have the Wall Street Wizard's fortune in my pocket. "Dex always wanted to transfer back, but I refused. I offered to transfer tonight to throw him off his game. I think it worked. He'll show up as me to conduct the two 'walk-ins' about now and his off-the-books transfer, so everything looks normal. Then he plans to go to my office for a drink. I suspect a bottle of whiskey he gave me is poisoned." *I understood who Marie gave the venom to: Dex. He's the man who gave it to Yvette for my coffee and her own death.*

"Do you know what three minus one is? The 'one' is the transfer for Dex and me. That leaves Dex only two—two transfers. Dex is going to be short a transfer. Since everyone has paid up front, Dex will have a hard time explaining why the Gizmo doesn't work. He won't be able to give a refund. "

"How did you know he was paid up front?'

It was my turn to laugh. "I'm familiar with *his* method of operation. Money on the table, no paper, no credit, no charges. I know his customers. They won't be happy with a man who took their money and didn't deliver the goods."

The marshal chuckled, "That was a longshot if ever there was one." Marshal Bennett turned around shaking his head.

The privacy window went up and I was alone with the deputy Marshal who looked like my Rosalie. I couldn't stop staring at her, especially after what the Doc reported. I didn't know what to say, or what to do.

She had something in her hand. "I've been looking for you for a long time, Mr. Warren. You haven't changed in looks much, just older." She handed me a photo that made me catch my breath. It was my senior prom picture with Rosalie Warren Smith.

"I can't remember ever being that young," I whispered.

"I know her mother sent you a letter while you were in the military saying Rosalie died in an accident. She sent you Rosalie's Promise ring as 'proof.' She wasn't honest with you, Mr. Warren. The accident was an unplanned pregnancy."

At this I choked, and my eyes teared up.

She took my shaking hands in hers. "Do you know who I am?" I nodded. "I've been looking for you my whole life, Dad."

Then I lost it. We wrapped our arms around each other and cried for minutes. I pulled out my copy of the photo from my portfolio. "I didn't know. I just found out tonight. I was coming to find you. I transferred with Dex hoping you would recognize me if your mom kept my photo." Relief and love quite unexpectedly flooded my soul. My heart began to beat again. *I know why I was still alive.*

After we each caught our breath, she cleared her throat. "We must talk about something important. After I tell you we will never speak of it again." She paused and looked down for a long moment, then raised her head and looked into my scared soul with kindness. "The reason Rosalie's father and your father didn't like each other is because they were brothers. Her father was given up for adoption. That's why their last names were different."

Brothers? Brothers? "Then that means…" I croaked out.

She nodded. "Yes, you and Rosalie were, in fact are, first cousins. That's why they didn't want you two dating. You didn't do anything wrong. Neither of you could have known. It's all finished now. Just to clear the slate, it also means you and I are first cousins once removed—as I understand it, but I will only call you Dad—if you let me."

My heart exploded. "Let you? Try and stop it. What's your name? Is it Rosalie?" I put my hand on her face and touched her to be sure she was real.

"Yes, but I go by Allie." She ran her thumb over my hand. "Dad, you have a serious cut here. There's a nurse on our plane. Ask her to look at it when we get on board." Allie kissed the cut, to make it better I guessed, and it did.

We sat close to each other for the rest of the ride to the plane, our hands entwined. I feared if I let go of her, she would disappear. I remembered Vic's note and took it out. It read "*Ad astra per aspera.*" *Through adversity to the stars.* I realized Vic understood a lot more about me than I ever did about him.

I recalled something I'd found out a year ago and chuckled: Vic hated fishing with a passion. The times he'd take my boat out he'd head a mile offshore where the water dropped off to four thousand feet deep. He'd eat some lunch, drink a few beers, and relax reading a book. When the coast was clear he dropped a weighted shape about the size of a body overboard. I guessed that's how he and Dex "handled it" when a couple of personal bodyguards went too far. I assumed that was how Dex was going to end up.

We were told the prisoner was secured on the plane as we boarded. I looked up and down the aisle and spotted two men sitting in the dimly lit aft section. I assumed they were guarding the prisoner. The taller man seemed familiar. I remembered I had seen him in the nightclub and by the pool. He was Jamie Justice's manager. "Mr. Bollar, I want to thank you for the great show your client put on for us." I proceeded to relate the story of Dex wanting to see Jamie do 'that Frankie girl from Jersey' when I noticed the other man's tie. It wasn't a tie, but a blue and red Hermès scarf folded and tied in a half-Windsor knot. Both men laughed at the Frankie story. I chuckled and looked the other man in the eye, suspecting he was Jamie Justice himself. "Perhaps your client might give us a return engagement in the future."

He winked at me and looked away. I realized they pulled off the best undercover assignment I could imagine. I stashed my coat and portfolio in the overhead and walked to the front.

The nurse had her back to me. "Excuse me, Nurse. Would you look at this cut?" I asked while examining my hand. I tried to picture what Dex did to earn this.

She turned around. "Certainly, sir. Let me see that." She wore a ring on her left hand.

"A Promise ring? I haven't seen one of those in a while."

"Yes, sir. I refused to give it up. My mom bought another to send to you, Skip," she stated simply.

My head jerked up and I was stunned. As her eyes met mine, I knew Rosalie Warren Smith was back in the game with me.

A word about the author...

I've been to 85+ countries and territories and around the world twice, once on an aircraft carrier. I am a globe-hopping retired engineering professor who loves to educate people as they read. I turned to writing novels after retirement to put my snarky mind to work to keep me out of trouble.

Thank you for purchasing
this publication of The Wild Rose Press, Inc.

For questions or more information
contact us at
info@thewildrosepress.com.

The Wild Rose Press, Inc.
www.thewildrosepress.com